HOME OF THE BRAVES

HOME OF THE BRAVES

DAVID KLASS

FRANCES FOSTER BOOKS · FARRAR, STRAUS AND GIROUX
NEW YORK

Library of Congress Cataloging-in-Publication Data
Klass, David.
    Home of the Braves / David Klass.— 1st ed.
        p.   cm.
    "Frances Foster Books."
    Summary: Eighteen-year-old Joe, captain of the soccer team, is dismayed
when a hotshot player shows up from Brazil and threatens to take over
both the team and the girl whom Joe hopes to date.
    ISBN 0-374-39963-8
    [1. Soccer—Fiction.   2. High schools—Fiction.   3. Schools—Fiction.]
I. Title.

PZ7.K67813 Ho 2002
[Fic]—dc21

                                                    2002019391

IN MEMORY OF MY FATHER, MORTON KLASS,
WHO CAME TO EVERY GAME

HOME OF THE BRAVES

I don't know how the legend started that Lawndale High School is haunted. I never believed it. First of all, I don't believe in ghosts and the supernatural. And even if I did, I've got to think visitors from some spiritual realm could find a more exciting place to hang out than the narrow halls and drab rooms of my suburban high school.

But you know how these suburban legends hang around. They get passed on from class to class, year to year. And just when they're losing steam and ready to completely fade out, somebody sees something, or hears a mysterious noise—a groan or a scream or chains being dragged—and the old myth has new life.

There's nothing at all special about Lawndale High. It was built thirty years ago, on a flat site near swampy land that borders Overpeck Creek. I admit that when the wind blows through the reeds of the swamp, it sounds like someone is sucking in a long breath of dry air over sharp teeth. But that's just the way swamps sound. And at night, during summer storms, I myself have seen flashes of lightning make irregular, improbable, downright creepy images flicker across the concrete walls of our school. But lightning storms are always creepy.

There's nothing special about me either, by the way. I'm not a brilliant student. Except for biology, which for some reason I do reasonably well at, my grades are mediocre. I'm a good athlete, but not exceptional. I think I'm a nice guy, but no doubt you could find a nicer one without looking too hard. I'd like to do something unusual or special with my life, but I seem to be lacking in the motivation and ambition department. I could probably get into a halfway decent college, but I'm not even going to apply—I've had enough sitting in classrooms for a while. So my future plans and prospects don't seem too bright. This is the story of a not very special guy beginning his senior year at a not very special high school that could probably be anywhere in America but happens to be in a small town in northern New Jersey.

Hundreds of years ago, the Leni-Lenape Indians roamed this part of New Jersey. One legend holds that our school was built on an old Indian burial ground, and that's why our sports teams are called the Lawndale Braves. The ghostly images and screams in the night are the spirits of long-dead Indians, outraged that their final resting place should have been violated to build the Lawndale High School, not to mention the football field, the soccer field, and the hard-surface tennis courts that stand at the edge of the creek.

Another variation of the legend says that a battle was fought on this site during the Revolutionary War, between George Washington's army and the British. The ghostly screams people claim to hear are actually echoes of the death agonies of American soldiers—really just boys our own age—who were bravely fighting for independence. Our sports teams are called the Braves to honor their brave final sacrifice.

Now, it is a historical fact that Washington's army did pass through Lawndale, retreating from General Howe. There are historical markers on Broad Avenue to show the route Washington's troops took, and Mr. Muldowney, our history teacher, has sketched the major campaigns of 1776 on a blackboard. But no one has ever, to my knowledge, demonstrated that any significant battle took place within our town limits.

So I think it's all a load of bunk. Every place that's not special has to make something up to pretend it is special and unique. There's a legend about a hill in New Jersey that you can drive your car to, turn off the engine, put the car in neutral, and the car will go uphill, defying gravity. There's a legend about a river in Hackensack that's so polluted with chemicals you can drop a roll of film in and the pictures will develop themselves. Sheer hooey. I don't believe any of this nonsense.

What I do believe is what I see and hear and feel each and every day. I see a normal, slightly shabby school, populated by eight hundred students, a hundred and fifty of whom are bused in. We study algebra and Dickens, flirt and fight, hang out and try to act tough, or slink along and try to hide, and generally muddle our way through the years between fourteen and eighteen.

That's all I see. And, when you think about it, that's plenty scary enough. Even scarier than ghosts and screams in the night, in its own unmysterious way.

1

The first word of the arrival of the Phenom blew into our school on a Tuesday with an October rainstorm.

Soccer practice ended just as the downpour started, and the twenty members of our team sprinted off the field with thunder crashing above us, and sharp harpoons of lightning forking out across the suddenly dark autumn sky. The rain went from a few isolated drops to a cold thudding cascade in about five seconds flat, and by the time we made it to the school and squeezed in through the basement entrance, in our dripping uniforms and muddy shoes, we were as wet as a soccer team can be.

I spotted Kristine in the basement hallway, near the band room, trying to not look like she was waiting for me. I tried to not look like I saw her not looking at me. I lagged behind the team and then, as they hurried noisily into the locker room for hot showers and dry towels, I made a detour toward her.

Kris and I lived across the street from each other, and I'd been friends with her ever since I could walk. But in the last six months our friendship had suddenly gotten very weird, and I wasn't sure whether it was me or her. Lately, when I talked to her, I couldn't figure out whether she was flirting with me or if I was reading it into everything she said. Some days I was certain she wanted me to ask her out on a date. Other days I was equally sure she considered me just an old pal from the same block who she could joke around with. The only thing I was clear about was that my old neighbor who I used to play tag with and chase around our backyards with a water pistol had grown up into a fun and very pretty girl with long sandy brown hair and sparkling hazel eyes.

"Hey, K," I said.

"You're a mess," Kris said back. Now, that's not normally a flattering comment, but she said it with a smile.

"Thanks," I said. "I don't know if you noticed, but there's a monsoon going on outside."

"Don't drip on me, Joe."

"It's okay," I told her. "It's not sweat or anything. It's just good, clean rain."

"I don't want to get wet with just good, clean rain. Keep away. You're flooding the hallway."

There was, in fact, a small puddle forming around my feet. I stepped back. "What's up?" I asked her.

"What do you mean what's up?"

"Why were you here waiting for me?"

"What makes you think I was waiting for you?" Kris asked. "Band practice just ended."

"And you're standing outside the guys' locker room."

"Coincidence," she said. "This happens to be the way I

walk from the band room to my locker. But since I'm here and you're here, I'll give you a hot tip, Mr. Soccer Team Captain. Unless you've already heard."

"Heard what?"

"Oh, so you haven't heard?" She sounded genuinely amused.

"Kris, for the second time, heard what?" I was getting exasperated.

"Congratulations," she said. "Your soccer team just got a whole lot better."

It was very strange, but even when she seemed to be saying something very directly, I couldn't understand her at all. "What are you talking about?" I asked.

"In fact," she said, "I think you guys might actually have a chance in the league play-offs."

"We've always had a chance."

"No, I saw you play on Sunday." She didn't need to tell me this. I had spotted Kris and some of her friends in the stands. I had been surprised and glad to see her there, and I wondered at the time if she had come to watch a soccer game in general, or me in particular. "No offense," she said, "but you guys looked pretty awful. In fact, you were awful because you had no offense."

"We had a bad game," I muttered.

"Joe, it's not your fault. You played great, but the rest of your team is a disaster."

I didn't say anything, because I didn't want to agree with

her, but I couldn't deny it. Being the captain and best player on a barely mediocre team is no fun.

"But now you have a chance of making the league play-offs," Kris said. "If not the state play-offs. If not the world play-offs. This is your lucky day, Joe. By the way, are there world play-offs in high school soccer?"

I stepped closer to her. "If you don't tell me what you're talking about by the count of three, I'm gonna shake my wet hair all over you."

"You wouldn't dare."

"One," I said.

"And this is the thanks I get for waiting outside your stupid locker room to give you a hot tip? That's it. I'm out of here."

I blocked her way. "Two," I said.

"Joe, you wouldn't dare."

"I'm warming up my neck muscles," I told her. "I hope that blouse dries quickly."

I have a big mop of curly black hair and it holds a lot of water. I think she saw that I was really about to shake it out all over her. "Okay," she said. "I guess you haven't heard about the new kid."

"What new kid?"

"The new kid who just transferred to our school."

"No. But so what? Kids leave. Kids come."

"Yeah, but they don't usually come from Brazil to New Jersey."

I felt my pulse quicken. "For your information, not all kids from Brazil play soccer," I told her.

"For your information, this one does," she said. "Or at least that's what I heard Mrs. Simmons telling Mr. Hart."

Mrs. Simmons is our head guidance counselor. Among her other duties, she helps new students get adjusted. It made sense that she might know something about some new transfer student. Mr. Hart is our athletic director. If Mrs. Simmons found out about a talented new athlete, it made sense that she would tell Mr. Hart. But, of course, I was still playing it cool. "For your information, not all students from Brazil, even if they play a little soccer, are any good," I told her.

"True," she said. And she paused. Again, that wicked smile. "And he doesn't look like a jock. He's not real muscular . . . and he's not as big as you."

"You've seen this guy?"

"He's in my calculus class. His name's Silva. Antonio Silva. He's real cute. Great hair. Even better eyes. He speaks real good English." She paused. It was a long pause. Her sparkling hazel eyes laughed at me. "And I hear he played for Brazil," she finally said.

"Don't you mean he played in Brazil?"

"No," she said, "for Brazil. I hear he was on the Brazilian national youth team or something. In fact, I think he was one of their leading scorers."

I just stood there. The blood stopped running through my veins, which is understandable because my heart stopped beating, and I believe my lungs also stopped pumping air. Everything just froze.

I guess Kris saw that her news had turned me into a statue, incapable of responding, so she kept talking. "Isn't Brazil the best soccer country in the world?" she asked. "I mean, don't they keep winning the World Cup, if that's what it's called? And he was one of the best young players in the whole country. I think he was a striker. Isn't that what they call the people who stay in front and score all the goals? Except on your team, where the strikers don't score any goals. Anyway, now he's at our school. So don't you think, Mr. Soccer Captain of a mediocre team with no offense, that you might want to check him out . . ."

But Kris never got to finish what she was saying, because I had disappeared down the hallway to find Antonio Silva.

1

The morning after I heard about the Phenom, I saw him for the first time, in a fight.

The bell for homeroom hadn't rung yet, so the hallways were still full of kids getting stuff out of their lockers and talking. But there's one part of our school complex that faces the swamps—the West Annex, we call it—that's kind of isolated. The gym and athletic department offices take up the entire ground floor of the West Annex. The chemistry and physics labs and science supply rooms are on the second floor, with a few rows of student lockers stuck in like an afterthought.

I was in the West Annex only because I had dropped a couple of practice jerseys off in the athletic office for Coach Collins. I was jogging back, heading for my homeroom in the main building, when a scared-looking sophomore came running down the stairs from the second floor, tripped over his own feet, stumbled down the last three or four steps, and crashed right into me.

I caught him as he fell. I could tell from his face that he had just seen something one level up that had scared him into panicked flight. "Take it easy," I said to him. "What's going on?"

"Some new kid is about to get his face rearranged," he said, and hurried off down the hallway.

Our school is a pretty tough place. I'd say there's about a fight a week, and newcomers and people who are different are usually the ones who are picked on. I figured it had to be Antonio Silva, the new kid in school. It sure hadn't taken him long to find trouble. I was sorry to hear that he might be getting his face rearranged, but to tell the truth, I was even more concerned that he might get his legs broken.

I hurried up a flight of stairs, toward the lockers on the second floor, where a bunch of guys and a few tough girls were standing around in a big circle, blocking the view and anyone who might want to escape. Jack Hutchings—one of the water rats, and a bully from a family of bullies—was shoving someone up against a row of lockers, and saying in a loud voice, "Last chance, jerkoff. Beg for mercy in Brazilian."

Then I saw the guy he was pushing. At first I thought it was a girl. I'm six feet tall, and Antonio Silva looked at least three or four inches shorter than me. He also didn't exactly have broad shoulders. In fact, he was kind of a splinter of a kid. And his big blue eyes and long curly blond hair, which fell several inches beneath his shoulders, gave his face a delicate, almost feminine look.

Except that he also had the quality.

I don't know if you've ever seen any pro athletes up close. I've seen a dozen or so. My dad owns a car wash, and after school I help out drying cars and tending the register.

Our town is between the Meadowlands Sports Complex and New York City, so a lot of people stop off on their way to and from sports events. Most of them are spectators, but occasionally we get a real live sports star. I've seen several world-class athletes don dark glasses and stand by themselves, trying not to be recognized, while their cars are washed and dried.

They weren't all seven feet tall or covered with muscles, but even if I hadn't recognized their faces from TV and the sports pages, I still could have identified them as professional athletes. They had the quality.

Sometimes I only have to see someone walk across the car wash parking lot to know they were born with a little something extra in the athletic genes department. And before they put on their sunglasses, or after they take them off, I can see it in their eyes. They have a confidence—a special toughness. "God gave me something you don't have" flashes out like a neon sign. It doesn't necessarily flash in an arrogant way, but it is still there in big letters, for all the world to see. I don't think I'm making this up. The quality exists, and I've seen it.

Antonio Silva had it, and I think that's one big reason why Jack Hutchings was picking on him. Jack did not have the quality. The Hutchings brothers—there seemed to be at least half a dozen of them—were not talented athletes. There was no grace to the way they lumbered through our high school's halls in baggy jeans and sleeveless T-shirts. But they were all big and mean, with the same odd way of smiling from one side of their face, and the same broad shoulders and enormous forearms.

Jack was shoving Antonio into the door of a locker, hard enough to dent the thin metal, but this thin Brazilian kid had terrific balance, and each time he was pushed, his body would fly back six or eight inches and bounce off the locker, but he wouldn't go down. He wasn't saying anything back. He had books in his hands, and he was just trying to walk past Jack and leave the situation behind him, but he had about as much chance of walking away from this mess as I did of making the Brazilian national soccer team.

"Hey, I'm talking to you, Goldilocks," Jack Hutchings said. "You trying to walk away from me?"

"He don't even know that you're there," one of Jack's friends said, egging him on.

"He's dissing you," a second voice added.

A third advised Jack, "You better teach him to show you some respect."

Jack Hutchings needed no more prompting. "I'll rip his head off, is what I'll do first." Sure enough, Jack made a grab for him. I knew exactly what was going to happen next. Jack was going to throw him down, and punch him a few times, until someone pulled him off, or Antonio started crying and begging for mercy.

But that's not what happened at all. There was a whirl of movement that was very hard to follow. Antonio's books flew in the air. Antonio shifted his weight onto his left leg and, in the same fluid motion, kicked out with his right one. It wasn't a soccer kick, and I don't think it was exactly a karate kick either. I know a bit about fighting because I wrestle in the winter, and I had never seen a kick quite like this before. It came from the side, powerful yet controlled, and it caught Jack just above the knee joint with a loud BAM.

He went down with a scream, holding his knee. I couldn't tell for sure if anything was broken, but from the way he was rolling around and yelling, Jack Hutchings would be limping down the hallways for quite a while.

Antonio bent down and picked up his books, and then he slowly walked around Jack as if nothing out of the ordinary had happened. The crowd that was blocking his way seemed, miraculously, to divide to either side so that a path out opened up. Antonio walked away through that path, showing no fear at all, looking neither to the right nor to the left, nor down at Jack Hutchings, who was writhing on the floor, cradling his damaged knee with both hands and making high-pitched gasping noises of pure pain.

Watching Antonio walk calmly away, his eyes straight ahead, his head held high, I couldn't help being impressed by his coolness. He was one tough customer, this Phenom.

I intercepted him about thirty yards down the hall. "Hey," I said, "that was pretty intense. It's Antonio, right? What did you do to him, Antonio?"

He barely gave me a glance. Kept walking.

"Was that karate? Kung fu? I'm Joe Brickman, by the way. Welcome to Lawndale High. Some of us are glad you're here." I held out my hand for a shake.

He ignored my hand. Kept walking.

"Whatever it was that you did to him, it wasn't that smart," I told him. "You just got here, right? You don't need to make enemies like that. He's a water rat."

Antonio slowed. "A water what?" Kris was right—he spoke very good English, with just a trace of an accent.

"He's not from Lawndale," I told Antonio. "He's bused in from Bankside. That's a town right on the banks of the Hudson River. A real tough place."

Antonio had stopped walking. "Tough how?"

"Every way. Lots of people out of work. There are gangs. And then there are all these extended family alliances that are even worse than gangs, because if you mess with the wrong guy from the wrong family, you might end up at the bottom of the river. Like I said, it's a tough town. They don't even have their own school. So the hundred or so kids from Bankside are bused in here, and they stick together real tight. We call them the water rats. You don't want to get on their bad side."

Antonio shrugged. The Phenom didn't spook easily.

"Even if you're a good fighter, you can't fight a hundred people," I pointed out. "But what I'm trying to tell you is that you don't have to fight them. Just show a little respect. If they ask you to say something in Brazilian, then smile and say something in Brazilian. You're new and different, so they're just establishing their home turf. Go with it. It's not such a big deal."

Antonio Silva looked at me like I was a fool. "There's no such language as Brazilian," he finally said. "We speak Portuguese."

"Fine. Then say something in Portuguese," I told him. "He wouldn't know if you made the whole language up. The point is to show a little respect."

The bright blue eyes fixed on me. "Why do you care so much?"

"I just want you to stay in one piece so that you can play on our soccer team," I told him.

His lips parted, and I thought he was going to give me a friendly smile, but instead he laughed right in my face, and started down the stairs. That wasn't exactly the response I had been hoping for, but I don't give up easily. Stubbornness is one of my core qualities. I followed him down, and caught up to him as he left the West Annex and headed for the main building.

"Hey," I said. "Wait up a minute. That was no joke. I was serious about you joining our soccer team. I hear you play pretty well. I think we could use you."

This time Antonio didn't stop or slow down, or even look at me. "But why could I use you?" he asked.

"We have a real good bunch of guys," I told him. "I'm the captain. Why don't you at least come out and kick the ball around with us? We're practicing this afternoon."

"No," he said.

We walked through the big double doors into the main building. The bell rang. We had one minute to get to our homerooms. Antonio Silva effortlessly speeded up. He didn't appear to be walking all that fast, but I found myself jogging just to keep up. Something told me that on a soccer field, winging toward a goal, the Phenom would be hard to catch. "Why not?" I asked him. "I hear you're a strong player. We have a team. I'm asking you in a friendly way to join us. Why not at least give it a try?"

Antonio Silva looked at me, and the quality flashed in his face, and maybe there was just a bit of arrogance there after all. "Because you don't play soccer," he said.

His answer amazed me. Maybe we weren't very good, but no one had ever accused us of not playing the game at all. "What do you mean we don't play soccer?"

"I have seen American high school players," Antonio Silva said. "It made me sick. Here, in my stomach. It is not soccer. It is a kind of . . ." His hands circled in the air for a moment as if he was trying to reel in a lost word. "Garbage," he finally said. "It is a kind of garbage. But thank you for asking. Goodbye."

He headed away. "You're welcome," I called after him.

And then I lost my temper. "*I said you're welcome. You arrogant, stupid jerk.* You sure know how to make friends."

"I don't want friends," the Phenom called back, and then he turned into a homeroom class and the door closed behind him.

The least-fun job at a car wash is the rag work. That's what I call the hand-drying process. Most of the water from the wash is sucked off in the vacuum hose or wiped clear by the three giant dry scrubs. But when someone pays good money to get their car cleaned, they also expect it to come back to them totally dry. And there isn't an automated drying system in the entire world that can get every last drop of water out of every little nook and cranny in an automobile. Under the fender. Inside the hood ornament. On the rims of the lights. Not to mention the grille slats. So the only way to do it is with a human crew, armed with rags.

At Brickman Car Wash we use three-man crews. The guys on the crews have been constantly changing ever since I can remember. It's hard, low-paying work, and people quit without even bothering to notify the boss, who happens to be my father. Rag men wander away on lunch breaks and never come back. Some stay for a week, some for a month, but they all eventually leave. The only one who has been doing the rag work for years is me.

I don't mean to complain too much. My dad pays me what he pays the other workers, so it's a good after-school and weekend job. And it keeps my arms in great shape. During wrestling season, when I lock up with opponents from other schools, I can tell how surprised they always are at my upper-body strength. They're probably thinking, "Wow, he must've pumped thousands of pounds of iron." They don't know that I've actually wiped the water and suds from thousands of Fords and Chevrolets and Toyotas.

The Saturday after the arrival of the Phenom, we had a big soccer game in the afternoon, against one of our archrivals, Carson High. Normally I would rest in the morning before a big game, but weekends are our busiest time and two of our rag men didn't show up for work that morning, so Dad pressed me into service for the first three-hour shift, from nine to noon. I brought along Ed "the Mouse" McBean, my best friend and the starting right wing on our soccer team.

Ed the Mouse is not a good rag man. In fact, he has the unique ability to wipe a clean, dry white rag over a car's hood, back and forth, for five minutes, and when he finally steps away, the car hood is still noticeably wet. I don't mean to pick on my best buddy, but the Mouse is also not a highly gifted right wing. When he gets what should be a breakaway chance, he rarely takes it down the sideline and chips it into the center, or busts past the central defenders for a brilliant solo scoring effort. Instead, he invariably gets his feet tangled up, and if there are no defenders to stop him, he's perfectly capable of tackling himself in the open field.

If you've never seen a soccer player tackle himself when

he's all alone with the ball in the middle of a soccer field, take it from me, it is not a pretty sight. And if you're wondering why Ed is our starting right winger, you have to remember that our team has never climbed above five hundred in the four years I've been at Lawndale High. And our biggest problem has always been our offense.

Ed's a small guy with a pointy nose and a voice that gets a bit squeaky and high-pitched when he becomes excited. But the original inspiration for his nickname had nothing to do with his appearance or his voice. He was named after the mouse that moves the cursor on the computers he has devoted himself to since about second grade. It's strange that we're such good friends—I barely spend any time on-line at all. Sometimes I think that if Ed could crawl into his computer screen and merge with his hard drive, he would have done so years ago.

You may be wondering why he's my best buddy. Well, the Mouse is not just very smart but also funny. He does perfect imitations of all our teammates and our coach, right down to their voices and facial expressions. And no one could be more loyal than the Mouse. If you call him up the day of a game and say, "I have to work the morning rag shift and I need company," Ed will come and dry with you, no questions asked.

So there Ed the Mouse and I were, with a third rag man named Fong who spoke almost no English, working a three-man shift on a Saturday morning at Brickman Car Wash. There were two other rag crews working, so every third car that came out of the rinse machines was our responsibility. Things slowed down a little bit, and Ed went inside for a Coke. When he came back he said, "Your dad's got a hot one on the line."

"New?"

"I never saw her before. You should go take a look at her. She's a real babe."

"That's okay," I said. "I'll take your word for it."

Dad was tending the register that Saturday morning, and presumably flirting with every attractive female customer. He had popped the Beach Boys CD in and cranked the music up pretty high. "Surfing Safari" was blaring from the twin out-side loudspeakers.

I didn't need to see Dad in action. I could picture him at the register, in his short-sleeve Hawaiian shirt open low to show his hairy chest, with his big smile flashing, and the huge biceps and triceps muscles on his hairy arms coiling and flexing as he worked the register and counted change.

The Mouse thinks it's very cool and funny that my father is such a pickup artist. I guess I miss the joke. My mom and dad divorced when I was five, and she ended up moving back to France, which is where she was originally from. She didn't fight my father for custody of me. She just let him have me, and she got the hell out of New Jersey. She visited

25

me twice when I was still young and she was still, I guess, feeling guilty. And up until I was about ten an expensive present would arrive from her, every year, on my birthday. Then the presents stopped. For all I know, she could be in Shanghai now, or Tahiti, or on the moon.

For all I know, she could be dead.

The door to the car wash office opened and Dad came out with a very pretty blond woman in her twenties. She looked familiar to me, although I couldn't place her. She was wearing a tan miniskirt and showing a lot of leg. Several of the rag men stopped drying and gave her long looks as Dad helped her into her car, which I had just finished drying. "Clean as a whistle," he said, thumping the hood. "And dry as a bone. You got the best service at Brickman. I got my own son working on your car. Joe, this is Dianne."

"Hi, Joe," Dianne said, and she gave me a little smile. There was something peculiar about that smile. It seemed to come from only one side of her mouth. Right away I knew who she was—a Hutchings, from Bankside. Dianne Hutchings. Oldest sister of all the big Hutchings brothers.

"Hi," I muttered back. I turned away to work on another car, but I could still hear their conversation.

"He looks like you," she told my father. "Except he's a little thinner."

"And he's got a little more hair on his head," Dad said with a laugh. "Actually, a lot more. So, you want to meet at the theater, or do you want me to pick you up?"

"Let's meet there," she said.

"Eight o'clock sharp," Dad suggested.

"Ten of. I want good seats. See you there."

She drove away. Dad looked around at the rag men. "Hey, what are you all gawking at? Haven't you ever seen a pair of legs before? Get back to work." You could tell by the tone of his voice that he was pleased to be the center of attention. "I'm not just the owner of this car wash," he was really saying, "I'm also the one who gets all the pretty girls!" And he sauntered back into the air-conditioned car wash office.

"Wow, that was a lot of blonde," the Mouse said. "Your dad is really something."

"Yeah," I muttered. "I guess."

"Maybe you could get him to teach you some of his techniques. And then you could show them to me."

"Keep drying, Ed. Come on, Fong. We're falling behind." We dried for about ten minutes in silence. I wondered what a young beauty like Dianne Hutchings saw in my father. Okay, so he was good-looking and youthful for a middle-aged man. And he owned his own business. And he was funny and outgoing. Couldn't she tell that his jokes had been recycled dozens of times on dozens of dates with dozens of women he cared as little about as he cared about her? Sometimes he would bring them home after a date, and they would disappear into his bedroom and the door would close behind them, and sometimes he would see them again for a week or two, but two weeks was his limit. Couldn't she tell?

We finished off a Jeep, and a rusty old station wagon, and we were just hitting a good rhythm when the next car came out into the sunlight, and at the same moment its owner stepped out of the office. The car was a classic Mustang convertible, powder blue, in terrific shape. Its owner was the Phenom. He stood there, like a movie star, wearing black pants and a purple polo shirt and reflecting sunglasses that hid his bright blue eyes.

"Hey, isn't that the Brazilian guy you tried to get onto our soccer team?" Ed asked me.

"That's him," I responded. "He's a real jerk."

"The jerk has a nice set of wheels," Ed observed.

"You dry them. I'm gonna go tell him he's a jerk."

"Do you really think there's anything to be gained by that?" Ed asked me.

"No," I said. "But I'm not trying to gain anything."

Tossing down my drying rag, I headed for the Phenom. His long blond hair had been blow-dried, and he ran one hand through it and stood there in the doorway like he was posing for a magazine ad or something. "You might want to close the door," I told him. "You're letting the cool air out."

He looked at me. I couldn't see his eyes through those reflecting glasses, but I was pretty sure from his reaction that he didn't recognize me. When I dry cars, I dress about as far down as I can go. I had a bandanna around my head, my jeans were more holes than denim, and the T-shirt I was wearing was so stained and ragged we would have thrown it in the bin if it had been a drying rag. "What?" he asked.

"Close the door, idiot," I said, enunciating clearly. And before he could react, I grabbed the door and pulled it closed.

He must have been surprised that a rag man in a car wash would talk to him this way. "What did you say to me?"

"Close the door, idiot," I repeated. "You don't recognize me, do you? I'm the captain of the soccer team that doesn't play soccer. You might be able to see better if you took off those ridiculous glasses."

The Phenom took off his reflecting sunglasses and studied me with his cool blue eyes. He really could have been a male model. "Joseph, right?" he said.

"My friends call me Joe. So you can call me Joseph."

"You're angry with me because I didn't want to play on your team?"

"I just got to thinking about if I was visiting Brazil, and some guy came up to me and in a friendly way asked me to join the local basketball team. And maybe that team wasn't so good. Still, I'd probably go check it out. And I sure wouldn't be rude to him."

"Our basketball teams in Brazil are good," the Phenom said.

"That's not my point."

"What is your point?"

"That you acted like a jerk," I said, looking right at him.

The Phenom shrugged. "You don't know anything about me."

"I don't want to know anything about you," I told him. "But I'll tell you something about myself. I didn't get to be the captain of our soccer team 'cause everyone likes me. I was Second Team All League last year."

"I don't know what 'Second Team All League' means," the Phenom responded.

"It's an honor," I told him, "and it's nearly impossible to get that kind of recognition when your team isn't so good." I probably should have walked away at that point, but I found myself speaking more quickly, and my voice got a little louder. "I've been playing soccer since I was six, and I fell in love with the game," I told him. "It didn't come that easily to me—my father was a football player when he was young, so I pretty much had to teach myself soccer. I may not have the best skills, but let me tell you something: I play good, hard defense. I'm not just the captain of our team, I'm the sweeper—the last guy back. I do what I need to protect my goal. You know what I mean?"

The Phenom replied softly, with a flat voice, but it was clear that on some level he was mocking me. "You think you're a good soccer player, Joseph."

"I think I am a soccer player," I told him. "A good, tough defender. I do what's necessary to stop the ball. Nobody gets by me without paying a price. Our team doesn't score many goals, but we also don't give up very many. I know you think you're hot stuff, and I haven't seen you play, but I don't think you'd get by me either."

The Phenom grinned. He didn't say anything, and he didn't need to. His amused grin told me I was crazy, and that I didn't know what I was talking about. "I see my car is ready," he said. "Excuse me."

"We're playing today at two o'clock," I told him. "Why don't you put on your ridiculous sunglasses and get in your flashy car and drive your rich, useless butt over to the field, and see if we're playing soccer or not. You might learn something. But I won't hold my breath waiting for you to show up. No doubt you have more important things to do. Like look at yourself in the mirror, and blow-dry your hair."

The Phenom put his sunglasses back on. "Nice talking to you, Joseph." He walked over to his powder-blue Mustang. Ed the Mouse opened the door for him, and the Phenom tipped him a dollar. I saw them exchange a few words. The Phenom got in, started the car up, peeled out loudly, and roared away across the parking lot.

The Mouse came over to me. "So," he said, "did you tell him he's a jerk?"

"He knows what I think," I muttered.

"Did informing him that he's a jerk make you feel better?"

"No," I admitted, "it made me feel worse. That guy really, really knows how to irritate me. How can anyone so young be so conceited and . . . arrogant?"

"Yeah, well, at least he's a big tipper," the Mouse said. "And he's a good-looking guy. And real friendly."

"What were you two talking about?" I asked.

"He wanted directions to our field. He said he might come to our game today, if he doesn't have anything better to do."

4

It was like the Alamo. We were under siege. That's my word for what happens in soccer when a defense holds up into the middle of the game, without much assistance from its midfield, and with no help at all from its forward line.

Carson High was attacking us in waves, winging it around the sides of our defense, juking and faking it through our midfield, and sometimes ramming it right down the center of our throats. Time after time our defense cleared the ball, either by long kicks or by a series of short passes. And then our midfielders would make a bad pass, or our forwards would get pushed off the ball, and the Carson High attack would come roaring back at us.

I was in the middle—the sweeper—the last man back. To my left, at left fullback, was Harlan James, black, stocky, a tough, physical defender who specialized in sliding tackles that toppled enemy forwards like so many bowling pins. To my right was Hector Martinez, a fast little sophomore with great ball skills. In front of me, at stopper, was Patrick Dunn, a tall, soft-spoken Irish kid whose job was literally to stop the Carson attack before it got started. His polite manners off the soccer field were misleading—Pat seemed to enjoy bone-jolting full-speed collisions, exchanges of elbows, and trades of crunching shoulder shoves.

But if and when they did get around Harlan, or over Hector, or through Patrick, it was up to me. The sweeper isn't assigned to guard one attacking player—he floats, sensing the threat as it develops, and then charging in at the right moment to snuff out the danger. If you guess right, you're a hero. If you guess wrong, you leave the goalie all alone, and pay for getting beat with the instant shame of the other team scoring and celebrating all around you.

I was guessing right against Carson. They had two very dangerous forwards—a tall, broad-shouldered Viking of a striker named Anderson, and a speedster named Conley who was an All League sprinter during track season. Twice they centered the ball to Anderson right in front of our net, but both times I managed to head it out of danger. When Conley sprinted past the rest of our defense in a brilliant solo breakaway, I stopped him with a sliding tackle that made a ZWOCK sound and ripped his soccer shoe half off his foot.

During breaks in the action, I couldn't help stealing a few glances at our mostly empty bleachers. The Lawndale football team draws four hundred fans for home games; our soccer team is lucky if we draw forty—almost all family members. I admit I was a little disappointed at not seeing Kris among our forty or so faithful fans, but I figured she had bicycled to our last away game, so I couldn't expect her to show up every time.

I tried to keep my mind on the game—or should I say the siege. I had no illusions: we weren't going to get any reinforcements, and a defense without a midfield or an offense is a losing proposition—ultimately it's going to crack apart. If there's one thing I've learned from playing on a team with no offense for three years, it's that if you can only play defense, you're setting yourself up for disappointment.

With ten minutes to go in the half, Harlan cleared the ball out of bounds. I followed the flight of the ball and saw her. Kris had just settled onto a bleacher with her best friend, Anne, and she caught me looking at her and waved back. She looked good—no, scratch that, she looked great. She was wearing jeans and a green sweater, and her long brown hair blew off her shoulders in the breeze. She waved and smiled, and even from across a soccer field I could see tiny sparks jump around in her hazel eyes.

Don't ask me to explain how or why, but at that moment, when I saw her smile and wave at me, I decided two things. First, Carson High was not going to score that day. And second, I was going to ask Kris out. Maybe not right after the game, but the next day, or at the very latest the next after that. I'd ask her to a movie, and if she suggested bringing some friends, I'd say, "No, let's go just the two of us." Or, "Kris, friends are fine, but I kind of think of you as more than that."

I would do it. Definitely.

Meanwhile, our defense was hanging on for dear life.

Carson High didn't want to go off the field at the half tied zero–zero. They pressed forward furiously, sending extra men up to join the attack, changing sides to create imbalances, working to open space, looking for an opening.

My shirt was drenched in sweat. The sweeper organizes the defense, and as I sprinted back and forth, I hollered out assignments, and ordered halfbacks back from midfield to pick up free men: "Harlan, watch the winger! Pat, two free in the center. *That's your guy, Murray! Stay right on him!*"

Those last few minutes of siege dragged by impossibly slowly, but the ref finally glanced at his watch, brought his silver whistle to his lips, and blew the first half to a close. Zero to zero. Our Lawndale Braves team wasn't winning, we weren't controlling play or generating any real threats, but so far our defense had kept the score even.

I jogged off the field with the rest of the team, over to our bench. Bottles of cold water were passed around, and I took one and filled up my mouth with a long squirt. I didn't swallow, though. I believe that drinking too much water during a game produces cramps. So I swished it around in my mouth and spat it out onto the grass.

Then I took a little shower. I pointed the squirt bottle at the crown of my head and squeezed, and in a few seconds streams of ice water were winding down through my forest of thick hair to form cooling cascades over my nose, shoulders, and back. I shook my head from side to side, creating a little rainstorm, and glanced up into our stands.

Kris was looking right at me, smiling. I must have looked like a shaggy dog, shaking off after a swim. She gestured to her forehead, and I touched my own. My hand came away dark with mud. I guess on one of my tumbles to the turf I had picked up a little bit of the soccer field, and I was carrying it around with me for all the world to see. I hosed my face off again with the squirt bottle, and tried to wipe it clean with my shirt. It wasn't exactly a clean towel. It had been white when we started the game, but sometime during the siege it had magically changed color. Now it was brown with sand and black with mud and green with grass stains and even red with a little dried blood.

I glanced back at Kris, and now she was really laughing. Her hazel eyes flashed merrily in the afternoon sunlight, and I don't think I've ever seen anything as pretty as her, in her jeans and green sweater, laughing at me and with me on a high bleacher, outlined against a cloudy October sky.

I laughed with her, till Coach Collins broke the moment by shouting, "LISTEN UP, EVERYONE." We crowded around him. His pep talks were never very inspirational, but then again there was nothing he could say that would do much good. "WE'RE LUCKY TO STILL BE IN THIS GAME!" he roared. "We're getting our butts kicked. WE'VE GOT TO CONTROL THE BALL . . ."

I listened to his instructions, but at the same time I knew they wouldn't do any good. It wasn't that Greg "Maniac" Murray, our excitable center half, who stood listening to

Coach while chewing on his upper lip as if it was a stick of gum, or Norm "Zigzag" Zigler, our center forward, who dribbled the ball in wildly erratic directions which at first seemed brilliant till you realized that he himself had little idea where his touches would end up, or Ed the Mouse, who was having another of his awful games at wing—it wasn't as if they didn't all want to trap the ball, find passes, and move the ball upfield in a controlled manner. They had all the desire in the world—they just didn't have the talent. When faced with the reality of the ball at their feet in a game situation with a rival player running at them, they would just kick it wildly and hope for the best. And nothing Coach Collins could say would give them the talent.

The siege was about to start again. It would be up to our defense. And with Kris in the stands, looking so lovely, I wasn't about to give Carson any easy goals.

The ref blew his whistle, signaling the start of the second half, and as I trotted back onto the field I suddenly found a new and unexpected source of motivation. A classic-model Mustang was pulling up in our parking lot. As we lined up for the second half kickoff, I just had time to see the door of the Mustang open and the Phenom get out.

He threw a casual glance at our field, as if he wasn't sure it was worth his while sauntering over to have a look. For a long moment he stood all alone in the parking lot, posing for an invisible camera. His blow-dried hair barely stirred in the breeze—maybe he used some kind of gel. He had the reflecting sunglasses on. Then he slammed the car door shut and headed for our bleachers.

The second half started, and as I turned my attention back to the game I felt a new tension in my gut, and an even stronger resolve: Carson High would not score that day.

I don't think I've ever played a tougher half. I never stopped moving, running side to side, shuffling, and back-stepping. I sucked down so many rasping breaths that I seemed to inhale the whole field—not the sweet green taste of midsummer but the dry, almost smoky grass smell of autumn that leaves your nose and throat parched and thick. They weren't going to score. Not now. Not today. Not with Kris watching my every step. Not in front of the Phenom, who had climbed our bleachers and now stood alone near the top as if he didn't even deign to sit because it would be an admission that we were really playing soccer.

Carson High penetrated into our half. Anderson sent a lovely through ball to Conley, their speed-demon striker, who split Pat and Hector like two lampposts on either side of a highway and came zipping right down the middle at me. Pat was sprinting back to try to help, but there was no way he was going to catch up. It was up to me.

I gave ground, watching Conley's feet as he dribbled toward me. He would touch the ball a few feet ahead with his right, and stride forward with his left. I waited . . . and waited . . . till he neared our penalty box and I could hear Charley "the Fish" Geller, our goalie, shouting at me, the panic building in his voice, "Too close, Joe. *Get on him!*" The one quality a goalie needs above all others is fearlessness, and, unfortunately, Charley the Fish was not exactly the bravest guy in the world. "*Stop him, Joe,*" he pleaded, his scream quivering. "*Stoooppp himm!*"

Still I waited, watching Conley's feet, till he touched the ball right, and then I made my move. When someone is dribbling at you at high speed, the instant they touch the ball forward is the moment when they have the least control till they can touch it again. As soon as Conley's right toe connected with the ball, I shifted direction, stopped backing up, and darted forward. Conley saw what I was doing and sprinted toward the ball, but my abrupt change of direction surprised him and I got there first. I knocked the ball sideways. Conley tried to jam on the brakes, but he skidded past me, slipped, and fell flat on his face on the turf.

I cleared the ball, and when it was safely out of our half I allowed myself a glance to see if Kris had appreciated that effort. She wasn't there! I spotted her friend Anne, but Kris had vanished.

Then I saw her. She was on the top bleacher, standing next to the Phenom, and neither one of them appeared to be watching the soccer game. I don't believe they had seen my brilliant defensive maneuver on Conley. They were looking at each other. And, dope though I may be when it comes to girls, I knew what it meant that she was on his top bleacher. He hadn't gone to her—she had come to him.

The rest of the second half dragged by for me excruciatingly slowly, like a nightmare in slow motion. I did my very best to concentrate on the game. I was seeing the flow of play very clearly, and continued to get to the right place at the right time and snuff out threats. But I couldn't help glancing up at the stands every chance I got. The Phenom and Kris were alone on the top bleacher, standing together, deep in conversation. I could have run off the soccer field and dove headfirst into Overpeck Creek and neither of them would have noticed.

Meanwhile, Carson High pressed the attack. They were a good team, and they had been held at bay for a long time. As the end of the game neared, they began sending extra men up—first halfbacks, and then even their fullbacks started making runs. They knew they deserved better than a tie. They came surging forward. It was the Alamo—it was Custer's last stand, and we were the ones surrounded, battling for our lives, under increasingly heavy fire.

With less than five minutes left, their right winger got around Harlan and made a strong run down the sideline. When our defense shifted over, their winger stopped on a dime and got off a lovely cross over the entire field to their left wing, who brought the ball down neatly and continued the run on our exposed flank.

I was the only man back, facing their winger, Anderson, and Conley. One defender cannot cover three attackers. I backed up, hoping their wing would give up the ball too early and take himself out of the play. But he held it, angling in toward our goal, and as he neared our penalty box I had to go out and stop him. I knew that he would try to pass the ball around me, to either Anderson or Conley, both of whom had taken up onside positions in front of our goal. As I ran out at their wing with my whole body exposed for a sweeping, sliding tackle, I guessed the pass would go to Conley, but their wing passed the ball to Anderson, who slotted it neatly past Charley the Fish into the upper left corner of our goal.

I couldn't do anything to stop it.

I just lay there, in the autumn grass, and listened to the cheers from their sidelines, and watched them celebrate.

One to nothing, Carson High.

Slowly I picked myself up off the sod.

A few minutes later, the ref raised his whistle to his lips and blew the game over. A couple of my teammates came over and offered some kind words. "Tough game, Joe." "You were a wall today." "You really played great."

"Thanks," I muttered. "You guys, too." But sweat and even a little blood were in my eyes, and the taste of dry grass in my mouth had turned bitter, and I just wanted to be off that field more than anything in the world.

We lined up at midfield and shook hands with the Carson team, and several of their best players went out of their way to let me know I had made an impression on them. Anderson gave me a good hard slap on the back and said, "No hard feelings. You hung tough in there. You were a monster."

"You guys are gonna win a lot of games," I told him.

And then we began walking off the field. I had a good view of our bleachers. Some members of our small cheering section remained in their seats to try to boost our spirits. There was a smattering of applause. A few pathetic shouts of "Good game, Braves." But the Phenom had not lingered to congratulate us on our hard-fought loss. He was walking across the parking lot, and he was not alone.

Kris walked next to him. As I watched, he said something to her, and she tilted back her head and laughed.

"Good game, Joe," Coach Collins said to me. "Looks like you're bleeding."

"It's nothing," I muttered. And it was nothing. Sweat and even a little blood were running down my forehead and into my eyes, and I kept blinking. The Phenom and Kris had reached the blue Mustang.

"She'll see right through him," I tried to calm myself. "You've known Kristine for years. He's known her for less than a week. She won't be impressed by his fancy car or his blow-dried hair. She'll look deep into his blue eyes and see what kind of a jerk he is and have nothing more to do with him. He might have her in his car now, but there are lots of things you can do later on."

But even as I tried to reassure myself, I saw the Phenom open the door for her, and then, when she was safely in, shut it gently and walk around to the driver's side and get in next to her. The tires moved, the Mustang galloped forward over the gravel parking lot, and then it was gone.

As I trudged through a gap in the fence with the rest of Lawndale High's weary and defeated team, heading for our basement locker room, no matter how much I tried to reassure myself, deep down I was keenly aware of a reality that is as true in other areas of life as it is in soccer: If you can only play defense, you're setting yourself up for disappointment.

5

My house felt like a cage.

I paced. Room to room. Living room. Ugly green couch and equally ugly black recliner facing big-screen TV. For Joe and Dad to lie back on and watch sports hour after hour. But I didn't feel like watching sports, and Dad was out on a hot date with Dianne Hutchings.

Dining room. Oak table-and-chair set that had been around longer than I had. My mother had eaten meals with my father at this table when they were a happy couple, back before recorded history. Even the grease stains in the wood bespoke a lack of manners, a growing disorder, a mounting chaos.

Up the stairs. Second-floor hallway. One bulb. Just enough light to distort faded patterns on yellowing wallpaper.

My bedroom. Sports trophies that mocked the defeated soccer team captain from their high shelves. A stereo and lots of CDs. Two of them from Kris—presents from last Christmas. Classical. Piano concertos. "I thought it was time you listened to something that actually sounds nice." Gifts from a friend? Teasing? Harmless banter? Flirting?

My computer. Send her an e-mail? And say what? "Don't trust the Phenom. He's a jerk. Even though I don't know him, I know that. Trust what you know, Kris. Be home. Be in bed. Be safe. Be mine."

Fish tanks along one wall. More than a dozen of them. Big ones, small ones. Freshwater and saltwater tanks. Tropical fish. Common fish. Angelfish. Red-tailed black sharks. I like the way they slide through water, as easily as we move through air; the way their eyes look back at you when you turn down the lights, and you can imagine them thinking that your room is part of their pond or lake or ocean. On this night all those fish seemed to watch me as I paced, to stare at me in my misery, to mock me because I was as trapped as they were.

Hidden things in my small bedroom. A few *Playboy* and *Penthouse* magazines. Why had I bothered to hide them? Dad would probably just have laughed. Which is, of course, why they were hidden. Cigarettes. Unsmoked because I was always in training. Truth be told, I wouldn't have wanted to smoke them. I just liked having them because I wasn't supposed to. A bottle of Jack Daniel's. Swiped from a liquor store on a dare. My one and only experience with shoplifting. Hidden away, not because it was a bottle of liquor, but because I was ashamed I had stolen it.

A photo of Mom, wrapped in a piece of cloth.

Why was it necessary to hide a photo of my own mother

with contraband and assorted items of shame? It was a tough question that I could answer only with other questions. Was it because I knew it would hurt Dad to see that I cherished a photo of the woman who had left him? Was I concerned that if I displayed the photo openly, on my desk or night table, I would have to look at her all the time, and she would be looking back at me? And if we established that level of intimacy through daily eye contact, was I worried that I couldn't keep myself from thinking about her, and why she wasn't around? Mom was a secret, infuriating, gnawing presence in my life, so it felt like the right thing to stash her away at the bottom of a drawer with cigarettes and dirty magazines, and other items I was ashamed to possess but reluctant to throw away.

I unwrapped the cloth. She must have been twenty-three when this image was frozen in time. Just before they got married. Photo taken at the beach. Probably the Jersey shore. Boardwalk in the background. Seaside Heights, if I had to hazard a guess. Beautiful young woman. Amazing body displayed by tiny bikini bathing suit. Dad has always been good with the ladies, and this was the one he tried to keep. Jet black hair and eyes. Mischievous, sophisticated European smile. What was a lady like her doing with my father in Seaside Heights? Slumming?

Mom. Wrap her up. Hide her away.

Back down stairs—two at a time.

Basement. I had built a little workout room down there. Chin-up bar. I did ten. Good for the upper body. Great for the back. Perfect form. Didn't help. Curling bar. Did twenty curls, sideways to the mirror, back straight, isolating the biceps. Upper arms pumping like pistons. Didn't help.

Phone. I ignored it. One good thing about phones—you don't have to answer them. It stopped ringing. Then it rang again. I didn't answer it. Another good thing about phones is that even if some persistent jerk calls you back, you still don't have to give in to him. You are the one in control. Then it rang a third time. I picked it up. "Yeah?"

"Didn't anyone ever teach you to say 'Hello' or 'Brickman residence'?" It was Ed the Mouse.

"Yeah."

"Why didn't you answer your phone. You sound weird."

"Yeah?"

"You stuck on 'yeah'?"

"Yeah."

"Look, it was just a stupid soccer game."

"Yeah."

"Listen, Joe, no offense, but I've had better conversations with a hair dryer."

I didn't say anything.

"So, what are you up to tonight?"

"Just . . . watching some sports," I mumbled.

"You sound like you need some fun. Charley the Fish and

I are gonna climb the fence and play a little night golf. Why don't you come with?"

The only golf course in Lawndale is private, and they lock the gates when the sun goes down. But, for years, kids from the high school have been scaling the fence after hours and hanging out in the lush fairways. Drinking and partying in the shadowy sand traps. This will give you an idea about Lawndale—the golf course at night is the most romantic and mysterious spot within town limits.

Night golf was a relatively new innovation. Ed the Mouse's father is a research chemist, and Ed has picked up a lot of knowledge from him, not to mention access to chemicals. About a year ago, Ed came up with a treatment that would make regular golf balls highly fluorescent, so they glowed bright orange in the dark. Ever since then, once a week or so, a bunch of us would scale the fence with a dozen balls, and try to play as far as we could before we lost them all.

Sometimes we didn't finish a single hole. Once we almost made it all the way around. We had two precious balls left, at the seventeenth tee, when Charley Geller, our team's goalie, drove both of them into the lake, one after the other, splash, splash. Same spot. We picked Charley up and threw him in the lake after the balls.

That's how he became Charley the Fish.

"Can't do it," I told the Mouse.

"Why?"

"Sore from the game."

"Since when has that stopped you?"

"Can't move."

"Brickhead, what gives?"

Of course, my name is Brickman, not Brickhead, but the Mouse was taking liberties based on years of friendship.

"Have a good time," I told him. "I have to take care of some things."

"What things? What are you . . . ?"

"Bye." I hung up. But of course there were no things to take care of.

So I paced.

Kris's house was directly across the street. I could see a light on downstairs. Probably her parents reading and listening to music. Their house was full of books, and they always seemed to be going off to concerts and recitals in New York at places like Carnegie Hall and Lincoln Center. Kris played first flute in our school band, and she'd also been taking piano lessons for as long as I could remember. Recently she'd taken up guitar.

And she sang. Pop. Folk. Country. You name it, she'd try to sing it. Even opera. Sometimes, on warm summer nights, I cracked open my window and could hear her singing as she sat on her second-floor balcony and played her guitar past midnight.

I'll be honest. Kristine didn't have the best voice in the world. But there were a lot worse ways to fall asleep on a sweltering Jersey night than listening to her sing.

She wasn't singing now.

Now the street was dark and quiet.

The best view of Kris's room was from the roof above my dad's bedroom. I turned out the lights so she wouldn't see me if she was home, opened the window in Dad's bedroom, reached up for the edge of the roof, and slowly pulled my body up. Seconds later I was standing on the roof. Unobstructed view. Kris's room looked dark. The shade was down almost all the way. Either she was asleep or downstairs with her parents. Or, the final possibility, she was out and about.

A Saturday night. A pretty girl. A Phenom with a nifty car.

By about ten o'clock I couldn't take it anymore. I was pumped from all the lifting, wound up like an alarm clock from all the pacing.

Ready to go off.

Ready to explode!

My house was a cage that could no longer hold me. I burst out, through the back door, and began to run.

6

It's better to run than to pace.

I flew down the long hill from my home toward the center of Lawndale, the stiffening night wind blowing around me, quick breaths rasping in and out of my lungs, my legs churning. Every time I felt like slowing down I speeded up, harnessing gravity, using the steepness of the incline to shoot myself forward.

Lawndale is a quiet town, and even on a Saturday night many adults go to bed before ten o'clock. I raced past dark houses where all signs of life had already been extinguished, TVs switched off, front and back doors locked, owners upstairs in their warm beds, reading books as their eyelids got heavy, putting down cups of tea on night tables, switching off bedside lamps, dreaming their safe, suburban dreams.

Most of the time I liked living in Lawndale. It was a safe, healthy place to grow up. But on this night, as I raced along, it seemed insufferable, boring, small, and confining. The whole town felt like a trap, on a larger scale than the house I had just escaped from.

An empty bench hunched in front of the bus stop on the corner of Broad Avenue—every hour a bus would pass by here, offering a forty-minute ride over the Palisades cliffs and across the Hudson River to Manhattan. I had taken that bus many times, with my dad, or with groups of friends, going into the city for a Yankee or Knick game, or a meal, or to buy something you couldn't get in Lawndale, or just to be there.

On a Saturday night like this, Times Square and the theater district would be hopping—thousands of people out and about, juiced up on noise and neon, living life to the fullest. Tourists from all over the world calling to one another in twenty different languages, trying desperately to keep family members close. Packs of young guys and girls hanging out, prowling Broadway for action, flirting and laughing and hurling curses at cabdrivers who considered red lights to be invitations to screech around corners. Old elegant couples and hip young lovers arm in arm, leaving Broadway plays for late night suppers.

And here I was, less than twenty miles from all that excitement, and the main street of Lawndale was as quiet and empty as a leafy path through an old graveyard. I hurdled the empty bus stop bench and turned right on Broad Avenue. A dog barked at me and I barked back. It was six blocks to the center of town. I broke into a full sprint.

Five, four, three, two, one.

I raced past the Empress Theater, where my father and Dianne Hutchings were no doubt sitting side by side, sharing a large popcorn and watching some stupid action movie. What could she see in him? He was almost twice her age, full of bad jokes on the surface and bitterness down deep over what my mom had done to him nearly two decades ago. Was there really such a shortage of stable, solvent men in the world? Did Dad have some charm that I couldn't discern? Or did Dianne just want to get her car washed for free for a while?

The center of Lawndale wasn't exactly Times Square, but at least there were people visible. Two bars were open less than a block apart. These were not "happening" night clubs with live music and beautiful people sipping exotic drinks and exchanging smart banter. These were sad little Jersey bars, where regulars sat on their appointed stools downing their customary drinks, a TV on a shelf above the bar playing ball games without sound, a pool table with rutted felt in the corner by the rest rooms and the back door.

A bunch of twelve- and thirteen-year-old punk wannabes were hanging out by the 7-Eleven. They spotted me run past, and one of them called out something that was swallowed by the night wind. I didn't have to hear him to know that he was asking me to buy him beer.

At the financial hub of Lawndale, two branches of different banks glared at each other across the main street, in head-to-head competition for Lawndale's inhabitants' hard-earned bucks. A travel agency and a funeral home stood side by side, capable of accommodating short-term or permanent trips. Mario's Brick Oven Pizza was still open for business, selling slices from the pies Mario baked for lunch and piled beneath the counter. By now the crust would have hardened, the cheese congealed, but two minutes in that brick oven would make them eatable once more.

I passed the grocery where I had worked for two summers as a bagger. Bagging groceries is one of the few jobs that's even more mindless than drying cars in a car wash. The drugstore that had sponsored my Little League team proudly displayed half a dozen large trophies in the window. Lawndale Hardware didn't have any trophies to show off, but it did have a window display of rakes, with a few colored paper leaves scattered around for artistic effect. Soon they would be replaced by snow shovels and fake snowflakes.

And that was it. The sights of Lawndale.

Four blocks of stores and shops.

No sign of Dad. No sign of Dianne Hutchings.

No sign of a blue Mustang with a Phenom behind the wheel and a cute girl with sandy brown hair mesmerized by his blue eyes.

Now I was moving away from the hub, toward dark and open spaces. I ran past the American Legion post and Memorial Park with its statue memorializing Lawndale's war dead going back all the way to the American Revolution. This was an old town, and there were families here living in three-hundred-year-old houses their ancestors had built. I passed the high school. The athletic fields were well-known night-time makeout spots, but they were empty. Either people were not in a loving mood on this autumn night, or they were being discreet.

As the houses became farther and farther apart, I speeded up, racing through the silent darkness. Every fifty feet or so I would reach a pool of light spilling down from a streetlight, dive through the golden glow with quick strides, and within ten steps the light would dwindle behind me and the blackness would take hold again.

Memories of Kristine. At a concert in Memorial Park, just last summer. I am sitting on the grass. Watching her walk forward in a light cotton dress to play a solo. It's mid-July and the temperature has been hovering above a hundred all day, and now the night wind gusts around her, picks up her long hair and blows it across her face so that she has to brush it back. Just as she starts to play there is a rumble of thunder, and then a flash of lightning, and then the deluge begins. It is as if a spigot has been opened right above the concert. Rain comes down in sheets, hitting the dry earth with enough force to make a hissing sound. All around me parents gather up blankets and stray children and run to find shelter.

Kris goes on playing, and I go on watching.

Her fingers fly across the golden flute, but the thunder and the rain soon drown out her music. Her cotton summer dress is slicked down by the torrential rain so that it clings to the curves of her body.

Lightning flashes out over the roof of the American Legion post and seems to touch the war memorial. The bronze soldiers come to life for a moment—they appear to be leading a retreat. The grassy park empties out at double march. The other musicians decide enough is enough and walk quickly out of the band shell, heading for shelter. BOOM, thunder rips, so loud the sky seems in danger of cracking open. The arc lights go out. The spotlight goes off. And still Kris goes on playing, and I can see her bathed in moonlight and strobed by lightning.

She finishes her piece. Takes the flute from her lips. And only then does she look around at the dark and empty field where two hundred music fans sat just a few minutes ago. Only a dozen or so remain—the die-hard music buffs, who have disappeared beneath their umbrellas like so many weasels into burrows.

I am sitting there, without an umbrella, soaking wet, and I start clapping. Kris spots me and laughs, and I laugh, too, and then she walks right out of the concert and into my arms. Well, not quite into my arms, but when she walks over to me she is shaking, and so I take off my shirt, and wring it dry, and drape it over her, and rub her shoulders to warm her.

"Ummm, that feels good," she says. The downpour has lessened to a drizzle, and I can smell her wet hair and I can feel her shoulder blades.

"I got to hand it to you," I tell her. "You really know how to get an audience reaction."

"Don't make fun of me," Kris says. "I'm soaked."

So we walk out of the park together, with the drizzle falling on my head and running down my neck and bare back, and with my hands still rubbing her shoulders, and we get some hot chocolate at the Broad Avenue Diner, and then when the rain lets up we walk home.

When we reach her house there's a moment when she stops, and thanks me for the hot chocolate, and I thank her for the great concert, and she giggles, and we're looking into each other's eyes, and all the long years we've lived next door to each other as teasing playmates and goofy childhood buddies suddenly twist up tightly into three long heartbeats— *ba*-BOOM, *ba*-BOOM, *ba*-BOOM—and we're looking right into each other's eyes and the moment is there and I know it's there and Kris knows it, too, and she is waiting.

All I have to do is kiss her. All I have to do is find the courage to reach through those years of being just friends and touch her cheek or lightly twist one of the curls of wet brown hair with my fingers, and suddenly, magically, everything will be changed.

But I do nothing. I let it pass. And then Kris is on her way up the steps to get warm and dry and I am on my way home, where I also get warm and dry, and then watch out my window as the light in her bedroom blinks off.

That night I lie awake for hours trying to figure out how

a guy who can seek out and even enjoy a teeth-rattling collision in a soccer game, or step onto a mat in front of five
hundred screaming people to wrestle one-on-one with the
strongest guy at a rival school, can be such a complete and
utter coward with someone who would never hurt him in a
hundred years.

But, I consoled myself that night, I had time. Kris would
be there, right across the street, just as she always had been.
The moment would come again. And again. Till eventually I
got it right.

And now I was in a full sprint through the autumn darkness, legs churning, arms pumping, and the security lights
around the golf course fence were swimming quickly toward
me through the murk. The lights were closest together near
the clubhouse, so when I reached the fence I headed east,
following the wall of wire, to the great expanse of the third
fairway, where the fence disappeared into a shadowy forest
of bushes and trees.

There was a pine right alongside the fence with low
branches to climb, and near it someone had bent back the
barbed wire at the top of the fence to create two handholds.
I can do thirty chin-ups without even slowing down, so it
only took me a few seconds to haul myself up among the
thin branches, with the sweet smell of the pine needles all
around, reach out and grasp the two handholds, and swing
myself over from tree to fence.

For a long moment I supported my entire hundred and

eighty-five pounds with my arms as I carefully shifted first one leg and then the other over the razor-sharp barbed wire. And it was during that long moment, as I rotated my torso over the knifelike barbs and prepared to climb down the side of the fence that faces the golf course, that I first heard the screams. They were distant and indistinct, blown and distorted by the night wind. They were pained and full of fear—someone was either being hurt or terrified. At least one of the voices was high-pitched—it could have been a girl screaming. Either that or my best friend Ed the Mouse McBean.

Instead of climbing down, I dropped ten feet to the soft ground, rolled to cushion the force of the landing, and came up running. I headed for the lake where, five months ago, Charley the Fish had been christened.

1

I don't know if you have ever run across a golf course in moonlight, listening to the screams of your best friend getting louder and louder as you get closer to him. The golf course, always mysterious in moonlight, seemed to grow more ominous as I ran forward. The dark fairway gaped wide as a sea monster's maw, odd, misshapen hillocks hunched like trolls in ambush, and sand traps and gullies popped open out of nowhere, as if the ground itself was trying to trip me up or suck me down.

Then the moon dipped behind a cloud and it was so dark I could barely see my own feet. I had to slow down, and veer out into the center of the open fairway to avoid obstacles. As I ran I imagined all kinds of awful scenarios of what could be happening up ahead.

There was a rumor that the Mafia actually owned this golf course, and that they didn't take kindly to local kids tromping all over the greens at night. Suppose they had decided to send in a few leg breakers to make an example of one intruder so the rest of us would stay away. Another often repeated rumor was that guard dogs were occasionally set loose on the course at night. I didn't hear any barking or growling, but that didn't stop me from imagining the worst as I neared the lake.

Words came to me clearly now, blown by the breeze. "Get off," Ed the Mouse was shouting. "Damn you, take your hands off me."

"Please, just let us go!" Charley the Fish wailed.

And what I heard in response to Ed and Charley's pleas made me clench my fists and run even faster, risking injury as I hurtled through the darkness. Not dogs snarling, not Mafia hit men threatening . . . but laughter. Someone was enjoying Ed's suffering. Using it as entertainment.

I heard voices I recognized from school, laughing and hooting and teasing, and a few girls' voices protesting that this was going too far. And I knew what had happened. A football team party on the golf course had turned ugly, and my buddies had blundered into the wrong place at the wrong time, and now they were paying for it.

As the moon emerged again, I saw the lake, the wind-stirred ripples on its surface glinting in the silvery light. Fifty feet ahead, where the bank made a broad sweep beneath some willow trees, I spotted two dozen kids—some from Lawndale but most from Bankside—standing in a semicircle facing the water. Every clique in our school has a nickname, and these were the "hard guys" and the chicks who hung with them. The hard guys played on the football team, pumped iron in the weight room, and hung out at their own parties where lots of beer was consumed and fights were not only common but considered part of an evening's entertainment. Even on this cool autumn night most of the hard guys were wearing sleeveless T-shirts to show off the results of those long hours in the weight room.

I spotted Charley the Fish first, and he looked okay. Two guys had twisted his shirt up around his neck and shoulders like a collar, and they were holding him there, preventing him from running away or going to the aid of Ed the Mouse.

Tony Borelli, the backup center of the football team, nicknamed "Jaws" because of his ability to open beer bottles with his teeth, was waist-deep in the lake, and at first I thought he was trying to drown Ed the Mouse McBean. He had him around the waist and by the back of the neck, and he dunked him and held him down, so that when he finally let him up Ed sputtered water before he started screaming. "Let me go, you Neanderthal. Or I swear to God I'm gonna—"

But Ed the Mouse never finished his threat because Jaws dunked him again, and held him down, thrashing and flailing but unable to raise his head, till I waded out in three or four giant, hurried, splashing steps. "That's enough," I said. "Let him go."

Jaws looked a little surprised to see me there, and I could tell he wasn't sure what to do. On the one hand, I wasn't one of the hard guys, and I played on the soccer team with

Charley and Ed, who they were in the process of roughing up. But, on the other hand, I wrestled on the same team as some of the hard guys, and if we weren't close friends, we respected each other. And there was one more thing: if push came to shove, I could kick Jaws Borelli's butt all over this golf course, and he knew it. "I was just giving your buddy what he wanted," Jaws said with a laugh. "He was thirsty, so I let him have a drink."

I grabbed Ed's feet and yanked him away from Jaws, and half carried, half dragged him out of the water, up the steep bank, where he managed a few stumbling steps and then collapsed, making retching sounds.

Charley the Fish broke away from the two guys holding him, who must have been distracted by my unexpected appearance, and ran off into the darkness. It wasn't very brave of Charley to flee like that, but I didn't have much time to think about it, because Jaws was wading out of the water and following us up the bank.

"Your buddy got what he had coming to him," he said to me. "He stole a beer—"

"I didn't steal anything, you fat liar," Ed the Mouse gasped. "Tracy gave me a beer. Ask her."

"Just be quiet," I whispered to Ed the Mouse, but it was too late.

"What did you call me?" Jaws demanded. " 'Fat liar'? Sounds like you need more time in the lake, little man."

I stepped between Jaws and Ed and raised my hands, but not as fists. Instead, I kept my hands flat, palms out, like two stop signs. And I forced my body to relax and I even tried to smile. "He's had enough of the lake," I said. "Why don't you go on partying and let me take my friend home."

"Since when is it your business what I do?" Jaws asked me. He didn't want to fight me, but he also couldn't back down.

"It's none of my business," I agreed with him. "Just go on with the party and let me take him home. This is over."

And I really thought it was. Because I sure didn't want to push it. And I had paid them respect, so they had no reason to push it. Even Jaws seemed to agree that it was over, because he shrugged and started to walk away.

Then a deep voice rumbled, "It's not over," and a hulking figure shuffled toward me through the gloom.

I knew who it was before I saw him clearly. His name was Slade, but everyone from Bankside called him "Slag." Maybe they called him that because he looked like a slag heap. He was about three inches taller than me, and he must have outweighed me by thirty pounds. The bad news was that it was all solid muscle. I believe there were muscles on the crest of his forehead. He had a neck like a fire hydrant. His shoulders and arms were so big it was tempting to think he was bloated from weightlifting, but he was one of the few hard guys who didn't haunt the weight room. This was just the way Slag looked. He was a co-captain of the football team, and he also boxed—he had made it to the state semi-finals in Golden Gloves. Oh, and one more thing. He was from a tough Bankside family, and was a cousin of Jack Hutchings.

"It's not over," Slag repeated. "Your friend is marked. The other guy, too."

So there it was. Exactly what I didn't want to hear. I didn't want this to escalate, but I couldn't let it stand. "They're not marked."

Slag stood there barely three feet away. "They have it coming to them," he said. "Your soccer team's been dissing us. I got my starting left tackle out three weeks to a month because one of your players kicked him in the knee. I got these two showing up at our party, stealing our beer, talking to our chicks. And I got this little punkass wising off to us in school and now calling Jaws a Neanderthal. Time to teach some respect. They're marked. Who are you to say different?"

Slag had moved two more short steps forward, close enough so that I was now in his swinging range, and even as I kept talking, nice and relaxed, I was watching his left hand because that was the one he would lead with, and I was also monitoring his feet for the weight shift that would be the only clue that the punch was coming. I knew that with his training in boxing, one clean punch to my face or body might take me out.

"I'm not disrespecting you, but you flat out have it wrong, Slag," I said as calmly as I could, under the circumstances. "Jack was picking on that new kid from Brazil. That new kid took it for a while, and then he busted up Jack's leg. I saw it happen and I couldn't blame the kid. But that's between you, Jack, and that new kid. He's not on my team, and he's not a friend of mine."

"I heard he was on your team," Slag growled.

"I asked him to join and he said no. I got nothing to do with him."

"He came to your game today," a hard guy named Donovan shouted.

I couldn't deny this. "He came to watch."

"And he's out banging one of your soccer chicks tonight," another hard guy lobbed in from the shadows. "Scotty saw them parked out by the boat landing, steaming up the windows of that fancy blue sports car."

For a minute my world rocked. Slag hadn't swung on me—he hadn't moved a muscle—and I still almost went down. "I don't know anything about that," I mumbled.

"Sounds like you don't know about a lot of things," Slag rumbled. "That new kid is gonna get his, whether he's on your team or not. And this little wiseass friend of yours has got to learn a lesson. You're marked," Slag said to Ed the Mouse, and the way he said it was like the pronouncement of a sentence by a judge. "Show respect or face the consequences. As for you, Brickman, time to put up or shut up . . ."

I knew I had to fight him then, and I knew I couldn't win. Even if I got through his punches and took him down, he had two dozen friends with him, any one of whom might jump on my back. Still, I couldn't do what Charley the Fish had done. I couldn't turn and run. It wasn't in my nature, and it would just postpone the inevitable. If I had to take a beating, I would rather take it now.

And that was when the sirens sounded. Someone must have heard the screaming and called the police. At least three squad cars were coming up the cart path at rapid speed, sirens blaring and lights flashing.

The party broke up at record speed. One minute there were thirty kids by the lake, the next minute there was empty grass.

Ed the Mouse and I slid back down the bank to the water's edge and then took off, skirting the bank. "Can you run?" I asked him.

"Yeah, I'm fine," he gasped. "Miller's hole?"

"Just what I was thinking," I agreed.

There were a half-dozen secret ways out of the locked and fenced golf course, and we knew them all. Miller's hole was an actual hole in the fence, nearly three feet in circumference—so big that you didn't even have to crawl to get through it. You just had to crouch and you could walk out.

The hole in the fence was on land owned by the Miller family, and the reason no one used it very often was because it was in a distant corner of the course, way off above the thirteenth fairway, with lots of thornbushes all around it.

But at the moment, the fact that it was so isolated seemed a big plus. Keeping behind bushes and trees, and moving farther and farther from the police spotlights that were sweeping the fairways, we hurried to the rough that bordered the thirteenth fairway, and then to the thick undergrowth beyond. Soon we were feeling our way around thornbushes, searching for the secret way out.

8

Ed the Mouse was shaking. As we walked up Grandview Lane
to the McBean house, his shoulders were jerking back and
forth in quivering, uneven hops. It was dark and he kept his
face turned away from me, so I couldn't tell whether he was
shivering because he'd been dunked in a lake and was now
walking through a chilly autumn night, or if something else
was wrong with him. But I thought I knew, even without
seeing his expression. After all, it wasn't *that* cold a night.
And I didn't hear Ed's teeth chattering. So I guessed something besides the cold was making my friend shiver. I figured
maybe he was crying, and that was why he kept his face hidden from me.

One thing was for sure: he didn't want to talk. I asked
him how he had ended up at that football team party, and
who gave him a beer, and I even tried to make a joke about
how we would have to rename Charley the Fish Charley the
Weasel because of the way he'd run off and left us. But Ed
didn't answer any of my questions and he wasn't amused by
my attempt at humor—he just kept walking uphill, with his
shoulders quivering and his head down and turned to one
side. So we climbed Grandview Lane in silence, keeping our
troubles to ourselves.

I had painful thoughts of my own to deal with. Strange as it may seem, I wasn't too worried about my confrontation with Slag. Oh, I knew my run-in with him might have dangerous and even violent consequences in the near future. Just for example, somebody might try to beat me up in school on Monday. But as I climbed Grandview Lane, I wasn't really worried about Slag or any of his buddies coming after me. What was torturing me, poking and prodding me, drumming through my brain over and over, was the words one of the hard guys had shouted out about the soccer chick getting banged in the blue sports car.

The Phenom's Mustang convertible was without any doubt the only fancy blue sports car around. And the soccer chick in question had to be Kris. The Boat Basin is a famous local makeout spot, down by the Hudson River. The Phenom hadn't grown up here—he would've never known about it. Kris must have taken him down there.

The thought of the two of them together was killing me. I felt betrayed, which was strange because Kris wasn't my girlfriend and she had made no promises to me. But I couldn't stop myself from thinking that promises had been made between us without words, woven into the long years of our friendship.

She barely knew him. This was their first date. The thought of his lips on her lips, of his hands on her body, made my fists clench hard as two rocks in the darkness. I wanted to scream, to hit something, to bash something down, but all I could do was keep climbing the long hill in silence.

Soon the McBean house came into view, surrounded by its landscaped yard. The porch lights were on, but all of the windows were dark, and it looked big and gloomy and empty. Ed's mom died of cancer five years ago, so Ed lived alone with his father, just like I lived with mine. But there the similarity in our situations ended.

I'm going to own up to something now that is not gonna sound very nice. But I did warn you, right up front, that I'm not the nicest guy in the world, and that you could find a nicer one if you went looking. So here's my confession. On some level, even though I felt terrible for Ed about what happened to his mother, I secretly couldn't stop myself from thinking that in one way, at least, he was kind of lucky. I'd had that thought many times in the last few years, when I'd visited Ed, or hung out at his house, or spent time with him and his father. I always felt guilty for thinking it, but I'm not sure you can be held responsible for something that keeps popping into your mind.

I know that Ed's mom went through sheer hell, and that her slow death was a tremendous blow to her husband and son. There was a six months' stretch when I was just about the only guy at school Ed would talk to. Twice I went with Ed to the hospital to visit his mom, so I saw her bravery and suffering firsthand.

But Ed's mother didn't leave him voluntarily—in fact, she fought mightily to stay with him for every precious day and hour that she possibly could. What she did was the exact opposite of what my own mother had done, fleeing New Jersey for greener pastures without a backward look. Mrs. McBean's tragic departure was a rejection of no one and nothing. Her final courageous struggle was a testament to how much she loved her family. If she was still alive, she would be in this house, watching over the ones she loved, and Ed knew that, and his father knew it, and so they could get on with their lives without guilt or self-doubts.

It was a big house, set on a bend of Grandview Lane, high above the town of Lawndale. From the astronomical observatory Dr. McBean had set up in the attic with an expensive telescope, to the Ping-Pong and foosball tables in the finished basement, it was roomy and filled top to bottom with fun stuff. Ed the Mouse had an enormous bedroom cluttered with books and gadgets and the most cutting-edge computer stuff his father could buy for him.

Dr. McBean was a research chemist who worked at a big pharmaceutical company in Rutherford, a few towns away. Don't get me wrong—I love my own father—but whenever I saw him next to Ed's dad, at a school function, it occurred to me that they were about the two most different fathers imaginable.

Even at school events, when he was on his best behavior,

my father was always on the prowl, telling bad jokes, dressing flamboyantly, and flirting with every young woman who would listen. I don't think Dr. McBean had ever even looked at another woman. Instead, he dedicated his life to his job and his son. I know it's an awful thing to envy a friend, but I couldn't help thinking that it must be great to have a father who hid his education and accomplishments behind gentle dignity—instead of one who flashed his ignorance and his biceps behind the counter of his car wash on a daily basis. And that it must be great to have the memory of a mother who had tried to stay with him as long as she possibly could, with that unbreakable, instinctive love that mothers are supposed to give their children.

So even though Ed wasn't much of a soccer player, and was picked on in school from time to time, and had lost his mom, I always thought the Mouse was a pretty lucky guy. As we reached his house, the pretty lucky guy who was also my best friend, and who had just been dunked repeatedly in a lake, slowed down and cleared his throat a few times, as if he was preparing for a brief conversation that he really didn't want to have. "Thanks for walking back with me," Ed said with his hand on his front door and his face turned away. "And for showing up at the golf course and everything. You, uh, don't have to come in, Joe."

"I want to come in," I told him.

"I'll be okay. Really," Ed the Mouse assured me, still not looking at me.

"I'm sure you will," I said, lying, "but I'm thirsty. I just need a drink of something and then I'll go."

His thin shoulders quivered and he took a few seconds. "Really, I'll be fine. Truly."

"I won't stay long. I just want a soda and I'm on my way," I told him. "Come on, Mouse."

He reluctantly let me into his house. It was dark and empty. Ed's father worked long hours three or four days a week and sometimes on weekends. He had a maid and a cleaning woman to look after the house when he wasn't there, not to mention the landscape gardeners, and the snow-shoveling service in the winter, so the house was always immaculate and Ed had virtually no chores and could spend hours on his homework, his video games, or whatever else he wanted to do. But sometimes, when I came home with Ed and the big house was dark and empty, it felt lonely to me. Ed never complained. We headed downstairs, to the finished basement, where we always hung out.

I can't tell you how many thousands of hours we'd wasted over the past ten years playing Ping-Pong in that basement. I even had my own paddle that I kept down there. It was made in China and had a specially padded surface and a leather grip. I almost never lost with it, but then Ed the Mouse wasn't much better at Ping-Pong than he was at soccer.

Ed opened the mini-fridge and fished out a can of soda for me. "Thanks. Drink one yourself," I suggested. "It'll make you feel better. And you might want to put on some dry clothes."

I didn't mean anything by my suggestions. I just didn't want Ed to catch pneumonia. But maybe I hit a nerve. Or maybe Ed was all nerves, and anything I said would have set him off. "Do me a favor," he said sharply. "Don't tell me what to do."

"Easy, Mouseman," I said. "It's just that your shirt is wet and you might catch a cold—"

"I said *don't tell me what to do.*" His voice started low, but it got louder and, at the same time, somehow more fragile.

"Okay," I said. "Chill. Don't drink a soda if you don't want. And you don't have to scream at your old buddy who just saved your neck."

Ed walked over to the Ping-Pong table and picked up a paddle. His hand was shaking. "And don't call me that."

"What?"

"What you just called me."

I had to think back. "Mouseman?"

"Mouse anything."

"But that's been your nickname since the third grade . . ."

"I didn't need you to help me tonight," Ed said.

"Sure," I muttered. "Whatever. Let's drop it."

"Let's not drop it. I can manage just fine by myself. And I don't need you to call me Mouseman or Mousehead or Mousedick or any other insulting name you can think of. And I don't need you to save my neck. I can handle things on my own. You got that?"

"Got it," I said. "Sorry. It's just that it looked to me like when you were handling things on your own, you were about to be drowned in a lake, and since you're my best friend, I felt like I had to do something—"

Ed threw his paddle at my head. I ducked, and it hit the wall with a loud CRACK. If it had hit me, it would have hurt. It could have broken my nose. He threw it that hard. I could see his face clearly now. We were looking right at each other. His eyes welled up and then the tears poured out. He brought the back of his hands up to his eyes as if they were two sponges and he could dab the water back with them, and then he gave up and lowered his hands and he just stood there and wept.

I don't know if you've ever seen your best friend start weeping so tears start sliding down his cheeks like raindrops down a windowpane, and suddenly he looks like a little kid again—the way you remember him from third grade—innocent and vulnerable and not able to hide anything.

Guys are not good at comforting guys. I wanted to put my arm around Ed or give him a shoulder to cry on or say something soothing. Instead I just stood there like a gawking gorilla and finally I heard myself mumble, "Jesus, Ed, pull yourself together. It'll be okay."

"How will it be okay?" he gasped through his tears. "How will anything be okay? You heard him, I'm marked. But I won't do it. I tell you now, I won't do it."

"Sure you'll do it," I told him gently but firmly. "And I'll tell you why you'll do it. Because it's nothing. It's just a silly custom and—"

"*It's a barbaric, emasculating custom,*" Ed blurted out. He was the only guy I knew who could use ten-dollar vocabulary words when he was so upset. "Everyone will see . . ."

"Yeah, but no one will care," I told him. "It's just for one week. Anyway, what choice do you have?"

"I have a choice," he said. "There's always a choice. I can go to Mrs. Simmons and tell her what's up." Mrs. Simmons was the head guidance counselor—a nice woman, trustworthy, and easy to talk to. "Or I can march into old Landisman's office and let him know what kind of delightful traditions are being observed at his beloved school." Mr. Landisman was our silver-haired principal, and I had to agree with Ed, the old fellow didn't have the slightest clue what was really going on in the hallways of the high school he was supposed to be running.

"You could do that," I said. "But . . ."

"But then I'd get my head handed to me, right?" Ed managed to look pathetic and furious at the same time, which was quite a trick. Tears were still streaming down his cheeks, and his nose was running, but he stood there glaring back at me with his hands on his hips. "It's so clear to you that I should just go with the flow and demean myself, isn't it? You don't have any such problems. Captain of the soccer team. Star of the wrestling team. Big man on campus."

I was shocked at his words, but I was even more surprised by the furious tone of his voice. I looked back at my oldest and dearest friend, and I whispered, "Ed, I'm anything but."

"No one's saying you're marked. Everyone respects you. You have no problems."

My mind flashed to Kris and the Phenom, down by the Boat Basin. "Sure," I muttered. "None at all. Okay, Ed, I'm done with my soda and I'll leave now. Hope you feel better."

I headed up the stairs. I got about halfway up before I heard Ed kick the weak leg of the Ping-Pong table so that there was a loud crash, which I knew was half the tabletop crashing to the floor. Then I heard breaking glass, which I think was Ed picking up one of the glasses from the down-stairs bar and hurling it against the wall. Then, as I neared the top of the stairs, I heard rapid footsteps as Ed started racing up behind me. I walked quickly to the front door, and I was very tempted to run out and leave him there, but I forced myself to stop and let him catch up.

"Sorry, Brickhead," he said in a very low voice.

"No sweat, Mousedick."

"I'm serious. Don't call me that."

"Listen, I'm gonna talk to Slag," I told him. "Maybe I can make this go away."

"How can you possibly do that?"

"Because he got it wrong. He's understandably pissed off about Jack Hutchings getting his knee busted up. The foot-ball team's in a race for the league championship, and now they've lost a key starter. Slag thinks the Phenom is one of us, and that this is the soccer team dissing the football team, and hurting its chances. And Jack is Slag's cousin, so it's also some kind of family revenge thing for Slag. But the Phenom's not on our team. I'll let Slag know that if he has a problem with the Phenom, he should settle it with him one-on-one. However he chooses."

"You're not a big fan of the Phenom's, are you?" Ed the Mouse asked.

"No, I'm not," I muttered. Ed gave me a curious look—he must have heard something in my voice that's not there very often. I have my bad qualities, but I don't hate many people and I'm not usually cruel or bloodthirsty. I shrugged. "Whatever they want to do to him is fine by me. Just so they understand he's not one of us and never will be. Now, why don't you put a dry shirt on before you catch pneumonia, Mousedick?"

"Okay, Brickface."

9

The Phenom came sauntering up to me first thing Monday morning, before homeroom, and flashed me a condescending smile. His blue eyes were beaming with self-satisfaction, as if he was thrilled at his own generosity for the favor he was about to charitably bestow. "I have great news for you, Joseph," he said.

It's amazing how a little thing like someone calling you by your full name, Joseph, when everyone else calls you Joe can really piss you off. I finished taking books from my locker and slammed it closed with enough force to rattle the hinges. "You're going back to Brazil?" I muttered.

He decided to treat it as a joke, and he laughed. "No, I like it here more and more. I'm staying in Lawndale. And the good news is that I want to join your soccer team." He said it as if he expected me to fall down on my knees and touch my forehead to the ground in gratitude.

I managed to reply in a low, polite voice that masked all traces of anger. "Thanks, but no thanks."

The Phenom's expression became incredulous. I guess not too many soccer team captains turned him down on a regular basis. "Why not?"

"Because we don't want you," I told him.

He studied me for a few seconds with those bright blue eyes. I got the feeling they didn't miss much. "Are you feeling okay, Joseph? You don't look so good."

"Thanks, I'm feeling fine," I told him. I didn't mention that I had been pacing around my room at 1 a.m. on Saturday night—actually Sunday morning—when his blue sports car had finally pulled into Kris's driveway. And that after I had watched her get out of his car and walk toward her porch, and then stop, turn back, and blow a kiss at his car and presumably at him, I had nearly put my head through my piranha tank.

Nor did I mention that while I was going crazy over Kris being out with him, it didn't help much that my father had been in his bedroom with Dianne Hutchings, door closed, baseball cap on the knob, which was a sign to me to keep out. He had his stereo cranked way up, but even so I heard them laughing together, and fooling around, and doing God knows what, till he walked her down the stairs a few minutes after Kris disappeared inside her house.

What happened to innocent first dates? What happened to people taking the time to get to know each other? How could I blame Kris for taking the Phenom down to the Boat Basin when my father and sole parental role model was setting a new speed record as a first-date Don Juan?

On Sunday I put in a half day working at the car wash, and hour after hour, car after car, I couldn't stop thinking about the Phenom and Kris. I didn't see her at all that day—maybe she was sleeping off her big date. Or perhaps she'd gone off somewhere with her parents. I didn't even want to think about the possibility that she and the Phenom were out on a second date, but I knew it was possible.

Sunday night I hadn't slept a wink, even though I was exhausted from drying so many hoods and hubcaps. I ended up getting out of bed, tiptoeing downstairs so as not to wake my dad, and working out in my little gym in the basement. It's not much fun to do sets of push-ups and sit-ups and chin-ups while the rest of the world sleeps. Nor do you get much lasting satisfaction at hitting a heavy bag in the same spot, over and over, with enough force so that the bag seems to groan and beg for mercy.

So my eyes were red and I'm sure I appeared a little tense as I stood in our school hallway looking back at the Phenom. I was confused and angry and jealous as all hell. To put it bluntly, I hated his pretty face. I hated his flirty blue eyes. I hated his mocking manner. Even though I barely knew the Phenom, every muscle in my body from my clenched jaw to my arched feet wanted to wring him like a sponge, to pound on him like a punching bag, to kick him all the way back to São Paulo like a soccer ball that has rolled onto the wrong field. "The team is doing fine without you," I told him. "Even though we don't really play soccer. So thanks, but no thanks. We don't need you."

"Kristine says you do need me."

It took a second or two to sink in that he was talking about Kris, my Kris, to me. I couldn't tell if he had any idea how I felt about her. She must have talked to him about me, if they had discussed our soccer team. Was he mentioning Kristine's name as a kind of challenge? Was this his way of telling me that she was his now—that he had taken possession? Or did he really want to join our team, and did he think that citing her opinion would help his cause?

"So what do I care what she says? I'm the captain," I told him evenly, "and I say we don't need you. Now, excuse me, I've got to go to homeroom."

The Phenom didn't step aside. In fact, he didn't move even an inch to get out of my way. "I saw your team play," he said. "You need me, Joseph."

I stepped forward and jabbed a finger into his chest with enough force to push him backward. "Get this straight, you stupid, conceited jerk. Stay the hell away from my soccer team." I wanted to add, "And stay the hell away from Kristine," but I didn't. Instead, I turned my back on the Phenom and stormed off down the hall.

I walked quickly, feeling those mocking eyes watching me from behind, sensing the slight smile on the Phenom's lips. Then I realized that someone was trailing me, trying to catch up with me. The faster I went, the faster the footsteps came behind me. When I felt a sharp tug on my arm, I whirled, ready for a more serious confrontation with the

Phenom. I started to say, "Get the hell away from me—" and then I saw that it wasn't the Phenom at all but rather my teammate Charley the Fish.

"Don't be angry at me, Joe," he whispered quickly, and his voice was so frightened it sounded like air escaping from a punctured tire. "I didn't do it. I swear I didn't. I need you to tell them that." Charley was never the bravest guy in the world, but just then he looked like he thought a bolt of lightning might snake in through one of the school's windows and strike him dead at any minute. His eyes were flicking around the corridor, from wall to wall and face to face. He was carrying a thick algebra book, which he held high and flat against his chest, like a shield.

"I'm not angry at you," I told him. "But if you're saying you didn't run away Saturday night and leave the Mouse and me hanging out to dry, then you're a liar."

Charley the Fish was about to reply, but then he saw something, and ducked his head and shoulders in a humble and submissive bow. Two junior girls watched him kowtow and giggled, and Charley tried not to look like he heard their laughter. A guy on the football team had just passed, and Charley the Fish was doing what a marked student in our school has to do. For one week, every time a football player passed him in school, or even outside, Charley had to bow to him. After a week, he would have paid his respect, and he would no longer be marked.

Charley the Fish straightened up and tried to act like nothing had happened. "Sorry I ran away," he said in a rushed, low voice. "I'm not proud of that, but you weren't there for most of it, Joe. They were ready to beat us up bad. Anything could have happened."

"Isn't that more of a reason to stick with your buddies?" I asked him. And then I took pity on him, because four football players passed, and poor Charley the Fish had to make four distinct bows, right at the most crowded part of the hallway. Grovel, grovel, grovel, grovel. People on either side of the corridor stared and laughed. Everybody knew what was going on. At our school, news travels like lightning. And there's a certain cruel fascination in watching a marked student humiliate himself. I have to admit, I've watched more than a few students bow and scrape over the years, and I've grinned to see it.

"Listen," said Charley, sounding a little more frantic, "I'm not talking about Saturday night—"

"Then what are you talking about?" I asked him.

"The police," he said softly.

I stopped walking. "What police?"

"They're here."

"Where?"

"Tobias's office."

"Doing what?"

"I don't know exactly," Charley the Fish said. "Because I didn't call them. I didn't tell them anything. I'm not that stupid." His quick black eyes searched the corridor. We were momentarily alone. His voice sank to a dry whisper. "But they know that something happened on the golf course Saturday night and they're calling in students. And if Slag talks to you, you have to tell him that I didn't call the cops and I don't know anything about this. Tell him that I accept being marked and I'm paying my respect. Okay?"

"Okay," I said. "But who did call the cops?"

"How should I know?" Charley the Fish whispered back quickly, as if even to speculate on such a question was to share a portion of the guilt. And then, as he headed away, he added an observation that I didn't like at all: "But the Mouse isn't in school today."

"So? What's that supposed to mean?" I asked.

"Nothing," Charley the Fish said. "But you have to admit, he's not in school. And the police are."

The news that the police were on campus, questioning students, created a weird energy at Lawndale High. Our school is a pretty tough place, but it's tough in very predictable ways. Students get bullied, and now and then they get beaten up, but rarely does something happen that's bad enough to bring the cops. And now Deputy Police Chief Coyle himself was here, in Vice Principal Tobias's office. Everybody was talking about it—wondering what had happened on the golf course, and why the police had come, and who was in serious trouble.

Since I had been on the golf course, maybe I should have

been worried. But I knew I hadn't done anything wrong, and I had other things on my mind. Kris and I often meet on the way to school, but I had missed her or she had missed me that morning. And we usually run into each other in the hallway before homeroom, but I had been busy with the Phenom and Charley the Fish. So as fifth-period advanced biology approached, my anxiety level kept rising. I wanted to see her, and, at the same time, I was kind of dreading it.

Kris is a stellar student and takes almost exclusively advanced-placement classes like calculus and world history, so we have never had too many classes together. But I've always been good in biology, and the head of the Science Department, Mr. Desoto, surprised me by suggesting I take his advanced class this year. It was fun being in the same class with Kris. We sat side by side and laughed and joked our way through the fifty minutes. We studied for tests together, and when a project called for lab partners, we paired off. We had already bred fruit flies and raised bean plants. Today we were supposed to dissect a frog together.

I walked through the bio lab door, and there Kris was, already suited up in a white dissecting smock, goggles, and rubber gloves. Beneath the ridiculous costume, she looked beautiful, as always. Her sandy brown hair was tied back in a ponytail, and her hazel eyes sparkled behind the thick goggles. She didn't seem embarrassed to see me, or guilty for having been out with the Phenom. Nor did the prospect of dissecting a frog appear to be making her upset or the least bit squeamish—if anything, she was raring to go. "So, Monsieur Brickman," she said when I walked in, "I believe the specialty *du jour* is frogs' legs."

I couldn't think of anything light or clever to say back. I guess I just wasn't in the mood. "We're not gonna eat it, we're just gonna cut it up," I muttered.

She dropped the French chef accent and switched to a backwoods drawl. "Okay, then, pardner, get out your buzz saw and let's slice and dice."

I pulled on a dissecting smock and goggles. This lab was optional—Mr. Desoto had told us that in his opinion there was no way to really learn the anatomy and physiology of an animal unless you literally took one apart. That's why medical students dissect dogs, and eventually human cadavers. But he also said he understood that some of us might have personal objections to dissecting a dead frog, so anybody who wanted to could opt out and spend the period in the library, doing some extra reading. Of course, nobody opted for the library. Not that we had a class of frog haters, but there was something about the word "dissection"—about goggles and scalpels and anatomy drawings with directions for incisions—that made us feel like doctors or mad scientists.

"You look like Dr. Frankenstein," Kris said with a giggle when she saw me with my goggles on.

Normally I would have returned the compliment, but I just said, "Where's our frog?"

"What's the rush?" Kris wanted to know. "It's not like

he's going to hop away or anything." And then, when I didn't laugh, or even smile, she asked, "Joe, what's wrong?"

"Nothing," I said, and went to the front of the room to get our frog. Now, I am not squeamish. A frog—living or dead—is no big thing to me. I've caught dozens if not hundreds of frogs in my life. I've snuck up on them in ponds and marshes, tiptoeing in from behind, and grabbing them around their fat bellies before they could hop away. In fact, once in fourth grade I believe I caught a particularly slimy specimen in Sylvan Park and brought it back and dropped it down Kris's shirt.

But when I went to the front of the room and Mr. Desoto handed me the dead frog that Kris and I were to dissect, I didn't feel so good. It was lying there stiffly in its bag, more like a piece of rubber than a frog that had once been hopping around chasing flies. And it stank of formaldehyde. For some reason, and I know this sounds crazy, I kind of identified with it. I felt like I was in a transparent bag, about to have all my nerves laid bare. "You and me, pal," I whispered to the frog as I carried it at arm's length.

I brought it back to our lab desk and handed it to Kris. "Here you go. Slice and dice."

She opened the bag and the smell of formaldehyde got even stronger. But, surprisingly, there was a sweet edge to this awful smell. Then I realized that Kris was wearing perfume. This may not seem like such a big revelation, but there are girls in our school who battle each other in the designer clothes and expensive scents competition on a daily basis. Kris wasn't one of them. But on this day, I noticed, she was wearing enough perfume for me to smell it over the formaldehyde. And earrings! Kris never wore earrings. But she was wearing hoop earrings today.

She felt me staring at her. "So, J, you wanna tell me what's wrong?" she asked again.

"Nothing, K," I said, responding in kind. "What's wrong with you?"

"Why should anything be wrong with me?"

"I dunno," I said, and I couldn't quite keep the anger from my voice. "Why don't you tell me."

"There's nothing to tell," she said. "Everything's cool."

"Great," I said. "Terrific. Me too. Cool. Never better." I dumped our frog out on the plastic dissecting board, turned it belly up, and began pinning its legs.

Kris watched me skewer the poor frog's limbs so that it was soon spread-eagled to the yellow plastic and I knew she could tell I was real mad about something. "So," Kris asked, "want to change gears and talk about something positive and happy for a while?"

I stuck a pin through the remaining leg. "Fire away."

"I hear your team has got itself a star player," she said with a big smile. "Congratulations."

I kept my eyes on the dead frog. "No we don't."

"Antonio." I didn't like hearing her say his name. She pronounced it like it was some exotic foreign dish she was ordering in a restaurant. A dish she had tried, and was eager to order again. "That guy from Brazil—"

"I know who Antonio is."

"He told me he wanted to join your team. And he's great. I mean, he's gonna turn your whole season around. If you win the rest of your games, you can still make the county tournament, and with Antonio I'm sure . . ."

That was when I lost it a little. I looked up at her—right into those pretty eyes. She saw my look and she knew enough to shut up. My words came fast and hard. "Kris, you go where you want, with who you want, do what you want, it's none of my business. But leave my soccer team alone."

Seconds ticked off silently, as Kris looked back at me and the dead frog looked up at both of us. "What the heck are you talking about?" she finally demanded. "For starters, what do you mean, go where I want, with who I want? What are you talking about—"

She was pissed off, but I matched her anger for anger. "If either of us is owed an explanation—"

And then we both shut up because the door to our bio lab opened and Mrs. Eckes, Vice Principal Tobias's dreaded aide and henchwoman, entered. She was a tall woman with a flint-hard face topped by a shock of hair dyed an ominous shade of flame orange. She was a feared figure in our school because she appeared in classrooms only to summon students to her boss for severe discipline. She spoke some quick words to Mr. Desoto, and they both looked at me.

"This is a one-of-a-kind lab that he won't be able to make up if he misses," Mr. Desoto told her. "I'll send him over as soon as we're done . . . ?"

"No. Now," she said. "They want him right away."

Mr. Desoto shrugged. "Joe, you'd better go . . ."

Everyone in the room fell silent. A summons to the vice principal's office is bad enough, but they all knew I was on my way to face a police interrogation.

Some of the anger drained from Kris's face and she even looked a little worried for me.

I looked back at her and said softly, "See ya, K. Good luck with the frog. Nice earrings."

And then I followed Mrs. Eckes out of the room, down the long and empty corridor, toward the vice principal's office.

10

Vice Principal Tobias was a big man with a big office. Facing west from the second floor, it looked out over athletic fields and tennis courts to a row of weeping willows that fringed the waters of Overpeck Creek. The office had been large to start with, and then he had knocked down a wall and taken over what used to be an accounting room. Since old Landisman, the principal, was doddering and missing from school for weeks at a time, Tobias had been running things day to day. From the ever-expanding size of his office, it was pretty clear he expected to be taking over completely in the near future.

The Vice Principal himself was more than six feet tall and must have tipped the scales at well over three hundred pounds. Not much of it was muscle—he was built like an enormous pillow, and every year the stuffing of the pillow seemed to sift downward a little bit, following the pull of gravity. He had a great bald head and enormous hands, and even though he always wore dark suits with the middle buttons done up, you could tell that his stomach jiggled like a tub of Jell-O when he walked.

When I entered his office, Vice Principal Tobias was sitting back in his big leather armchair, sipping coffee and talking to Deputy Police Chief Coyle and a young policewoman who I didn't recognize, about the fish mounted on his office wall. He didn't stop talking when I came through the door, so I stood there uncomfortably, waiting for them to acknowledge me, as Tobias finished describing how he had caught this trophy largemouth bass. "So then I said to Martha, 'To hell with eating it, this one belongs on my wall 'cause it's more than a meal, it's a damn work of art,' " Tobias finished.

"Well, you got that right," Deputy Police Chief Coyle said, studying the mounted fish as if making a calculation. "How much they charge you to stuff it?"

"Twenty-five bucks."

"You got ripped off," Coyle said. "I got a nephew who would've done it for fifteen. But it's a fine fish anyway."

The policewoman didn't say anything about the fish. She was young—maybe twenty-five, with short black hair and a pretty face that she kept pointed at the screen of a laptop computer on the desk in front of her. I didn't blame her for keeping quiet—if I were a pretty young woman alone with Tobias and Coyle, I would keep my mouth shut, too. I guessed Deputy Police Chief Coyle had brought her along to take notes and make himself seem more important. I figured he was probably also hitting on her every chance he got.

You can probably tell that I didn't have a very high opinion of Deputy Police Chief Coyle. My father washes all police cars for free. Before he became the deputy chief, Coyle used to be a regular patrolman and he would pull his cruiser into our car wash twice a week, even if it was perfectly clean. Now, police cruisers are more work and they take longer to dry than just about any other type of car, because of the overhead flashers. Coyle used to walk slowly around his car when I was done, inspecting it from the hubcaps to the flashers. As often as not, he'd call me back with a loud "Hey, Car Wash Boy. Sloppy work today. Come on over here and get your rag out again."

I didn't relish being called Car Wash Boy. Especially when we were washing his car for free. And I didn't appreciate being tipped a quarter for a police cruiser, when most people tip a dollar for a regular car. Each time I vacuumed the inside of his cruiser, I saw the *Penthouse* and other magazines that Coyle kept under the dash. He had a pretty extensive collection. I figure what a person reads is his own private business, but at the same time I like to think that police, on duty, aren't reading flesh mags.

So when Coyle looked down from the fish on the wall to me, and stared at me hard for a moment as if he was calculating how much it might cost to have me stuffed, I looked right back at him, meeting his gaze head-on. We didn't like each other, and we both knew it. But whatever I thought about him, he wore the badge, and I knew I had to be real careful.

"Sam, Lisa, this here is Joe Brickman," Vice Principal Tobias said. "Good kid. Wrestling star. Captain of the soccer team, too. Not a discipline problem either, least up till now."

"Joe and I know each other," Coyle said. "We're old buddies. Right, Joe?"

"Yes, sir."

"Joe used to wash my car," Coyle said, with a little grin for the benefit of the policewoman. "Did a pretty good job, too. Pretty handy with that rag."

I felt her glance at me, as if trying to imagine me holding a rag. I just stood there with my arms dangling, and didn't say a word.

"How's your father, Joe?" Coyle asked, not that he could have cared less.

"He's okay. Thanks for asking."

And then, quickly, "You play golf, Joe?"

The unexpected question caught me off guard. "Not really," I said. "I mean, I play all sports a little."

"Lot of wrestling," Coyle said. "Soccer captain." The knuckle of his index finger ran back and forth over his thin, rust-colored mustache. "Why not a little golf? You own your own clubs, Joe?"

"Old ones."

"So you like to hang out on golf courses?"

Now I knew where he was going with this. "Not particularly. Like I said, I only play a little."

"What about Saturday night? The town course, about 11 p.m.?"

I stood there awkwardly, looking back at him, and knew

that he knew perfectly well that I couldn't answer what he was asking. It's not that I don't respect cops. My father brought me up to trust police, and to tell them the truth, so even though I didn't have much personal liking for Deputy Police Chief Coyle, I would have liked to answer his questions. All I had done on the golf course on Saturday night was to intervene to stop violence, and to rescue a friend. But of course there was no way I could tell them that. Because once I admitted I had been there, I would have to provide details, and name names.

There's a code of silence in our high school that you just don't break. Never. Ever. Kids don't rat on other kids to adults. Lawndale kids don't rat on Banksiders. Soccer team players don't rat on hard guys. It was simply out of the question. On the other hand, I had to say something. And I didn't want to tell an outright lie. "Wish I could get in to play. The town course is locked at night," I said. "And fenced off. Barbed wire at the top."

Coyle scratched his nose. "So, if someone said they saw you running away from the golf course on Saturday night, they'd be lying?"

"Did someone say that?" I asked.

Suddenly he was leaning forward and his tone was hard. "Answer my question."

"Sure I was running near the golf course," I admitted. "I always run at night, to stay in shape for soccer. I run in the winter, too, for wrestling."

"The golf course is three miles from Laurel Street," Coyle pointed out, letting me know he considered this serious enough to have taken the time to find out where I live. "Pretty far for a late night jog."

"Sometimes I run five, six, seven miles," I told him. "Once I get going I don't notice the distance."

"So on Saturday night, when you were running near the golf course, who else did you see? I'm collecting names, Joe. Someone gave me yours. If you help me add to the collection, I can let you out of here."

"Sorry. I was concentrating on running."

Coyle looked back at me. "So that's the way it's going to be," he said. There was a long, uncomfortable silence during which they all looked at me and I didn't make a sound. "Lisa," he finally said, "tell Joe about Red Flag."

The young policewoman looked up from her computer screen. "Red Flag is a new system," she said, and it sounded like she was quoting from a public relations brochure she had memorized. "It was developed at the state level as an interface between school and law enforcement. Crimes involving teens, and reports of violence involving teenagers, and certain other types of incidents and information get flagged automatically onto our system. And when we start to see patterns and increases that we think might be warning signs, we come to the school and get involved."

"Sounds like a good idea," I said.

"It is a good idea," Vice Principal Tobias said. "But it requires the cooperation of students. What happened on the golf course on Saturday night, Joe?"

For a minute I looked right back at this big man who would soon be taking over our high school, and I thought to myself, almost angrily, that he was no fool. He was not old and naïve like Principal Landisman. He had gone to school here himself, years ago. He knew all about the bullying. He knew about the fights—he could see them on the athletic fields from his window. He knew about the feuds between Lawndale and Bankside that went on day to day, week to week. And he sat there in his big leather swivel chair looking at his stuffed fish, and he did nothing. So what did he want from me?

"I wish I could help more, sir," I said. "I was really just out for a run."

11

One of the things I love most about sports is how, when things are going from lousy to awful, or are getting so confusing you're not sure why you bothered to get out of bed that morning, you can completely lose yourself in sprinting around a grassy field till your lungs burn and your legs ache. There's nothing quite as effective at clearing a troubled mind as a hard sliding tackle or a SLAMMING, BAMMING chest-to-chest collision.

That afternoon, as I sprinted toward the practice field, I tried to forget all about Kris and the Mouse and golf course brawls and police interrogations, and just enjoy racing down the gravel path and then out along the grass of the practice fields as an autumn breeze blew off Overpeck Creek, straight into my face. It was a whistling breeze that sometimes swelled to a howling roar as it thrashed willow branches and smacked waves against the bank.

Most of my teammates were already on the field, stretching or kicking balls back and forth in pairs and triangles. Usually Coach Collins is out there, too, in his faded blue sweatpants and tattered Rutgers University shirt. He always wears the same silver whistle around his neck, and when he sees me run up he raises the whistle to his lips and blows a shrill blast, and the team circles up around me to begin stretching.

On this afternoon, Coach Collins was late. He must have been held up at a faculty meeting or something. No problem—I could start the practice on my own. *"Okay, bozos, circle up!"* I shouted. And soon I was taking the team through warm-ups, from the first groin stretches to the final leg raisers. There were the usual bad jokes and stupid banter. "Hey, Zig," Harlan called out to Norm Zigler, our flaky center forward, "did you step in something or is that just the way you smell?"

"You wish you smelled like me," Zigler shot back.

And then other teammates joined in, and it became a crude free-for-all. "No, Zig, he's right. You stink."

"Breathe deep and enjoy, guys. This is the way a man smells."

"You're wilting the grass. I swear, dead fish smell better. Why don't you try taking a shower every month or so?"

"Why don't you get your girlfriend a new leash?"

"At least I have a girlfriend."

"You don't think I could get a girlfriend if I wanted?"

"I don't even think your right hand would go on a date with you."

It was funny and I enjoyed it, although I missed the Mouse. He was the funniest guy on the team by a hundred miles, and every now and then I wondered why he hadn't come to school that day. Was he sick from the late night dunking? Afraid of being marked? I tried to put all such worries out of my mind and just enjoy the routine of soccer practice. I led them through push-ups and sit-ups at a rapid clip, and we were just finishing our leg raisers when Greg Maniac Murray shouted out, "Hey, Brickman, I hear the police called you in to Tobias's office. You been robbing banks again?"

For a moment, everyone stopped stretching and stared at me. "No, they wanted to arrest all of you losers for impersonating a soccer team," I told them, "but I talked them out of it." There was laughter, and before anyone could ask me any more questions I shouted, *"Last set of leg raisers, six inches, to the death!"* Everyone knew what I meant—we would all begin at the same time and the last guy who could keep his heels six inches above the grass would win.

It wasn't really a contest. I'm the only guy on the soccer team who wrestles, and years of wrestling practices have given me steel stomach muscles. I can do seventy-five sit-ups on an inclined board with a fifty-pound weight strapped to my chest. We lay there on our backs in the grass, with the bugs crawling over our faces and through our hair, our legs straight out and our heels six inches above the ground, and after about a minute the groans started. One by one, teammates gave up and lowered their feet.

After two minutes, there were only three of us left, Patrick Dunn, Maniac Murray, and me. The Maniac let out one of his trademark high-pitched bellows that had earned him his nickname—"YA-YA-YYYAAAHHH"—and dropped his feet in surrender. Then there were just two of us. Pat was a tough kid. We had played defense side by side for years, and I knew he would swim through boiling oil before giving up. With my heels six inches from the ground and my legs locked in place, I did a half sit-up and looked over at him. He was starting to cramp, and his face was turning red. "Don't put yourself through this," I advised him.

"I'm enjoying this," Pat managed to spit back, through gritted teeth.

"Good, because I can go on forever."

"Me too. Longer than forever."

"You're in agony. Give up."

"Never."

Pat's cramps got worse, and he started beating on his stomach with his fists, to try to pound out the knots. But of course this never works—once you start to cramp, you're a goner. Finally he had to lower his heels with a disgusted "Brickman, you're not human."

I kept my feet up for fifteen seconds more, to enjoy the burn that I was starting to feel from my ribs to my thighs, and to remind those bozos who their captain was. Then I rocked up and popped to my feet. *"Two miles,"* I announced. *"Last four to finish take down the soccer nets after practice."*

Off we went in a thundering herd. No one wants to stick around after practice, so there was lots of incentive not to lose. I'd helped hang the nets up dozens of times, not to mention liming the field, and doing whatever else was necessary. But I made it a point never to lose the run and have to take the nets down. Taking them down was a kind of punishment, and therefore unfit for the captain of the team.

I can't tell you how much I enjoyed that run. My stomach was still burning from the leg raisers, so I didn't push it. I stayed in the middle of the front pack, chin up, elbows pumping, sucking air as I ran right into the teeth of the wind. We skirted the edge of the football practice field where the varsity team was out sweating and bleeding and pushing tackling sleighs and running plays as they prepared for their next game in what was one of their better seasons in recent memory. I saw Slag, looking like a cement truck with his shoulder pads on, ramming a tackling sleigh like he was trying to break it in half. And I heard Mr. Bowerman, the ferocious and truly disgusting head football coach, shouting at one of the substitute quarterbacks, "YOU CALL THAT A SPIRAL? I'VE PULLED BETTER-LOOKING THINGS OUT OF MY NOSE!"

As the distance and the effort of fighting the wind began taking their toll on the leaders, I moved up to the front of the pack. We passed the tennis courts, which were empty. No one could play with such gusts of wind—a lobbed tennis ball might take flight and never come back to earth.

Then we were in the home stretch, running along the muddy bank, where the footing was slippery and gusts of wind scooped up creek water and doused us with unexpected cold showers. I loved it! I loved the sudden, numbing spritzes of icy creek water, and the dull SQUISH-THUMP, SQUISH-THUMP of footsteps on the muddy earth, and I completely lost myself in the mindless rhythm of a two-mile race as all around me my teammates gasped and strained to keep the pace. It was only when I turned toward the soccer field, for the final hundred-yard sprint, that I saw the crowd.

Coach Collins was there, standing next to Athletic Director Hart, who was not a big soccer fan and rarely if ever attended one of our games. I couldn't believe he had come out to a mere practice. Mrs. Simmons, our head guidance counselor, was talking to him. She was a nice lady, but not known as a giant sports fan. A tall blond man in a leather jacket and dark glasses, who I had never seen before, stood apart from the rest of them and turned to one side, silhouetting himself against the late afternoon sun. And standing in the middle of the field as if he owned it, wearing a Lawndale Braves soccer uniform, was the Phenom.

There were fifty yards to go. Hector Martinez was in the lead, running hard, trying to finish first. Normally, I would have let him. I had won the leg raiser contest, and it's not such a good idea to win at everything. But when I saw the crowd, I picked up the pace.

I spotted fans in our bleachers. This had never happened before at any soccer practice in all of recorded history. But Kris was sitting up there, and next to her was Jewel Healy—easily the most popular girl in our entire school if popularity is measured by the number of guys who wanted to go out with her, and the number of girls who wanted to be her. It didn't make sense for Jewel to be sitting there with the wind blowing her perfect blond hair—what was she doing at a soccer practice? Even football practices were beneath her. Even football games were beneath her. And what was she doing hanging out with Kris, and vice versa?

When there were thirty yards to go, I pulled even with Hector. He was running a great race for a sophomore, but I was a senior and the team captain, and jogging in the evening for years had given me an extra gas tank. Step by step I moved ahead of him to finish first by a good five yards. Hector sank to the ground, gasping for air, but I stayed up, hands on my hips, looking right into the face of the Phenom.

He didn't have to say anything. We both understood the situation. That very morning I had told him no way in hell he was joining our team. And now he was on my field, standing next to my coach, wearing my team's soccer shirt.

I also figured out pretty quick who the tall guy in the leather jacket was, now that I was close enough to get a good look at him. Even though he was wearing reflecting sunglasses, I could see the family resemblance. The Phenom had brought his father, who looked like a big and arrogant jerk in his own right.

"Okay, guys, circle up," Coach Collins called out with a big smile as the rest of my teammates ran up. "Over here. Come quickly. I have great news. *Outstanding news!*" I had never seen Coach Collins in this kind of mood before. He's a pretty low-key, even-tempered guy. He has sat patiently through a lot of soccer debacles that would have given other coaches white hair and high blood pressure. But now Coach Collins was grinning as if he had just discovered a gold mine in the middle of our soccer field. "Guys, we have a new teammate. Some of you may have met him already. This is Antonio Silva."

He said it like he expected applause, or maybe a thunderclap. Instead, there was an awkward little silence. My teammates were busy trying to figure out our coach's almost drunkenly happy mood, and they were also evaluating the presence of the guidance counselor and the athletic director at a soccer practice, to say nothing of the most popular girl in the school, or the blond man in the leather jacket who seemed to be posing for an unseen camera, as if he was starring in a movie that the rest of us didn't know was being shot.

I broke the silence. "Coach, he can't play with us."

The Phenom looked back at me. Coach Collins blinked and sounded like he might choke. "What? Why not?"

"League rules. Transfers aren't allowed in mid-season."

Athletic Director Hart wasted no time in correcting me. "Transfers aren't allowed in mid-season from one school *in America* to another," he agreed. "But Antonio has never been registered in an American school, so he's like a new student. I checked with the league office, and there's no problem."

"There you go!" Coach Collins said joyfully. "No problem! *Bingo!* Now, why don't we welcome our new teammate by running some drills. We'll go half field, offense against defense. Antonio, I hear you're a goal scorer, so why don't you start the drill at center forward. Norm, since the Mouse is out today, why don't you slide over to right wing."

In less than thirty seconds I was at my sweeper position, with Pat in front of me, Harlan on one side, and Hector on the other. It was just a practice drill, but at the same time it was a hell of a lot more than practice, at least for me. "They don't score," I growled to my defense. "No matter what we need to do, they don't score."

And they didn't. Not the first time we ran the drill, when the Phenom passed the ball to Zigzag Zigler at right wing, who zigged and zagged to the sideline and then gave the ball away like a Christmas present to Harlan James.

And not the second time, when the Phenom passed the ball to "Canoe Feet" Cavanaugh at left wing. Now, you don't get a nickname like Canoe Feet by being graceful. Sure enough, Cavanaugh couldn't make up his mind whether to try to dribble or to pass it back to the Phenom, so he ended up stopping short and tripping over his own remarkably large feet, and then falling flat on his face on the soccer ball, his mouth wide open, as if he planned to swallow the ball whole.

The Phenom watched this with a look of disbelief. I don't think he had ever seen this particular move on a soccer field before. I'm not sure in the whole proud soccer history of Brazil it had ever even been attempted.

"Okay, let's run it again," Coach Collins shouted, a little embarrassed that he was being exposed as the coach of a team of dorks. "Antonio, this time hold the ball if you need to." What Coach was really saying was that Antonio should forget about passing and try to dribble through our defense on his own. Coach Collins blew his whistle.

And that was when I learned something about life. It's not a very nice lesson to have to swallow, but it's a true one. Life can be just plain unfair. Desire can count for nothing. Training and conditioning can count for even less. And if you don't think what I'm saying is true, you've never gone up against a player the soccer gods have smiled on.

It happened like this. Antonio veered left, and Hector Martinez came out to tackle him. The Phenom head-faked left and then darted right, and in an instant he was by Hector and sprinting for the middle. This Phenom could move! No way Hector could catch him from behind.

Pat moved up to stop the dribble, and I knew Pat would at least take a piece out of the Phenom. The tough Irish defender went for a sliding tackle that was designed to get the ball and a little leg, too, but Antonio flipped the ball expertly into the air with his toe, and jumped right over the sliding Pat, like a hurdler. He came down light as a feather with the ball at his feet and Pat flat on his back behind him.

Antonio could have gone for the goal then, and I was ready for him. But instead he danced sideways, the ball sticking to his feet like it was glued to the toes of his soccer shoes. Harlan came roaring in from the left side, and he meant business. He was fast on his feet, a terrific athlete, and a very experienced defender. But just when it seemed that he had gotten directly in front of the Phenom, Antonio faked left, then right, then left again, in three lightning jukes. Harlan was fooled by the first fake, and confused by the second one, and so flummoxed by the third that his body seemed to get pulled in three different directions at once and he ended up falling on his butt, contorted like a Gumby toy, one leg sprawled awkwardly behind him, one sockless foot twisted up in front of him, literally faked out of his shoe.

Then the Phenom turned toward the goal, and headed right at me. Behind me, I could hear Charley the Fish hitting the panic button. "Stop him, Joe. *Get on him. Joe, don't wait!*" It would be nice to play with a brave, courageous goalie behind me, but instead I had Charley the Fish, one of the

biggest cowards ever to stand in front of a net. "HE'S GET-
TING TOO CLOSE, JOE! STOOOPPP HHIIIIMMMMM!"

Most strikers need to glance down at the ball as they
dribble and have a tough time fixing on the defender coming
out to stop them. The Phenom didn't watch the ball. He
treated it as a part of his body, a third foot that the soccer
gods had grafted on. So he watched me as I came out to stop
him, and I watched him. Just by the way he ran, I knew I
couldn't risk playing the ball. He was too quick, and he had
too many moves. I had to play his body, and if necessary
bring him down.

Then he was in front of me, about twenty-five yards
from the goal. He stopped on a dime, the ball between his
feet, so that he could go either way. I was in a classic defender's position right in front of him, knees bent, arms out
wide for balance, ready to anticipate him to either side, or to
dive in and take him down if he gave me the chance. He
didn't—he immediately went right. Or at least his whole
center of gravity shifted right, so that I stepped wide with
my left foot to stop him. But it was only a fake—a faster, better fake than I had ever seen before. He reversed direction in
the blink of an eye and went left, and I stuck my right foot
out to cut that direction off, too. And in the frozen heartbeat
when I had my legs splayed out to either side, he tapped the
ball right between them in a move called a nutmeg, which is
about the most embarrassing thing that can ever happen to a
defender.

The ball rolled between my legs. The Phenom flashed back right, and around me, and I dove at him with everything I had, ready to mash him to the grass, even if I had to grab him and throw him down with a wrestling move. But I was a microsecond late, his first step was so fast that I barely made any contact—not nearly enough to knock him off his feet—so I went sprawling face first, and tasted grass and turf, while the Phenom ran to the ball he had tapped between my legs, and faced Charley the Fish one-on-one.

Antonio shot from fifteen yards out, his right foot striking the ball with a startling *ka*-POW. The ball zoomed like a targeted missile into the right upper corner of the goal, ripped the netting from its nail on the back of the goal, and continued for another thirty yards before it finally rolled to a stop.

I got up slowly, first on my elbows, and then on my knees, not quite believing what had happened, and also not quite believing what I was hearing. It was applause. Coach Collins was clapping on the sideline, shouting to no one in particular, "Did you see that! *Man, did you see that!*" And Mr. Hart and Mrs. Simmons were also clapping. All around me, my own teammates were clapping! Even Pat and Harlan and Hector—my humiliated fellow defensemen—were clapping and patting Antonio on the back! And from the high bleacher where they were sitting, Kris and Jewel were on their feet, clapping, and I heard Kris yell out, "Way to go, Antonio!"

The rest of soccer practice was a miserable blur. It seemed

to flash by with me standing to one side, watching the Phenom show off. He could dribble the ball with just his right foot. With just his left foot. With just his forehead. He could make Zigler and Cavanaugh and Maniac Murray actually look half-decent by giving them great passes, and by getting so open that even they could pass the ball back to him. He could score at will.

Finally, mercifully, it was over. We circled up in midfield. "Thank you for coming out today," Coach Collins said to Antonio. "I don't know what to say, except that you've shown us how this game should be played. We hope you'll stay with our team. Everybody, let's give Antonio a big hand." And they gave him one more big hand. And then practice was over, and the team jogged off toward the locker room.

Kris climbed down off the bleachers and intercepted me on the sideline. "Hey, J, I told you your team would get much better."

"Yeah, well, thanks," was all I could manage.

She looked at me. "Want to walk home? I'll wait. Maybe we should talk."

"Another time," I mumbled. "Don't bother waiting. I gotta help the guys take down the nets."

12

"Talk to me, Mouseman," I said. "I've been here for half an hour and you haven't looked up from that computer."

The Mouse was in his super-large bedroom, hunched over on the very edge of a swivel chair, so that his face was a few inches from his computer's screen, and images from the game he was playing flashed across his cheeks and forehead. It was a violent, first-person shooter game, and each time he reached a new level he got to select a new weapon. He had gone from a submachine gun to a plasma gun to a grenade launcher, and now he was firing tank shells. When the shells "exploded" on-screen, blowing flashing targets to smithereens, his state-of-the-art surround-sound speakers rendered realistic KA-BLAMS that seemed to shake the room. "I'm almost to level five," he mumbled.

"Who cares. That's just a stupid game. My troubles are in the real world, Mouse."

"Last night I made it to level six." He was so intent on the game his eyes never seemed to blink. His right hand jerked the joystick back and forth to aim, while his fingers pressed different buttons to duck and fire.

"You've been playing this at night, too? When do you sleep?"

"I didn't last night. Wasn't tired."

"Not at all? That's not healthy. How many levels are there?"

The Mouse jerked the joystick, but too late. There was a particularly loud explosion. "AAAHHH," he screamed. "GOT ME!" He finally looked away from the screen and said almost angrily, "Couldn't you see I needed to concentrate?"

"Yeah, I could see that. But I've been pouring my guts out for half an hour and you haven't listened to anything I've been saying."

The Mouse turned away from the computer screen. "Sure I have," he said. "So, is he really that good, or did you just have an off day?"

"He's really that good," I admitted. "He's arrogant, and he's a jerk, and he brought his father to practice, but when it comes to playing soccer . . . I can't touch him. I don't think there's a high school player in the state who can. I've never seen anything like it. It's unbelievable."

"What's unbelievable is that Jewel Healy came to our practice," Mouse said.

"Yeah. With Kris. What do you make of that?"

"You should have asked Kris out long ago," the Mouse told me. "Didn't I always tell you that?"

"You never told me that." And he never had. Kris, Mouse, and I had done lots of things together over the years, from snowball fights to going to movies, so he had seen how close

Kris and I were. There had never been a need to discuss it directly. Until now. "So what do you think I should do?"

"There's nothing you can do," the Mouse said, and maybe it was sleeplessness, but there seemed to be a new note that rang sharply in his voice every now and then—an angry note, almost a mean note. "You blew it. He's great-looking and he's a soccer star and he's got the best car in the school. You lost your chance. You're history."

"Thanks," I said, getting up from my chair. "I'll be going now. I appreciate all the comfort and support."

"You wanted the truth, right?" the Mouse said. "Who said life is fair? It's not fair. It sucks. It's twisted. It kicks you in the balls. But you have to face facts."

"And your way of facing facts is to stay home from school and play this stupid video game all day and all night?" I asked.

"No," he said. "I just needed a time-out. I'm going to school tomorrow."

"So you're going to accept being marked? Good decision. It's just for five days and then it'll be over."

"I'm not going to accept anything," the Mouse snapped, and again I heard that sharp note in his voice.

"You mean you're going to go in and tell the Guidance Department and the principal about what happened on the golf course, and about being marked?"

"No, that would be suicidal. I'm not that dumb."

"So what are you going to do? There's no other choice."

"There's always a choice," the Mouse said. "I'm not going to bow to anyone. And no one's going to hurt me, either."

"How do you figure?"

"Because I'm not going to act like a victim anymore. See, I've been reading this stuff on the Internet, on self-defense and personal empowerment. And everyone agrees that victims make themselves victims. They act weak. And that's the way I was acting. That's why I got dunked in the lake. And all the other stuff that's been going on for years. But that's not going to happen anymore."

"But what if it does?"

"It won't. Because people will realize that I refuse to be a victim, and that if they pick on me there will be consequences they won't like. Don't ask me any more stupid questions." He swiveled around and clicked the game back onto his screen.

"Mouse, you're my best friend and I don't think you've thought this through—"

"Yeah, well, you can think whatever you want. And you can deal with your Kris problems however you want. I've made my decisions for myself. And now I'm going to get to level six, if I can have a little peace and quiet," the Mouse said, and the joystick was back in his right hand.

So I left him there, hunched over his computer screen,

and I headed down the long hill. The windy afternoon had given way to a drizzly, blustery evening. I didn't have an umbrella or a raincoat, and I didn't care.

I came down the hill and turned onto Main Street. Windshield wipers slapped back and forth on the passing cars, and their lights cut twin tunnels through the rainy darkness. I could still taste the soccer field from when I had gone down, face first, after being nutmegged. It was the kind of bad taste that might linger for weeks, or even months. I had replayed the moment in my mind a hundred times.

What could I have done differently? He was just a much better soccer player than I was. He was too quick for me. If I could get him on a wrestling mat, I could slow him down. I could put him in a cross-face and apply more and more pressure till he screamed for mercy. Maybe I should have forgotten about soccer and given him an elbow in the ribs. Or maybe I should have popped him in the nose. That's the best place to hit someone. I've seen dozens of fights, and I've been in more than a few myself over the years, and no matter who it is, no matter how fast or how tough or how mean, if you smash someone right in the nose, he goes down. And he doesn't get up. BANG, he bleeds, it's over.

I didn't realize I was throwing punches till a car honked and flashed its lights. I had been throwing imaginary lefts and rights at raindrops, trying to break the nose of a windstorm. I lowered my fists, feeling a little embarrassed, and went to see who had caught me acting like an idiot. It was a bright red foreign compact sports car that I knew I had seen before. But I see hundreds of cars down at the wash, and I can't always put a name or a face to a hood and a fender.

The driver-side window rolled down, and a very pretty blond woman smiled at me. "I thought it was you," Dianne Hutchings said. "Is the fight over?"

"Between rounds."

"Want a lift?" she asked. "I'm going your way."

"No thanks."

"It's warm and dry in here."

"I like it wet and cold."

"Please," she said.

So I got in. It smelled good in the car. Dianne Hutchings must have used some kind of shampoo or conditioner in her long blond hair that wasn't as strong or sweet as perfume but had a nice clean smell. Now that I was sitting next to her, I could see how pretty she was. How could someone with such beefy, brawny brothers look like her? And then she smiled at me, that peculiar smile on one side of her face, and I saw that she was a Hutchings after all.

"So," she said, "thanks for drying my car the other day. You work there a lot?"

"When my dad needs me."

"It's nice that you and he get to work together. My father runs an auto detailing business, and my brothers work for him sometimes. You probably know some of them—you guys must all be in school together."

"Yeah, sure," I said. "Jack is the same year as me. I know Ray—we wrestle on the same team. Lou is three years behind. And I know your cousin Slade, too."

"Poor Jack," she said. "It was terrible that he got his knee busted up."

"Yeah."

"I'm a nurse, and I got him in to see a specialist at our hospital. He may have to miss the whole rest of the season."

"Yeah, that's tough," I muttered. And then to change the subject, "Is that a good job, being a nurse?"

"I like it," she said. And then, mischievously, "So what's your father like?"

"Is that why you picked me up? To pump me for information?"

"That's exactly why," Dianne Hutchings said.

"He's how he seems," I told her. "What you see is what you get."

She drove in silence for a few seconds, thinking this over. We were nearing my block, and she seemed to be slowing down, as if she wanted the chance to talk more. Then she came right out with "What happened to your mother?"

"She took off when I was young," I told her, watching the raindrops bounce off the windshield.

"Took off where?"

"Europe. France."

"So she doesn't come back to visit every so often?"

"You don't have to worry about her," I said.

"I'm not worried about her."

"Good. Neither am I."

Dianne Hutchings slowed and then stopped. "Are you pissed off about something?" she asked.

"What makes you think that?"

"I really like your father a lot. I'd like to be friends with you."

Rain drummed on the top of the car. I looked back at her. "You really want some advice from me about my father?"

"Yes. He doesn't talk much about himself."

"Okay, here's some advice. Don't like him so much."

"Because? Come on. Because?"

"Because he hates women," I told her.

Dianne Hutchings looked back at me, and then unexpectedly laughed, and it was the kind of amused, fearless, devil-may-care laugh that was kind of hard not to like. "He sure doesn't act like he hates women," she said.

"I guess not."

"So it's because of your mom leaving? That's why he hates women? That's what you're saying?"

"That might be one good reason. I don't really want to talk about this anymore. You asked for advice. I gave you advice."

"Okay," she said. "Thanks for the warning." And she drove the rest of the way to my house in silence and pulled into my empty driveway. "Looks like your father isn't home yet."

"I can let you in."

So we ran through the rain, and onto the front porch, and I unlocked our door and let her in. I brought her a towel to dry off with. "I'm gonna go upstairs," I told her. "Make yourself at home. My dad will probably be here any minute."

"Okay, thanks," she said, drying her face. And then, in a soft, friendly voice, she said, "Joe, I'm sorry if I hit a raw nerve. I mean, that's really sad about your mom leaving. Sometimes I ask too many questions."

I already had one foot on the stairs. "You didn't hit a raw nerve."

"But I can understand about your father. It sounds like he got his heart broken. That's a good reason to have a lot of anger, even years later. Do you understand that?"

"No. Not really."

"That's because you've never had your heart broken," she said with a smile.

I looked back at her, and through the window behind where she was standing, I could see the lights of Kristine's house. "No doubt."

Her voice dropped a tiny bit. "I've been through something like that. So I can understand a little bit. But to keep anger for too long . . . is like a trap. I believe that people can break out of those traps. People can break patterns of bad behavior, if they try hard enough. Don't you think so?"

"I don't know," I told her. "My dad's patterns are pretty well fixed. For example, he comes to my wrestling matches and shouts himself hoarse, but he considers soccer a wimpy sport, so he's never come to even one of my soccer games, in all the years I've been playing. I've let him know that I would like it if he came, but he never has and he never will, and that's just the way he is. What you see is what you get. I gotta go upstairs now and do some homework."

"Maybe one day he'll surprise you and show up at a soccer game," Dianne said. "I know things can change for the better. Look at me and your dad going out. I mean, that's breaking a pattern. Given the history between our two families."

I was on the third step of the stairs, but I turned back. "What history?"

"Well, your father and mine were in school together. On the same football team. That was the year they won the state championship."

"Yeah, I knew that. I've seen pictures."

"They were the two toughest kids in the school. And they hated each other. Senior year they went out to the War Zone, and they had a fight that people still talk about."

"You mean a fistfight? The two of them?"

"I'm surprised your father never told you."

As if on cue, car headlights sailed up the street and turned into our driveway. My father was home. I heard a car door slam.

"Who won the fight?" I asked.

"I'm not sure anyone won," Dianne Hutchings said. "But I know they damn near killed each other."

13

Kris was waiting for me the next morning, sitting on the front steps of her house, looking across the street at mine. When I came out the front door with my bookbag over my shoulder, she stood up with a smile. I hadn't been expecting to see her there, but I managed to smile back, and I walked to meet her in the middle of the street.

"Hey, J," she said, her usual greeting.

I tried to banter casually. "Hey, K. Did you hack that frog apart without me?"

"Yeah, I shredded him," she said. "It wasn't pretty."

I noticed that Kris seemed to be dressed up more than usual. She was wearing a powder blue tube top and a matching blue cardigan, and little silver earrings. I believe I smelled perfume. This was the girl I had known for so long, yet she seemed completely different.

We started off toward school together. "So what did the police want?" Kris asked.

"They were looking into some fight on the golf course," I told her. "They wanted to know if I knew anything about it."

"Did you?"

"Nothing I wanted to talk about."

Kris got the message and didn't press further. We walked in silence, side by side, our feet rising and falling in unison. We had walked to school together, exactly this way, for more than ten years. Don't ask me why, but we always walked on the east side of the street. Don't ask me why, but we never stepped on the cracks in the sidewalk—we shortened or lengthened our strides to skip right over them. So on one level it felt very familiar to be walking next to Kris, matching step for step the way we always had, and on another level, everything felt different. We walked for two whole blocks without saying a word.

"So," she finally said.

"Yeah?"

"I guess we should talk. I mean, don't you think?"

"Sure," I said. "Let's talk."

"I hate having you mad at me, Joe."

"I'm not mad at you," I said.

"I thought you'd be grateful to get a good soccer player on your team. I mean, you care about that team so much. And you're so good. And the team was always so bad—"

"I don't want to talk about that." I cut her off.

"What do you want to talk about?"

I gathered my courage. "Friday night."

"What about Friday night?"

"There's a new movie opening at the Empress." I felt my heart thumping in my chest. "I thought maybe we could go."

Kris looked surprised and confused. She opened her

mouth to answer, and no words came out. She closed it and looked back at me. "Sure, it would be great to go to a movie," she finally said. "Friday's not good, but maybe Saturday, or the Sunday matinee. I can ask Anne to come, and maybe Ed will want to come, too—"

"No," I said. "I don't want to go with a crowd. I want to go with you. On Friday. Just the two of us."

She looked down at her feet. "Joe . . ." she began, and stopped. The way she couldn't look at me when she spoke my name told me more than anything she might have said. "Joe, I have plans for Friday night. I'm sorry."

"Plans with Antonio?"

We had stopped walking and stood beneath an old maple tree whose low-hanging branches we had climbed and swung on since we were six years old. Kris raised her eyes and looked at me. "Yes," she said. "We're going into the city, to a concert. He's already bought the tickets. I—"

"Kris, don't do it."

"Don't go to New York?"

The words came out low and hard. "He's no good, Kris."

"What are you talking about?"

"I don't know anything about a lot of things," I told her. "I don't know anything at all about girls, that's for sure. Sometimes I think I must be the dumbest guy in the whole world when it comes to that."

"No, Joe," she said, "you're not—"

I talked right through her. "But I can judge guys. I've played on enough teams and been captain and team leader, and had a lot of friends, and . . . I just know what makes guys tick." Her hazel eyes begged me not to go on, but I said it anyway. "He may be smooth and look great and have a fancy car and all the moves, but down deep he's a bastard."

Kris's beautiful eyes narrowed in sudden anger. "You think I like somebody 'cause he has a fancy car?" she snapped.

"Well, you seemed pretty eager to take a ride in it."

"Meaning what? Come on, meaning what? Say it."

"You think I don't know about going down to the Boat Basin?"

She slapped me. I had never been hit by a girl before. It feels very different from being hit by a guy. And then she started crying. It's a strange thing, that she should hit me, and then *she* should start crying. I didn't know what to do. "How dare you," she said. *"How dare you spy on me?"*

"I wasn't spying on you," I told her. "Look, Kris, stop crying. Some guy on the football team saw you guys down there . . ."

"Oh, great," she said. "Great."

"I probably shouldn't have mentioned it. I'm sorry . . . but . . . he's no good, Kris."

Tears were running down her cheeks and she didn't try to brush them away as she looked right back into my eyes and said, in a soft but strong voice, "Don't say anything else, Joe. Because . . . I think I'm in love with Antonio Silva. And I don't want to talk to you anymore." Then she ran away from me, crossing to the west side of the street, the side we never walked on. As if she still wasn't far enough away, she veered wildly up the driveway of some house we didn't know, and disappeared into some stranger's backyard.

Somehow I made it to school that morning. But I was in a daze, almost sleepwalking. My homeroom teacher said something to me and I nodded, but I had no idea what she'd said. The morning announcements played over the intercom, but I heard only bits and pieces—something about a Spanish Club meeting, and a few jumbled fragments about the volleyball team. My mind kept swinging back to my conversation with Kris, that had turned into a confrontation, and then a disaster.

I had meant to let her know how much I cared for her, and to ask her out on a date. Instead, I'd insulted her and she'd run away crying. And for the life of me, as I sat on that plastic chair in homeroom and waited for the first-period bell to ring, I couldn't figure out what had gone wrong. The one thing I was sure of was that I had managed to say exactly the wrong thing to her. And I didn't know if I could ever fix it.

The bell finally rang, and I was off that chair and out of that classroom in about two seconds. It felt better to be standing up, in the hall, moving around. I passed Ed the Mouse, and I have to admit, he was being pretty successful at not looking like a victim. I won't say he was swaggering down the hallway, but he looked relaxed and even happy to be back at school. He certainly didn't look like a marked man. "Hey, Brickhead, how goes it?"

I heard myself mumble in reply, "It goes."

"You okay?"

"Yeah, sure. Never better."

"Then why do you look like death warmed over?"

Two football players passed by, Jack Hutchings, limping, and Tony Jaws Borelli. Everyone in the hallway turned to watch Mouse, waiting for him to double-dip in humble repeat bows. But the Mouse stood straight and tall, as if he didn't even see them.

"Hey, little man, aren't you forgetting something?" Jack Hutchings said.

The Mouse turned to look right at Jack. He took a half step toward him, raised his right hand, and pointed a finger at him. This must have been something Ed the Mouse had read about on one of those empowerment sites on the Internet. He spoke very loudly and succinctly. "LEAVE—ME—ALONE." It wasn't a plea—it was more like an order.

Jack Hutchings looked a little surprised. I think he and Tony might have responded immediately and violently, except that it was a crowded hallway, and a teacher was headed our way, not to mention that I was standing there next to Ed. So Jack Hutchings smiled slightly and shrugged, and said in a low voice, "Okay, little man, you'll get yours." And then the two of them walked on down the corridor.

"Mouse," I said, "What are you doing? I can't protect you."

"No protection necessary," Ed responded, calm and cool as a plate of clam dip. "What just happened is called assertive confrontation. It's a defusive strategy—one of the key steps to avoiding being a victim." I don't know what nonsense Ed the Mouse had been reading on the Internet, but it was clear he had swallowed it hook, line, and sinker. "They got the message, that I won't be messed with. Now, what's wrong with you?" he asked.

"Nothing," I said. And then, because Ed kept looking at me, "I had a confrontation of my own. But I wasn't assertive. Or maybe I was. I don't know. I don't know anything. All I know is I'm my own victim, which is pretty damn stupid, huh?" I pivoted sideways and punched a locker so hard I dented the metal. The few kids still in the hall moved away from me. My hand throbbed. I opened it and closed it: nothing broken.

"Why don't you just bash your head into the wall?" Ed the Mouse asked. And then my best friend since third grade said, "C'mon, Joe, what happened? Who'd you have the run-in with?"

The warning bell rang, and I was grateful. I didn't want to talk about it. Twenty more seconds and we would be late. "Gotta go to class. See ya, Mouse. We'll talk later."

Biology is normally my favorite class, but I was dreading it that day as fifth period got closer and closer. I was dreading walking into Mr. Desoto's classroom and seeing Kris. What can you say to someone you love, who you made angry enough to slap you? I was pretty sure she wouldn't speak to me. I imagined us sitting side by side in stony silence, listening to a lecture about the mammalian circulatory system. I don't normally chicken out of confrontations, but I admit I thought of leaving school early—of escaping and just going on a long bike ride. But it turned out not to be necessary. After fourth period, the unexpected happened. School left me.

Fourth-period history class was just dragging to a close with Mr. Muldowney detailing the political repercussions of the Alien and Sedition acts when an unexpected crackling came over the school intercom, and the voice of Vice Principal Tobias sounded. "Hello, students and teachers. First, let me assure you that there is absolutely nothing wrong."

We sat there, listening, and even in my dazed state I realized that he wouldn't have said this unless something was very wrong.

"Fifth period and the rest of classes today are canceled. Repeat, there will be no more classes today. You should all remain in your fourth-period classrooms until someone from the front office comes to escort you to the auditorium. We will be summoning you by grade, starting with seniors. There will be absolutely no talking in the hallways. Teachers, please enforce this." A stern note of warning crept into his voice. "You will all be on your best behavior and do exactly what you are told." It took him a second to shift back from his harsh, disciplinarian voice to his warm and fuzzy voice. "Thank you for your cooperation, Lawndale students. See you soon."

We were one of the first classes to be summoned. Mrs. Eckes, her face looking even more flinty and severe than usual, came for us and led us to the front of the auditorium. As I sat there, and watched the vast hall fill up with the eight hundred students of our school, I tried to guess what had happened. There were at least five cops in the auditorium, and then I saw Deputy Police Chief Coyle walk in with Vice Principal Tobias. So I figured something had happened that morning that registered on the Red Flag warning system. At first I worried about Ed the Mouse, but then he came in with the rest of his fourth-period calculus class. So I gave up trying to figure it out and just waited silently, as row after row of seats were filled, and finally Vice Principal Tobias climbed onto the stage, his stomach jiggling with each step.

"Good morning," he said. He was such a big man that standing there in his pin-striped suit, with his great bald head shining in the light, he looked larger than life. Deputy

Police Chief Coyle stood on one side of him and a thin man sporting a bow tie, who I didn't recognize, stood on the other. "I'm going to keep this brief," Mr. Tobias began. "An incident occurred this morning that we don't have to go into right now." He glanced at the thin man in the bow tie, who seemed to nod in agreement. "Except to say it was an unfortunate, unpleasant incident . . . and one of a chain of such incidents involving students of this school that I intend to put a stop to here and now."

There was a complete, almost unnatural silence in the auditorium. No one was shifting around or coughing or whispering. Maybe it was the presence of the police, but everyone was paying respectful attention.

"Since Principal Landisman is away, I'm responsible for this school and all of you, and I'm not going to drag my feet. I would rather err on the side of being too safe than not do enough. So, starting right now, we're adopting a zero tolerance policy when it comes to violence and inciteful behavior at this school. There will be no more fighting. No more bullying. No more teasing. No more drinking or drugs. No more stealing. None of it. It will end *here and now.*" He repeated the three words again, looking out at us as if he were warning each one of us personally. "Here and now." He had started to sweat, and he wiped his enormous forehead with the back of his right hand. "If you're a troublemaker, and you're sitting there thinking that what I'm saying doesn't apply to you, I have some simple advice for you. Don't test me. Because you will be suspended or expelled from this school faster than you can say Lawndale or Bankside. Are there any questions?"

For a long moment, no one said anything. Then Patty Margolis, a senior cheerleader from an old Lawndale family, called out, "Yeah. What exactly happened this morning?"

"Maybe you didn't hear me the first time, but we are not going to go into that now," Tobias almost growled at her. He glanced at the thin man in the bow tie and seemed to read a message there that he should not end things on such a gruff note. So he forced himself to smile at us. It really was an awful, thin, uncomfortable smile—it seemed to slither onto his big sweating face and unfold itself reluctantly, like a snake emerging from a dark hole. "What you need to know is that this school will be safe. All trouble will end here and now." He rubbed his hands together nervously, and a bead of sweat slid off his forehead and ran down one side of his nose. "There's absolutely nothing to worry about," he assured us. "The situation is one hundred percent completely under control."

14

One problem with Vice Principal Tobias's decision not to go into specifics about what had happened at our school was that it opened the door to all kinds of speculation.

Rumors began flying even before the auditorium emptied out. Some said a threatening e-mail had been sent to the school. Others whispered about a fight between a student and a teacher. Some pointed out how many cops there had been in the auditorium and said that a large stash of drugs had been discovered in a locker. And then there was the story that I first heard as I walked home from school that Tuesday afternoon with a bunch of my soccer teammates—the one that turned out to be true.

It had nothing to do with Ed the Mouse, or friction between the soccer team and the football team, or anything else I would have predicted. Instead, it involved one of the least likely people imaginable. His name was Carson Feeble, and he was as wimpy as his name sounded. Think of a fifteen-year-old boy as skinny as a stickball bat, with a big mop of uncombed black hair that he tucked beneath a Mets cap. Maybe there were shyer kids at Lawndale High than Carson, but if so, they must have been hiding in their lockers.

The only reason I knew him was that I had taught a junior lifesaving class at the town pool the previous summer, and Carson's mother had made him sign up. He swallowed too much water during the first class and threw up in the pool. Throwing up in the pool is not a great way to make your fellow swimmers like you. Ditto for your teacher. Carson was so embarrassed at what had happened that he never came back for another lesson, which didn't seem to me to be such a bad decision. Certain people are not cut out to be lifeguards.

Carson was a nerd's nerd and spent most of his free time in our school's computer lab. "Computer lab" sounds impressive, but actually all we have is a dozen old computers that were donated four years ago by some rich guy in town. Ed the Mouse used to hang out there to play computer games, but his father bought him much better equipment, and now Ed never goes there, so I don't either.

There was a girl from Bankside who went to the computer lab once in a while to write papers. Her name was Tara and she was cute and popular. Whenever Tara had a problem with one of the computers, Carson would come over and help her.

I guess he got a big crush on her, and he started to bring her small, nerdy presents. Tara's boyfriend Mitch, a J.V. football team member, found out what was going on and thought it was hilarious. Until he thought about it some more, and then it pissed him off. He taunted Carson about it right in front of Tara, and during gym class he yanked Carson's shorts down to his ankles, and I even heard that one day after school he made Carson eat his own Mets cap, or at least chew on it while he stood over him laughing.

Tuesday morning, Carson snapped. He stole a gouge from shop class, and during gym class, when Mitch began shoving him around again, Carson pulled the tool from his shorts and tried to stab Mitch in the face with it. Mitch got a hand up to block it, but the gouge punctured his right hand. The guys I talked to who saw it all happen said the tool went right through Mitch's palm, and there was lots of blood.

Mitch started screaming and rolling around on the grass holding his hand. Mitch's buddies from Bankside went after Carson, who ran to the gym teacher and wrapped his arms around the teacher's legs, and then the police were called.

So that was what had happened, to push us over the edge into zero tolerance territory. I think it was foolish of Vice Principal Tobias not to just come out with all these details. As I've mentioned before, at our school news spreads like wildfire. Enough kids in the gym class saw the stabbing so that even though they were all sternly cautioned not to talk about it, there was no way to keep it quiet.

I first heard the story from Hector, from my soccer team, and then other information began to complete the picture. By Tuesday evening, as phone calls and e-mails circulated between friends, all the little details like the computer lab flirtation and Carson's past humiliations became known.

The next morning the Bergen *Record* ran a front-page story about a violent incident at Lawndale High, with details of the new zero tolerance policy. The article included an "un-substantiated account" of the stabbing from an "unnamed source," and a description of hundreds of worried parents calling the school's switchboard with questions. Apparently, the demand for more information was so great that a public town meeting had been scheduled for that Friday evening.

My father read the paper at breakfast, which for him is always a Pop-Tart and a cup of coffee. "Jesus, you guys are screw-ups," he said. Apparently he wasn't one of those worried parents who were burning out the switchboard. "In my day we knew how far we could push things."

My regular breakfast during a sports season is a cup of juice and a piece of fruit. I took a bite out of my Granny Smith apple and said, "Yeah, I heard you and Mr. Hutchings pushed things once upon a time."

My father looked over at me and grinned, which is what he does when he hears something he doesn't like. "Where'd you hear that from?"

"Your girlfriend."

"Dianne? She's not my girlfriend."

"She thinks she is."

"She can think whatever she wants. We're just having fun together. And she shouldn't be telling you such things."

"So it's not true?"

My father took a big bite of Pop-Tart. "Yeah, we had a fight."

"Why didn't you ever tell me?" I asked him.

" 'Cause I'm not that proud of it."

"I don't see why not. He didn't whup you, did he?"

"That's not it," my father responded slowly. He chewed for a while, and then swallowed. "Did you ever wonder why I never graduated from high school?"

"I figured you were a dumbass. Just kidding."

"That was why," he said.

"You got expelled for fighting?"

"We both did. Three months to go in our senior year."

"How did they find out? If you had the fight off school grounds . . . ?"

"It wasn't the kind of thing you could hush up," my father said. "And Kevin Hutchings and I both had lots of souvenirs we couldn't get rid of so easily." My father touched the tip of his crooked nose with his index finger. I had always wondered where he had broken it. Then he tugged on his left earlobe, and I could see where a tiny piece had been bitten off. I had always thought he just had a funny-looking ear. "Must have been quite a fight," I said.

"Like I said, I'm not proud of it. So are you going to this meeting on Friday night?"

"Maybe," I said. "Probably."

"Maybe I'll go, too."

"Don't you and Dianne have a date Friday?"

"No," he said. "I may be cooling things off with Dianne." He glanced down at the paper. "Friday night I'll be at that town meeting."

"Why?" I asked him.

"Because it's going to be a real barn burner." And then, as he turned the newspaper to the Sports Section, he added, "And, of course, I'm concerned about my son's safety."

"Right, of course," I said. "Or maybe it'll be a good place to pick up chicks."

"Maybe." He nodded, and took another bite of Pop-Tart.

"Guess it's about time to find a new one. I mean if you're cooling things off with Dianne."

"Any time is a good time," my father answered. " 'Bout time you found one, too, Joe."

If there was one thing I didn't want to do, it was talk to my father about girls, and girlfriends, and the lack thereof in my life. I drained my juice. "I'm looking," I told him. "Now I'd better head for school. See what else they've got in store for us, to keep us safe."

"By the time I was your age, I'd gone with lots of girls," my dad said.

I was already standing up, moving away from the table, getting my books together. "I bet you were quite the stud."

"It's no big deal," my dad said. "Getting chicks is pretty simple. Anytime you want me to explain it to you, let me know. I can tell you everything you need to know in about five minutes."

"Okay," I said, heading for the door. "I'll keep that in mind."

15

I never believed that Lawndale High School was haunted, but Wednesday morning, when we all returned to school, I felt an odd, almost eerie tingling, as if some kind of dark spell had been cast over our familiar halls and classrooms.

First, there was the metal detector that greeted us at the front door. It wasn't that big a deal, I guess—just two sensor bars that we had to walk between, single file, to enter our school. But it was a search, just as if they had made us strip off our clothes, or held us upside down and shaken us. We knew it was a search, and we also knew that the reason we were being searched was because someone had decided we were not trustworthy. We constituted a threat, to each other and to ourselves.

Then there were the cops. I guess one of them was assigned to our school on permanent patrol, and three or four others were there to help out with the metal detector and to make sure there were no disturbances on our first day back. One cop might be a safety measure, but five were a show of force. Seeing that many cops at our school didn't make me feel safer. It made me feel like our school had been invaded and occupied by a foreign army.

Lots of other small and large changes waited for us that morning. Metal grates were going up over our first-floor windows. Two new security cameras had already been installed in the main front hallways—more were soon to follow in other school gathering places. Homeroom was extended that Wednesday for fifteen minutes so that our teacher could explain the details of the new zero tolerance policy. She told us what objects we could no longer bring to school because they might be mistaken as weapons, what words we could no longer use because they might sound like threats, and what the penalties were for breaking the new rules. She also told us how many second chances we would get if we did break the rules—zero. Zero tolerance meant automatic suspension or expulsion.

It was strangely silent by the lockers, as kids got out their books and glanced up at the two new security cameras overhead. It was also quiet when we changed classes, even when the police weren't patrolling nearby. You could sense everyone looking around, taking the security measures in, digesting them, as we realized that something quite serious had changed in our school. And even for the students who had felt threatened or victimized in the past—and I know there were more than a few such kids—I think there must have been a sense of sadness. Nobody wants to see metal detectors and grates and bars in doors and windows of a school. It felt like we were losing something that we might never get back.

Something had changed between Kris and me also. No bars or grates had gone up between us, but we had also lost something that I doubted we would ever get back. We sat next to each other for all of fifth-period advanced biology without exchanging a single word. Several times I glanced at her, and thought of writing her a note or whispering something to break the ice, but each time she seemed to look away. So I just sat there and listened to Mr. Desoto's lecture on the difference between cold-blooded and warm-blooded organisms, and Kris and I stayed as still and silent as two lizards on a cold rock.

The summons came for me right after fifth period. This time it wasn't a summons from the front office but rather from Slade and the hard guys. I had been expecting it since Monday morning, so I wasn't surprised when a senior bodybuilding goon named Chris Coleman lumbered up to me as I left the bio lab and said, "Slade wants to talk to you."

"Where?" I asked.

"Subbasement bathroom."

"Fine."

Now, you might think I would have been afraid to go down there all alone, but I wasn't. For one thing, I didn't think Slade would try something violent on school grounds on the very first day of zero tolerance, when there were police all over the place. And for another, I've just never been scared of these kinds of confrontations. I've always found I can take care of myself, and the best way to face danger is to meet it head-on. So I headed right down to the subbasement to hear what he had to say.

The subbasement bathroom is off by itself in a dark corner of the least-used floor of the school. It's not really a floor at all—just a dark and narrow hallway that seems like an extension of the stairwell, with the school's boiler rooms and furnaces, and locked storage closets, and what looks like a windowless brick cave that the Photography Club has turned into a darkroom. There were no security cameras down there, and no police walking around. The light bulb nearest the bathroom had either burned out or been busted on purpose, so it was semidark and deserted. I opened the door.

Slade was inside, sitting on a sink. Half a dozen other hard guys were there, including Jack Hutchings and Tony Jaws Borelli. I let the door close behind me. "Hey," I said, "what's up?"

"What's up with you?" Slade asked. He was wearing a tight black T-shirt, and he looked bigger and wider than the swinging door to the one bathroom stall.

"Not much," I said, relaxed and easy, with a shrug. "You wanted to see me, right?"

"Right," he said. "You been talking to someone you shouldn't, Joe?"

"Like who?"

"The police have called me in twice," Slade said. "They

wanna know about Saturday night. Somebody gave them my name."

"They called me in, too," I told him. "Coyle and Tobias grilled me."

"How did they get your name?" Slade asked.

"I have no idea. They said somebody saw me running near the golf course. They wanted me to name names."

"And what did you tell them?" Jaws Borelli demanded.

"I told them I couldn't help them. What did you tell them?" I shot back.

"He didn't tell them nothing," Slade said, "but somebody sure did. They know I was there. They just can't prove it. And they know details about what happened. I don't like it."

"I don't like it either," I said. "I didn't like getting called in any more than you did."

"So what about your friend the Mouse," Jack Hutchings said.

"What about him?" I asked.

"Maybe he's the one who talked to the police."

"No," I said. "First, that's not his style. I know him from way back, and he would never do that. And, second, whoever gave your name gave my name. Mouse is my friend. He'd never get me in trouble."

There was silence in the little bathroom as they thought that over. I knew that what I'd said was true, and made perfect sense, but I also knew that they were pissed off, and anything could happen. Two of them had edged near the door, and if they decided to block it, no way I could fight my way out before the rest of them grabbed me. I stood there, nice and relaxed, hands away from my body, waiting for them to decide. And as I waited, it occurred to me how strange it was that this was happening on the same day that all the new security measures were clicking into place all over the school. Clearly things weren't as secure as Vice Principal Tobias and Deputy Police Chief Coyle wanted to believe. I wondered if they ever would be. I wondered if any school, anywhere, can be made completely secure.

"Clear out," Slade said, looking at me.

Without a word they all left. It was just him and me. He stood up from the sink and took a step toward me. I'm used to looking down at people, but he loomed about four inches above me. "You say you know your buddy, and it's not his style to go to the cops?" Slade asked.

"I guarantee it."

"But he's marked, and he's not paying respect."

"He does respect you," I said.

"Then why isn't he showing it? He knows what he has to do."

"It has nothing to do with not respecting you. He doesn't bow because . . . of pride," I said.

"Pride?" Slade repeated the word as if he was chewing on it and finding an unexpected taste. "That little pimple has pride?"

"Yes, he does," I said.

"He's cruising for a bruising. A real bad one. You'd better warn him."

"You already gave him the bruising," I said. "You guys dunked him in the lake. Nearly drowned him. That was the bruising for not showing respect. You already got him."

"It doesn't work that way."

"It could work that way if you say so," I pointed out. "This isn't the time to push things, with police all over and the whole school messed up. Just let it go, Slade. As a favor to me."

A grin flashed across his face, and then he unexpectedly took another step closer, and I thought to myself that if he threw a punch I should get down low as quickly as possible, and try to get inside and wrap up his legs. That's the best way to fight a boxer. Don't stay outside and punch with him, because he'll kill you at long range. Get inside and tie him up. But Slade didn't throw a punch. "You told me that new guy who hurt Jack wasn't on your soccer team," he said. "But he is. He's practicing with you guys."

"Coach wants him on the team. It's out of my control."

"So you were wrong?"

"About him, yes. But not about Mouse."

Slade studied me carefully, and I couldn't read his expression. He looked like he was trying to figure something out. "What do you weigh?" he asked.

"One eighty-five."

"I don't see no body fat."

"There's some," I assured him.

"I've seen you wrestle. And I can tell just by the way you're standing there, with no fear at all. It's the two of us, ain't it?"

"I don't know what you mean."

"Yes you do. Those guys out there"—and his eyes flicked to the door, behind which I knew half a dozen of the hard guys waited—"are pumped up with muscles, but you'd take them apart. In this school, it's you and me. Ain't that right?"

"That's right," I said.

"So? Which one of us? I'm just asking."

"You," I said. "I'm just a little guy who's too dumb to be scared."

Slade's grin flashed again. "You ain't that little," he said. "How come you never played football? You woulda been a natural. I hear your father was a warrior. We coulda definitely won the county with you. Maybe even the state."

"Never liked football," I told him. "I like soccer."

"Why?"

"It's a beautiful game."

"It's a pussy game," Slade said.

"Each to his own. I gotta get going. I'm already late."

"Go," he said. "I'm not keeping you."

So I turned toward the door, and even though I didn't see him, I sensed him step toward me from behind. He moved incredibly fast for a big man. I ducked away, but it was too late—his hands gripped me for a split second, and then his shove propelled me into the bathroom's metal door with a loud BAM. I spun off the contact, and whirled to face him, low in a wrestling stance, but Slade was just standing there grinning.

"Just playing around," he said. "When I'm serious, you'll know. Go. Get out of here."

16

"I think it's terrific," Ed the Mouse said, as we jogged to the soccer field. He nodded toward a police car that stood on a corner of the school parking lot. The big cop who had parked the cruiser there was patrolling the pathway between the school and the athletic fields, keeping watch as students walked home. "It's about time they stepped in. I feel safer already."

I didn't want to burst Ed's bubble, but I thought I'd better tell him what I had heard. "I hope you're right. But, listen, I talked to Slade this morning."

"You can talk to anyone you want," Ed the Mouse said, "but don't tell me about it." He put on a burst of speed.

I caught up with him in three long strides. "Listen, Mouse, you should hear this. Slade said—"

He cut me off. *"No I shouldn't.* I couldn't care less what he said."

"But he said I should warn you. You should at least hear—"

"NO, I SAID NO," Ed the Mouse blurted out really loud, really fast. "Don't try to make me a victim, Joe. I don't want to hear any of that stuff. Okay? *Okay?"*

"Suit yourself," I told him.

We ran on in silence. The soccer field came into view. A few of our teammates were already out there, dribbling balls. Coach Collins was there, too, in a brand-new blue sweatsuit, looking a lot more enthusiastic than usual. He had been Lawndale's soccer coach through many long and losing seasons, and I guess he was savoring the prospect of a true star joining our team. He was barking commands and encouragement even though practice hadn't even started yet.

And we had fans. Not just Kris and the perfect Jewel Healy. Jewel had brought Laura Weston and Jennifer Mackenzie, two friends of hers from her clique of "super-popular prettiest girls in the school." Even from a distance, I could see cardigans and scarves and a hat with fur trim. They had chosen a corner of the highest bleacher, and they sat up there as if they were conducting a private little fashion show, talking among themselves as the wind tugged at their cottony scarves and blew their feathery hair.

"What's with the beauty pageant?" I asked Mouse.

"Kris must have brought them," he said. "She's really different these days."

We reached the edge of the soccer field and headed for the knot of players in the center circle. "Different how?" I asked, and slowed down so that Mouse could answer before we reached our teammates.

Mouse began to walk, and we trudged across the freshly

mown grass side by side. I could tell he didn't want to hurt me. "Go ahead," I said. "Different how?"

"I guess it's no secret she and Antonio are an item," Mouse said. "She's not exactly trying to hide it."

"What do you mean?"

"I saw them holding hands in the hall the other day," Ed the Mouse said. "But here's what I don't get. Kris and I have lunch fourth period. She used to eat with her friend Anne, and sometimes with me and Zigler, or Rory. Or wherever there was an empty seat, Kris would just plop herself down. But she doesn't sit with us anymore. She and Antonio sit at the 'popular table' with Jewel and her posh pals and Andy Powell and his stuck-up suck-ups. They've got this table by the window, and they all sit there together like royalty. Kris doesn't even say hello to us anymore. She doesn't even wave. What gives?"

We neared the circle of soccer players. "I guess she's made some new friends," I muttered.

"Yeah, well, it's weird for someone to change that fast," Mouse said, and then he ran off to retrieve a stray ball.

For a fraction of a second I couldn't help glancing up. Ed the Mouse was right—Kris didn't wave, or even smile back. Nothing. Then I realized she was looking toward me, but not at me. She was looking over my head and beyond me, to where Antonio was loosening up in a corner of the field.

He was keeping the ball in the air with just his knees and his head, each touch a work of art. The ball never seemed in any danger of taking an awkward carom and hitting the ground. It took great skill to juggle a ball in the air like that, but he was also showing off.

Then I saw the cameraman, and Antonio's father. The Phenom's dad stood about twenty yards from his son, in his expensive leather jacket with a bright yellow scarf tucked into the neck. Next to him was a fat man who toted a big TV camera on his shoulder. As Antonio skillfully kept the ball in the air, the cameraman pivoted to follow his movements.

When we circled up to start stretching, the man with the TV camera walked onto the field and stood about ten feet from us. Now that he was closer I could see a decal on his camera—he was from a local cable news station. As we did warm-ups, our players kept glancing over at the guy, checking to see if they were being filmed. "Coach, could you ask that guy to stay off the field," I finally said.

"Don't worry about it, Joe," Coach Collins replied. "It'll be great publicity. Just put it out of your mind."

I wasn't sure why our soccer team needed publicity, but I tried to ignore the cameraman, and to lead the guys through warm-ups and calisthenics the way I always had. When I got to the final set of leg lifts, I shouted out, *"Last set, make it hurt. Six inches, to the death . . ."*

Coach interrupted me, with a nervous glance toward the TV cameraman, who had just walked back to the sideline. "Joe, you can't say that."

"What?"

" 'To the death.' You can't say anything like that any-more."

"But I always say it. Everyone knows what I mean . . ."

Coach Collins walked over and stood above me. "No mention of death. No mention of causing pain. The new policy is really clear. If you say it again, I'll have to report you. Don't put me in that position."

The guys were all looking at me. I wanted to argue, but I didn't know what to say. It was preposterous. I wasn't threatening to hurt anyone. They were just leg lifts, and Coach knew that as well as I did. I couldn't believe he was threatening to report me, in front of my team.

"Why don't you just do the run?" Coach Collins suggested. "We can talk about this later."

"Okay," I said. And then to the group: *"Everybody up. Three miles, to the road and back. Last four losers to make it back take down the nets after practice—"*

"No." Coach Collins cut me off again. "Students are not allowed to penalize or punish other students, or call them losers. That's hazing under the new policy, and it's strictly forbidden."

I looked back at him. "This is the way I've always run practice. We never had a problem."

"I didn't make these rules, but I have to enforce them," Coach Collins told me. "And so do you, as captain. Right?"

"Right," I repeated. I took a deep breath. *"Okay, every-*

body. We're going for a run, for fun. If you get tired, take a break. Slow down to a jog, or even walk if you need to. Don't worry if you lose, there's always another race tomorrow. Let's go."

A few guys laughed. Then, as we started running, guys began having a little fun at my expense. I had always tried to run a tight ship as captain, and push the team to their limits, and now the guys were testing me. "Hey, I'm feeling winded," Maniac Murray said. "I might need to walk. That okay, Brickman?"

"Do what you have to do," I told him.

He didn't walk, but he did slow down noticeably. A couple of the guys slowed down with him.

"Three miles seems a little long," Zigler pointed out. "What about two miles? Two miles feels like enough today."

"Run as far as you want," I said. "I'm going three."

Most of them turned back long before the road. I ran the full three miles, sprinting the final hundred yards as my lungs burned. But even though no one passed me, I wasn't the first one back. The guys who had run two miles had already finished up, and were kicking balls around as I sprinted up, gasping for breath.

Practice was miserable for me that day. I kept getting distracted by the cameraman, who roamed up and down the sideline following the Phenom. Antonio seemed to be making a personal highlight film as he shredded our defense time and again. When he sank a ball on a beautiful bicycle kick, all four girls on the high bleacher clapped.

Coach Collins finally blew his whistle three times, signaling that we were done for the day. "Great practice," he said. "Antonio, you were super. Monday we play Emerson. We have to beat them to make the play-offs. Well, we have to beat just about everybody to make the play-offs. The way you guys looked today, I think we're gonna give them a run for their money."

He had to be kidding. Emerson was one of the best teams in the county, and they had always beaten us by three or four goals. We weren't in their class—we weren't anywhere close. I figured Coach's new sweatsuit must be too tight and had cut off circulation to his brain or something. "Joe," he said, "hang out for a minute. We should talk."

My teammates headed back toward school to shower up. Coach Collins exchanged a few last words with the Phenom's dad and the TV cameraman, and then he walked over to me. "Listen," he said, "I didn't mean to embarrass you out there. I know you didn't mean anything bad during warm-ups. I myself think some of these new rules are a little . . . excessive . . ."

"I would never insult or punish or haze anybody on this team," I told him. "You know that."

"Sure I do. That's why you're the captain," he said. "Everybody respects you."

"Then why do I have to change the way I've always run practice? How can we have a team race without winners and losers?"

"Maybe we can't have any more team races," he said. "At least, not with penalties."

"Races make people run faster," I argued. "If they run faster in practice, they'll run faster in the game. Taking down the nets never hurt anybody. It's good for discipline . . . it makes everyone try harder."

"People are trying hard," Coach Collins said. Then he smiled, an unexpected, big, gaping, hopeful smile, like a man lost in the desert who sees rain clouds gathering. "Joe, great things are going to happen to this team. This could be the beginning of a success story for soccer at Lawndale. You should be proud—no one's worked harder for this team than you. I want you to think about something—an idea I had."

"What idea?" I didn't like the sound of this already.

"Antonio—he's really special," Coach Collins said. "I'd like to make him feel welcome here. And acknowledge that he's a unique talent. I want to give him a role on this team that befits his soccer experience and abilities. He has a lot to teach me as a soccer coach. And obviously he has a lot to teach you guys. So . . . what would you think about making him co-captain?"

"He's only come to a couple of practices," I pointed out in a low voice. "I've busted my butt for four years."

"Just think about it," Coach Collins said. "You guys would be great together. Lots of teams have two captains."

I squared my shoulders and looked Coach Collins right in the eye. "Not this one," I told him. "This team will only have one captain. The day he puts on a captain's armband is the day I take mine off." I turned and started away.

"It was just an idea, Joe," he called. "You should at least consider it. Where are you going?"

"To take down the nets," I shouted back at him. "Because no one else is gonna do it. Nobody lost the race, nobody stuck around after practice, and the nets have to come down. So let me do what I need to do, as long as I'm still the captain of this team."

I took down the nets myself, and rolled them up, and stuffed them into their sacks. Each net weighed forty pounds. I slung the two heavy sacks over my back and started toward the school, and I was so angry at Coach Collins for what he had just suggested that I barely even felt the weight.

Then I saw Kris. She was saying goodbye to her new girl-friends, and as they headed off in one direction, she walked across the field to intercept me. "Hey, J," she said, "you look like Santa Claus after his reindeer deserted him."

"I don't feel very merry," I muttered. "What's up?"

"I have to practice a piece in the band room, so I'll be there after you shower," she said. "Maybe we can hang out, and have a talk, and walk home together."

I couldn't stop myself from asking, "Wouldn't you rather drive home in a sports car?"

Kris looked back at me for a few seconds. "No," she finally said. "Today I feel like walking."

"Wouldn't it be more fun to hang out with your new friends?" I glanced at Jewel, Laura, and Jennifer as they gingerly picked their way across the grass in their expensive shoes, as if trying to avoid patches of quicksand.

"I kind of want to hang out with an old friend," Kris told me. "Even if he's in a lousy mood. That is, if he still wants to hang out with me."

17

As I showered and started dressing, I found myself moving more and more slowly. It's a strange thing—I hadn't been scared to meet Slade in the subbasement bathroom and risk getting beaten up, but I was afraid of this talk I was about to have with Kris. I must've spent ten minutes combing my hair and thinking of things I should and shouldn't say to her. Finally I couldn't delay any longer, so I walked out and headed for the band room.

The conductor's platform was pushed off to one side and the wooden band shell was empty, but the lights were on, and I could hear flute music coming from one of the practice rooms. I followed the music to the closed door, and knocked twice. Kris let me in, and the door swung shut behind her. We were alone in the small practice room. "I'm almost done," Kris said. "That must have been the longest shower in history."

"I was dirty," I told her, which sounded so stupid when I heard myself say it that I grinned, and followed it up quickly with the equally goofy "But now, as you can see, I'm clean."

"Yes, you do look cleaner," she said with a nod and a smile. "Do you mind waiting?"

"Go ahead and finish. I've got nothing to do."

The practice room held only one chair and one music stand, so I sat on the floor, with my back against a wall, and watched as Kris glanced from me to her sheet music, and slowly raised her flute to her lips.

I can't tell you how pretty she looked as she started to play. I sat there and watched her, and remembered why I had liked her so much for so long. And I could feel that as she played, Kris was aware of how close I was sitting to her in the tiny room, and of the intensity of my gaze. She didn't seem uncomfortable with it. In fact, I sensed that she was kind of enjoying it. A strange, charged energy bounced around the room. Her fingers moved expertly across the keys, her lips kissed the silver mouthpiece and let it go, only to kiss it again, and her hazel eyes flicked over the bars of music as if she was looking for hidden secrets.

As I watched her, and listened to the beautiful music she was making, I kept asking myself variations of the same question, over and over. How could I have let months and years slip by without telling her how I felt about her? We had had many good times as friends, but we should have been girlfriend and boyfriend long ago. How could something that was so clearly meant to be not happen?

Kris played a last few dazzling, silvery notes and was done. She lowered the flute and looked at me. "So, was that awful or what?"

"I've listened to more painful things," I told her. "Kris, I thought it sounded great."

"That shows what you know about music."

"I know what I like."

She began putting her flute in its case. I continued to sit there and watch her. The room was totally silent. She felt my gaze and glanced down at me. "What?"

"Nothing. Just . . . you look really beautiful when you play," I said in a low voice.

I had never paid Kris a compliment like that before. Our relationship had always been based on mutual teasing. She looked like she didn't know how to respond. "Thank you," she finally said, and blushed, which made her look even more beautiful.

"I'm sorry for what I said last time we talked," I told her. "It was rude of me, and none of my business, and I deserved the slap."

"It's okay, Joe," she said. "What you said hurt me, but I got over it."

"I would never hurt you, Kris. I felt so bad afterward. Truly."

She snapped the top of the flute case closed, but neither of us made a move to leave the little practice room. I guess we both realized we had found a good private spot, and that there were things we needed to hash out. "I know I hurt you, too, Joe," Kris said. "This is a really awkward situation. We should talk about it, and we need to be honest no matter how painful it is. You wanna go first?"

"Not really," I admitted.

She grinned. "Me neither," she said. "Maybe we need some small talk."

A few seconds of awkward silence ticked by. "What do you think of all the cops and metal detectors and cameras?" I asked her.

"It's spooky," she answered. "I don't think it's necessary. Our school's not so dangerous."

"That town meeting on Friday's gonna be a real zinger," I said. "I read in the paper that they're expecting a few hundred people. Are you gonna go?"

She hesitated, and then shook her head. "My parents are going. They'll fill me in."

Then I remembered. "Oh, yeah. You already have plans for Friday night."

"So much for small talk," Kris said. "Yes, I do have plans on Friday."

"Where is he taking you?"

"This famous Spanish guitarist is playing a concert in Manhattan," she said. "He rarely performs. I've wanted to hear him play for so long."

"So, going to hear him was your idea?"

"No," she said. "It was Antonio's idea. He's very into the music scene. Joe, do we have to talk about this?"

"See, that's what's wrong with me," I muttered. "I would never think about asking you to a concert by a Spanish guitarist in a million years. I guess I don't have that much culture. I just wouldn't think of it."

"Joe, don't do this to yourself . . ."

"And I know I'm not that good-looking, or even a soccer star . . ."

"Please, please, don't do this."

I'm not sure if I would have had the courage to go on if I hadn't just had the clash with Coach Collins. But I was still furious about what he had suggested, and somehow my anger at him made me brave enough to speak the truth to her: "But I have feelings for you, Kris, that have been growing for fifteen years."

"*Stop*," she said loudly, and tears brimmed in her eyes. But those tears made her eyes look even more tender than usual, and she was looking right back at me. She didn't pull away when I moved toward her. I reached up very gently to touch her hair. It sifted out of my fingers—as if too delicate to be held in a hand that had washed ten thousand cars. My fingers moved up farther, and I grazed her cheek. She trembled when I touched her, but she didn't pull away. Instead, she raised her own hand and put it over mine. Her touch was warm and soft, and suddenly we were looking deep into each other's eyes. I don't know whether she drew me to her, or whether it was my idea, but a second later we were kissing.

I can't be sure how long it lasted, but I do know it went on for a few seconds, and it wasn't just me doing the kissing.

And I know that that long kiss with Kris was the best and most honest thing I'd ever felt in my entire life.

Then she pushed me away. "No," she whispered.

Our faces were inches apart. "Why not?" I asked her. We were both breathing hard.

"Because . . ."

"That's not a very good reason."

"Because I have a boyfriend," she said.

"Who you've known for two weeks, and gone out with once or twice. Big deal."

"That's not the point," she said. She was retreating. I could feel her pulling back, drawing away from me, as she said, "Friday night, I'm going out with him again, and . . ."

"Yeah, fine," I said. "So Saturday night you can go out with me. And Sunday and Monday and Tuesday."

"No," she said more firmly. "No, Joe."

There were tears brimming in my own eyes now, and I don't cry very often. "K," I whispered, "we were meant to be a couple. You can't just erase all the time we've spent together. Tell me why not? You're gonna have to tell me—"

"Damn you." Kris didn't slap me with her hand again, but her voice was a slap, her words were a slap. *"You can't do this to me now. That's not what you wanted, Joe."*

"You're wrong. That's what I've always wanted."

"No you didn't. I waited and waited and there were a million chances, and if you had wanted it, it would have happened." She wiped tears away. "But you didn't. Not when we

were freshmen. Not when we were sophomores. Not even for our junior prom."

"You always said dances were silly."

"They are silly. So what? Didn't you think I wanted to go to my own junior prom? I dropped hints and waited for weeks for you to ask me. I even had a dress picked out. But you never asked me . . ."

"We went to a restaurant that night, with Anne and Ed and Rory, and we had a good time . . ."

"And I came home and cried. I wanted to go to the dance, Joe. I wanted so much to go with you."

"Why didn't you tell me?"

"I did," Kris said. "Maybe not directly, but a hundred times, in a hundred ways. I waited and waited. And you never asked . . . because you didn't want it."

I looked back at those hazel eyes and I said, softly, "I want it now, Kris."

"Now it's too late," she answered. "I still have feelings for you but it's like . . . I crossed a bridge. And I'm not gonna cross back."

I saw that she meant it, and I put my fist through the wall of the tiny practice room. I didn't even realize I was throwing the punch, and then WHAM, my knuckles exploded through plasterboard and foam core. The shock of the punch broke the tension between us.

"Joe, you just put your hand through the wall," Kris said.

"Yeah." I took a couple of breaths. "Sorry."

"You okay?"

I gingerly pulled my fist back through the hole it had made. There were three or four cuts, and a little blood on my knuckles. "Don't worry, I'll pay for whatever it costs to fix it."

"It's not a really big hole," Kris pointed out. "Maybe no one will even notice. And if they ask me, I'll say it was here when I started practicing. This might not be such a good time for you to admit to punching walls and destroying school property, Joe."

I saw what she meant. "Okay." I shrugged. "But if you get in any trouble, put the blame on me. I'll just tell them I heard something in the band room I didn't like much."

Kris stood up, and I stood up, too, clenching and un-clenching my hand. "So, are we still walking home together?" she asked.

"Up to you," I said.

"Go wash the blood off," she suggested. "I'll meet you at the side entrance in five minutes."

I went to the bathroom and ran icy-cold water over my hand. It throbbed, but the pain was kind of welcome. I splashed cold water on my face and tried to calm down.

Kris was waiting for me by the side entrance. We started home, walking in complete silence, but we didn't get very far. There was a bench beneath a willow tree that overlooked Overpeck Creek. When we passed it, Kris veered over to it and sat down, and I sat down next to her.

The sun was sinking behind the cattails of the marshes

on the far side of the creek, and a breeze rippled the smooth surface of the water. "So," I said, "what do we do, Kris? Where do we go from here?"

"Friends," she said hopefully.

"We can never be just friends."

"Of course we can," she said. "We've been friends for years."

"We can't go back. Not after today."

"That would be a shame," Kris said. "Old friends are the best friends."

"You're the one who's giving up your old friends," I told her.

She didn't like that. "What do you mean?"

"Anne. And Rory."

"They're still my friends."

"Ed says you never sit with them at lunch anymore. You always sit at the popular table."

Kris tried to control her anger. "Well, things change."

"Yeah, but you're changing awfully fast. Ed says you don't even wave hello to him anymore."

And then she stopped trying to control her anger. "Joe, Ed is a social zero."

I was shocked. "Nobody's a zero," I told her. "And he's been my best friend since third grade."

"*We're not in the third grade anymore*," Kris snapped. "Don't take this the wrong way, but when are you gonna grow up?"

I looked back at her. "Is hanging out at the popular table with a bunch of jerks in designer clothes growing up?"

Kris stood up off the bench, and I stood up also. "Your friends are the same friends you've had since third grade," she said. "Your hobbies—those stupid tropical fish, I'm sorry, Joe, but they were cute when you were ten. You're not even applying to college—"

"A lot of people don't go to college."

"So are you going to work in a car wash all your life?"

"My father's done that. He's not a bad man."

"No, he's not," Kris said. "I didn't mean that he was. But you could be so much more. You could do so much more. You've got to take chances. It's part of growing up." She paused for a second and looked at me, and the breeze blew her hair. "Just like asking someone out on a date, before she got involved with somebody else, would have meant taking a chance, and risking the old for the new. You should have taken that chance. Joe, you've got to grow up."

I was getting pretty tired of hearing her tell me that. "Thanks for the advice, Kris. I may not have my future mapped out too well, but at least I know who I am. Good luck with your new friends and your new clothes and your new boyfriend. I hope it all makes you happy. But somehow I don't think it will."

"I do," she said to my back as I walked away. "I've never been happier in my life."

18

They finished putting up security cameras in all the main hallways by Friday, just in time for the big meeting that night. The Mouse said the cameras made him feel safer, but they made me a little self-conscious. You couldn't pick your nose or scratch your butt or give some teammate a playful shove in the back without worrying that your actions were being recorded, and that an alarm would go off, and cops were going to thunder down the hall to arrest you.

There were rumors that there were other cameras, too, secret ones. Some said sensitive smoke alarms had been installed in the bathrooms in case anyone was dumb enough to try to sneak a cigarette. Others said microphones had been hidden in the locker rooms—always a source of threats and bad blood and violence in our school. I didn't believe those rumors, but I did feel I was being watched all the time, by police, by office workers who were patrolling the halls morning and afternoon, and by the security cameras.

Iron-mesh grates had been bolted to the outside of all first-floor windows, and several second-floor windows, too. One of my favorite views of Overpeck Creek, from the second-floor science room, was now crosshatched by iron mesh.

Soccer practice was weird that Friday. The local cable news network had run their spot on Antonio on Thursday night. The clip was thirty seconds long and showed him juggling a ball in the air, while a voice-over explained how an international youth star had joined the Lawndale team. More soccer lovers must have seen it than I would have guessed. We had several dozen people in the stands for our Friday practice. Half of them were adults I had never seen before—maybe they were soccer fans, or scouts from local teams, or journalists.

Our team reacted to the unexpected attention by playing better than usual. Antonio was so good that he made everyone on the offense look better. Time and again his crisp passes found open players and created space. Surprisingly, guys like Zigler and Canoe Feet Cavanaugh and Ed the Mouse started looking to make passes themselves, or at least tried to get the ball back to Antonio. Several times during practice our offense moved the ball all the way downfield, changing sides and making short, controlled one-touch passes that I wouldn't have believed possible from this collection of goofballs.

I guess I should have been appreciative. Coach Collins was right—I had worked harder for our team than anyone else. But I kept thinking that after the Phenom showered up, and blow-dried his hair, and dressed in one of his natty outfits, he would be taking Kris to New York to hear a Spanish guitarist. And I would be stuck in Lawndale, hanging out with Greg Maniac Murray, and Ed the Mouse, shooting pool at the rec center.

Some of Kris's words to me must have hit home. I have to admit, all during the pool game at the rec center, and later at Mario's Pizza, I was conscious of watching my buddies and listening to their boneheaded banter in a way I never had before—as if sizing up whether or not they were indeed social zeros. While I knew this was an awful way to think about old friends, it was as if Kris had planted a dangerous seed in my mind, and I couldn't stop it from taking root.

Ed the Mouse and Maniac Murray decided to find out who could eat a slice of pizza faster without using hands. They got down on their knees in front of our Formica table and practically licked their slices off the paper plates. Shirts got covered with cheese and tomato. Crusts slid into collars. Red pepper got into Maniac Murray's eyes, and he let out one of his patented howls and flushed it out by pouring a pitcher of ice water over his face. I thought about Kris and Antonio at some elegant Manhattan restaurant, dining by candlelight. When I blinked and looked around, it seemed like I was trapped in a Three Stooges movie.

As it got close to seven, we headed down to the high school for the big town meeting. Even before we reached the school, I could tell that the newspaper had been wrong— there would be a lot more than a few hundred people. The parking lot was already full, and police were directing cars to side-street parking, three and four blocks away.

Our town's entire police force must have been on duty that night. They weren't just helping with the parking and directing traffic, but were also on guard in the school, making sure that everyone walked through the metal detector at the front door. I could tell that it felt as strange to our parents as it felt to us. "I don't mind walking through one of these at an airport," I heard an elderly woman complain. "I understand the danger at an airport, so I'm happy to cooperate. But just to get into a school?"

The meeting had been moved from the auditorium to the gym to accommodate the overflow crowd. The gym bleachers hold a thousand people, and they were filling up rapidly. Mouse, Maniac, and I found seats in a middle bleacher, near a lot of other students. I saw kids from Lawndale and Bankside, hard guys and nerds, popular kids and loners. My father had been right—this was the big Friday night event of the year, and no one wanted to miss it.

At the front of the gym, our town's movers and shakers milled about, pressing flesh and smiling for news cameras. I spotted Mayor Garsons, and Police Chief Keller, and School Board President Hamilton. But even though these bigwigs wanted to be seen, apparently they didn't want to be heard at such a controversial meeting. When the lights dimmed and people started to quiet down, all of them quickly took seats.

Deputy Police Chief Coyle was seated up on the platform, near the microphone. Vice Principal Tobias was there, too, in a brand-new pin-striped suit. He had a pocket watch on a gold chain, and he kept pulling it out and looking at it, as if impatient for this big show he had produced to get under-way. Sitting between Tobias and Coyle was the thin man I had seen for the first time at the school assembly, sporting what looked like the same polka-dot bow tie. He kept glancing at a pad he had brought, as if cramming for a big test.

But when the moment came to open the night's proceed-ings, neither Tobias, nor Coyle, nor the bow-tied mystery man made a move. Instead, it was old Principal Landisman who limped slowly and unsteadily to the microphone, and tapped it with his finger. "TESTING, TESTING," he said. "CAN YOU HEAR ME? I don't think the darned thing's turned on."

There was some laughter, and people called out, "It's on, say something worth listening to," and "Get him out of there before he electrocutes himself."

Out of the corner of my eye I saw something small fly through the air near my head. I thought it might have dropped from the ceiling, but then I saw another tiny pellet fly by and hit Mouse in the back of the head. He turned, and I also pivoted. Tony Borelli, Jack Hutchings, and Chris Cole-man were sitting two bleachers behind us. They had a bag of popcorn, and they grinned at us. "What are you looking at, Mouseman?" Jack Hutchings asked.

"Cut it out," Mouse said back to him.

Meanwhile, someone got the message to old Landisman that he was coming through loud and clear, and he stopped thumping the microphone with his finger and looked out at us. He must have been more than seventy, and he didn't look in very good health. In fact, as he stood there, peering out at a thousand or so of us, on row upon row of bleachers, he looked very frail. He reached out and held the microphone stand, as if for support. The crowd quieted.

"Welcome, all of you," he said. "I won't be doing much talking tonight. I've been a little under the weather. In fact, I broke doctor's orders to come. But I wanted to be here. In my school. Talking to all of you, students, parents, members of the community. I know we're all here because we care. That's the way it's been for many years."

He cleared his throat, and it sounded like an old car trying to make it up a steep hill. "Many years," he repeated. "I started as a high school teacher more than fifty years ago. Do you know why I went into education? Heck, I knew I wasn't going to make a lot of money. But I believed that there was no higher profession on this earth than being an educator. I believed that girls and boys are fundamentally good at heart, and are curious, and soak up what they need to know like sponges. And I'm not just talking about book learning. I'm talking about good behavior, too. Fifty years."

Old Landisman broke off for a second. I thought he

might have forgotten what he wanted to say next, but then again, maybe he knew exactly what he was doing. Maybe he was speaking to us with his silence. He just stood there for ten or fifteen seconds, and the thousand people in the gym waited.

"Fifty years is a long time," he finally said. "Too long. I'll be stepping down as principal at the end of this term. Vice Principal Tobias is more than competent to run the school. The board may decide to bring in somebody from the outside. That's up to them. All I know is I'm tired . . . and a little confused. So I won't be talking much more tonight. These new changes . . . the security measures . . . this emergency . . . frankly, it's all beyond me. It's not what I understand about being an educator of good girls and boys."

His hand, holding the microphone rod, shook, and the mike rattled. "What has happened to change things in our peaceful community?" he asked. "What is this new danger, this fear . . . this violence . . . this . . . phenomenon?" The crowded gym was silent—his question hung in the air.

A faint squeaking came from two rows behind us. And I heard whispers: "Mouseman. Mouseface. Mousedick. Yeah, you, Mouseboy."

Next to me on the bleacher, Mouse tensed up but did not turn around. He was watching Landisman, as if waiting for an answer from the old man, and he didn't even flinch as another piece of popcorn hit the back of his head and lodged in his hair.

"I'm sure the vice principal will be able to answer your questions," old Landisman finally said, and for a moment he seemed to look right at us, right at Ed the Mouse, with a slightly sad, almost apologetic expression. "I know I can't. So I'm going to walk away now."

But the old man didn't walk away. He just stood there, and finally he smiled a tiny but wonderful little smile, and he said, "Forgive me, I was just remembering a scared twenty-three-year-old teacher, fresh out of college, who faced a class of high school students for the first time half a century ago, and let me tell you, were his knees knocking that day! He looked around at a bunch of teenagers who were looking back at him, and he thought to himself, 'Here you are, old boy, you'd better try to teach them something worthwhile, because they're good kids, with hearts of silver and gold, so give it your very best shot.' " Old Landisman took his hand away from the microphone rod, stood up straight and tall, and said, "It's been a real honor. Thank you all very much."

A chair had been set for the old principal on the stage, but he headed for the stairs instead, and descended into semidarkness. There was a strange silence in the gym, and then somebody started clapping, and in a minute applause rolled through the gym like a thunderstorm. Vice Principal Tobias walked to the microphone, but the clapping didn't end. So he stood there, a bit uneasily, clapping himself, and he waited. I saw him steal one quick glance at his pocket watch.

The applause slowly died, and the big man on the stage adjusted the microphone to his commanding height. "Good evening," he said. "I'm Stephen Tobias, the vice principal. Those were wise words from Principal Landisman, and I'm sure we're all very sorry to hear him announce his retirement." Tobias paused, and licked his lips, as if anxious to taste a meal he had waited a long time for. "I'm the one who set up these new policies and security measures, so I can speak to you about them. My purpose tonight is to tell you what we've done, why we've done it, and how it's working."

A tough-looking man near the front stood up and shouted, "HEY, BIG SHOT, WHAT'S WITH MAKING ME WALK THROUGH A METAL DETECTOR? WHY DON'T YOU TALK ABOUT THAT?"

There was nervous laughter at the show of disrespect.

"Sir, I fully intend to," Vice Principal Tobias replied with dignity. "Why don't you sit down and give me a chance."

The man sat down, and Tobias began detailing the new zero tolerance policy. Then he described some of the security measures that had been installed, from the cameras to the police patrols. There were more than I knew about. Windows and doors had been secured all around the school. Direct hot lines had been set up with the county police, and with a School Violence Rapid Response Team from the state police. There was a new School Evacuation Plan, and in addition to fire drills, we would soon have a School Emergency Evacuation Drill.

All during the recitation of safety measures, I kept hearing squeaks from behind me. Popcorn strafed us. The three hard guys behind us weren't just squeaking and calling names, they were whispering messages now, too: "You know what you have to do, Mouseman. You don't show respect, you know what's gonna happen. You're cruising for a bruising. It's your choice."

"So, that's the gist of our new security measures," Vice Principal Tobias finally finished. He glanced at Deputy Police Chief Coyle. "Anything I left out?"

Coyle looked like he might say something, but a tall woman from the audience beat him to it. "WHAT ABOUT EDUCATING OUR CHILDREN?" she shouted. "YOU HAVEN'T TALKED ABOUT THAT AT ALL."

Tobias smiled at her. "You're absolutely right. Principal Landisman reminded us of the joys and challenges of being an educator. I agree with him, and with you, ma'am, that's why we're here. To educate our kids. But we also have to make sure they're safe. That's our first priority. Nothing I've done goes against education. Everything is for the purpose of protection. In order to educate, we need to protect—"

"WHAT I WANT TO KNOW IS WHO ARE YOU PROTECTING THEM FROM?" a big woman in a blue dress rose to demand. I recognized her from the town pool. She was the mother and grandmother of a huge Lawndale family and was always shouting at some kid or grandkid to put on lotion, or stop fighting, or get out of the water.

"You tell him, Mary," a woman near her shouted.

Mary didn't look like she needed encouragement—she forged ahead. She had a voice like a foghorn: "WHERE'S THE THREAT?" she demanded. "WHO'S THE THREAT? IS IT THE TOWN? THE PARENTS? ARE YOU PROTECTING OUR KIDS FROM THEMSELVES AND THEIR OWN FRIENDS? I'VE SENT SIX KIDS THROUGH THIS SCHOOL, AND THEY TURNED OUT JUST FINE."

"I'm sure they did," Vice Principal Tobias told her. "You're just the kind of concerned parent who should appreciate what we're trying to do. There isn't one specific threat. These are general, preventative safety measures—"

She shouted him down. "YES, BUT DID YOU EVER STOP TO THINK WHAT MESSAGE YOU'RE SENDING KIDS, WITH ALL YOUR METAL DETECTORS AND BARS ON WINDOWS? YOU'RE TURNING THIS SCHOOL INTO A JAIL, A WAR ZONE. BE CAREFUL, IF YOU BUILD IT, IT MAY COME! AND YOU MAY BRING IT!" She sat down, to loud applause.

Vice Principal Tobias pulled out a handkerchief and dabbed at his forehead. "The suggestion, that I built this . . . that I'm creating this problem . . . is the opposite of the truth," he said. "I didn't find this problem . . . it found me. Deputy Chief Coyle, why don't you tell them about Red Flag."

So Coyle walked to the microphone and told the crowd about Red Flag, and how a sophisticated state-of-the-art prognosticating tool had determined that Lawndale was facing mounting teen violence, and was considered high-risk.

"HIGH RISK OF WHAT?" a bald man near the front demanded.

"We don't know what," Coyle admitted. "We're trying to take the proper precautions . . . so we don't find out."

"WHAT'S HAPPENED SO FAR?" the bald man shouted back. "WHY DON'T YOU TELL US ABOUT THIS MOUNTING VIOLENCE SO WE CAN JUDGE FOR OURSELVES HOW SERIOUS IT IS?"

"I wish I could," Coyle said. "But it's not in your best interest for me to do that."

People whistled and stamped on the bleachers and shouted that they could decide what was in their own best interest. The meeting was getting out of control.

A hand reached down from a bleacher behind us and flicked Ed on his earlobe. He jumped up, and whirled around, but the hand had been withdrawn. Ed the Mouse glared up at the three hard guys, who grinned back at him.

"Ed, maybe we should move," I suggested.

"No way," he said, sitting back down. "I'm not going anywhere."

Deputy Chief Coyle shrugged at all the jeers and foot stomping, and glanced toward the thin man with the bow tie, who got up and walked to the microphone.

Tobias introduced him. "Ladies and gentlemen, please let's be civil. This is Dr. LaFarge, an expert in the study of school violence and a professor of sociology at New York

University. Professor LaFarge is writing a book on how schools like ours can prevent violence, and he's been retained by our school system as a consultant. Professor . . ."

LaFarge looked a little nervous. "Yes, well," he said, "umm, yes, well." He glanced down at his pad, and blinked. "The question was posed why we don't detail the recent acts of violence. Chiefly, we want to prevent notoriety, which can lead to emulation and escalation."

"Speak English," somebody shouted, and there were hoots of laughter.

LaFarge shifted uncomfortably. I got the feeling this wasn't his usual type of audience. "Well, in plain English, then, there's such a thing as a copycat effect," he said. "If we publicize acts of violence, students may envy how other students became famous, and may decide that they want to become famous, too. And they may think they can become even more famous by doing something even worse. And that can lead us to some very bad places, where none of us want to go."

There was an uneasy silence.

The president of the School Board, Mr. Hamilton, stood up in the first row, and he didn't have to shout out—someone brought him a portable microphone. "Professor," he said, "I wonder if you could answer for us the question that our principal posed early on: why is this . . . phenomenon . . . appearing now? Why here, in our peaceful community?"

LaFarge rustled a few papers. "This is an area of some dispute," he said. "Many factors have been cited. They include the stresses of being an adolescent these days, violent media culture such as action movies and video games—"

"Yeah, but when I went to school there was a cold war and we were building bomb shelters," Board President Hamilton pointed out. "That was pretty stressful. And we had our share of violent games back then. But we didn't need a metal detector in front of our school, or bars on the windows."

"Yes, well, hmm," LaFarge muttered, and glanced back at his pad. He continued with his laundry list of possible causes: "Access to firearms and incendiaries, TV news coverage of graphic violence and acts of international terrorism, the Internet, lack of parental supervision—"

That was as far as he got. There were loud jeers and boos and hisses, and an enormous man in a faded T-shirt reared up near the front, and roared, "THAT'S ENOUGH, POINDEXTER. I DON'T KNOW WHERE YOU WENT TO HIGH SCHOOL, BUT YOU DON'T KNOW SQUAT ABOUT THIS SCHOOL. AND IF YOU BLAME US PARENTS, SOMEBODY'S LIKELY TO TIE YOU IN A KNOT, AND IT MIGHT BE ME." He half turned and smiled at the audience, as if silently enlisting our support.

I recognized the big man immediately—he looked about the size of a rhino, and the strange smile out of one side of his mouth was unmistakable. This was Kevin Hutchings, father of Jack and Dianne, and uncle of Slade.

"I'm sure you don't mean to publicly threaten a man who came here to help us," Vice Principal Tobias said. Deputy Police Chief Coyle stepped up right next to him, for support.

"ONE THING I DON'T NEED IS FOR YOU TO TELL ME HOW TO BEHAVE," Kevin Hutchings shouted back. His physical presence, and sense of menace, brought silence. He looked around at us all, and his rumbling voice seemed to carry to all corners of the big gym without effort. "I'LL TELL YOU WHAT THIS IS ALL ABOUT. ONE WORD. RESPECT. WE ALL KNOW WHAT HAPPENED AT THE SCHOOL—SOME BOY WAS BEING PICKED ON, AND INSTEAD OF FIGHTING BACK LIKE A MAN, HE GOT A SCREWDRIVER AND STABBED SOME OTHER KID. THAT WOULDN'T HAVE HAPPENED IN MY DAY. WE KEPT EACH OTHER IN LINE. WE TAUGHT PEOPLE HOW TO ACT."

"YOU NEVER TAUGHT ANYBODY ANYTHING." I thought I knew the voice, and then the man stood up near Kevin Hutchings, to challenge him, and I felt a wave of cold shock as I recognized my own father. "YOU COME TO OUR GYM, IN OUR TOWN, TO THREATEN OUR SCHOOL OFFICIALS, AND YOU TALK ABOUT RESPECT? WHY DON'T YOU SHOW SOME?"

"WHY DON'T YOU SHUT YOUR MOUTH AND GO WASH SOME CARS," Kevin Hutchings rumbled back ominously.

I know this may sound strange, but until that moment, I had never realized how big a man my father was. I knew he was tall, and had big arms, but now, as he squared his shoulders, and put his hands on his hips, he looked every bit as massive as the man who glared back at him. They were like two bull moose who had fought each other years ago as bucks, and now had wandered into the same forest glade, and were circling.

"I never let you tell me what to do, and I'm not about to start now," my father said. "Why don't you go back to Bankside."

Kevin Hutchings began moving toward my father, and he was no longer shouting, because it had become personal: "Why don't you find a wife your own age, so you can keep your hands off other people's daughters."

Meanwhile, somebody had picked up on what my father had said, and shouted, "YEAH, BANKSIDE'S THE PROBLEM. THEY ONLY CAUSE TROUBLE." More voices joined the chorus: "YOU'RE ALL THUGS!" "GO BACK TO BANKSIDE." "GO BUILD YOUR OWN SCHOOL."

Bankside parents rose to shout back, "YOU TAKE OUR TAX DOLLARS." "IT'S OUR SCHOOL, TOO." "WHY DON'T YOU TRY TO GET US OUT OF HERE?"

There were screams, and a punch was thrown, and suddenly pandemonium broke out. I heard Vice Principal Tobias at the front, begging: "EVERYONE, PLEASE, SIT DOWN, PLEASE . . ." And I saw Deputy Police Chief Coyle give a signal to some of his men, who blew whistles, and began to make their way up the bleachers.

187

A sneaker whizzed down and hit Ed the Mouse in the back of the head.

"Let's get out of here," I said, and tried to pull him away.

But he picked up the sneaker, turned, and whipped it back blindly, but at high speed. As luck would have it, the sneaker hit Tony Jaws Borelli right in the nose.

Jaws went for Mouse, but chaos had erupted, and a half-dozen people got in between us. I managed to get Mouse safely down from the bleachers, and find our way to a side exit.

I looked back once and saw at least a dozen men fighting near the platform at the front of the gym, while police blew whistles and tried to break them up. I spotted Vice Principal Tobias trying to crawl underneath the stage platform, looking for a safe spot to hide. The last thing I saw was old Principal Landisman standing on a chair, waving his thin arms back and forth, and shouting, *"Stop it, stop it, all of you, this is our school, our community."* And then someone bumped into his chair, and the old man tottered, and fell to the gym floor.

19

Our school was a mixed-up, nutty, out-of-whack, off-kilter, discombobulated place on Monday morning.

The near riot in the gym had gotten a lot of press coverage over the weekend. Some kids decided to stay home for a few days, till things cooled down. Others had to endure the unheard-of embarrassment of their parents walking them to school. Some of these concerned parents paused to exchange strong opinions with Vice Principal Tobias, who was standing outside the front door with an expression that was more wary than welcoming. I watched some parents shake his hand, and others shake fists at him.

When all the students were safely inside the school, and all the nervous parents had departed, there was an attempt to return things to a normal state. The riot in the gym wasn't referred to in the morning announcements. Our homeroom teachers didn't mention it. Clearly, a decision had been made that our school day should be business as usual.

But that was impossible. Guys were bragging about whose father punched out whose father, and whose mother got arrested for kicking a cop. Dozens of Lawndale kids—including ones I wasn't even friends with—came up and congratulated me on my dad's standing up to Kevin Hutchings, as if I had done something brave or noteworthy. The surging crowd had kept the two big men apart, but I got the feeling everyone wished my father and Kevin Hutchings had had a chance to duke it out.

I could feel the anger and watchfulness between Lawndale and Bankside kids bubbling over in every class, and seething near the boiling point in the corridors. No one did anything violent because of all the cameras and police. Three uniformed cops with pistols in their holsters and billy clubs in their belts patrolled our school's halls, looking a little self-conscious as they whispered into headsets, and tried to avoid knocking into open locker doors, or getting tangled up with hurrying students. Everyone at our school—teachers, students, and even the cops themselves—seemed angry, upset, and uncomfortable. Nothing made sense.

That feeling of things not being normal—of the familiar having been thrown wildly off balance—continued after school, as our soccer team prepared to take on Emerson. Half an hour before game time, as I led our team through stretching, I glanced at the stands and saw fifty people already seated.

It didn't make sense to me that soccer had become a big spectator sport at Lawndale—but then nothing made much sense anymore. The two cops who took up positions in front of our bleachers didn't make sense. Vice Principal Tobias trudging across the field in a suit to watch the first soccer game he had ever attended didn't make much sense. Though I was no longer surprised to see Kris and Jewel Healy show up, I was surprised to see a dozen of the most popular and beautiful trendsetters of our school. Lawndale High soccer had suddenly become the hot ticket in town.

The Emerson team arrived in their bus, ready to crush us, as they always did. We had twenty players on our squad, but Emerson had forty, and they were big guys—some of the best athletes in their school. They bounded off their bus, and began walking across the parking lot. You could tell from their relaxed, smiling faces that they were ready for a romp, a walkover, a couple of rounds with a punching bag. The last time we played, they had pounded us six to nothing. And then they slowed and started glancing around, noticing the noise volume, and the number of fans in our bleachers. I think they were wondering if they were headed for the wrong field. Because there were two hundred people in our stands, and a TV camera crew was filming their entrance.

I was standing next to Coach Collins, who was so excited he was hopping from one foot to the other. "That's Channel Five!" he said. "And that's a reporter from the Bergen *Record*! They might want to interview you after the game, Joe."

"Why me?"

"You're the captain," he said, as if that explained it. "How's the team? Are the guys ready?"

"Ready as they'll ever be."

"It won't be six to nothing today," Coach Collins muttered. We watched the forty Emerson players troop onto our field. "Look how smug they are. They'll never know what hit them."

"Don't be too disappointed if things don't work out," I cautioned him.

Coach looked at me. "You don't think we can beat them?"

"One player doesn't change a team."

He thought about what I said, and for a moment his shoulders sagged as if a heavy weight had just been lowered onto them. Then he shrugged it off and smiled. "Just play hard defense," he told me. "Give us a chance. Give our secret weapon a chance. Uh—'scuse me, I've got to go do a quick interview before the game."

I wasn't sure if the Emerson guys had seen the news spot on Antonio and knew what all the fuss was about. Then I decided they must have seen it, because as we took the field, several of their guys talked trash to him. "Hey, superstar," their center half, a big, mean-looking guy with tattoos on both his arms, said to Antonio, "you're hot stuff, huh? I'm gonna cool you off, man."

Antonio didn't say anything back. But, as I told you early on, the Phenom had this quality. There was something about the way he walked onto a soccer field that spoke volumes. The Emerson center half saw it, too. He kept talking trash, but I could tell he was a little spooked.

The ref blew his whistle to start the game. Emerson's forward touched the ball back to the center half. Antonio was on him in a flash, and when the big guy held the ball a split second too long, looking for the right pass to start the attack, Antonio stripped the ball away, and started a solo run.

He didn't mess with passes or fancy dribbling—he just streaked straight for the Emerson goal, and his speed caught their defense by surprise. He made the transition from midfield to deep penetration in five lightning strides, and as he neared their fullback line he kicked himself a twenty-yard through ball—a perfectly placed pass to himself, if he could catch up with it. He burst between their left back and their sweeper to chase the ball down.

Then it was just a contest of acceleration and a test of speed, a pure footrace between their two defenders and Antonio. He started out even with them, but by the time he reached the ball he was four steps in front. He let loose a bazooka blast of a shot from thirty yards out. The ball SMACKED the right upper corner of the crossbar, and bounced down and into the net.

One to nothing, Lawndale. I don't think ten seconds had ticked off the clock.

There was a stunned silence, then applause that swelled louder and louder, till it became wild cheering. I glanced at our sideline and saw Kris standing on a high bleacher, clapping and shouting, "*Way to go, Antonio!*"

The Emerson goalie dove for the ball, and landed hard.

He got up slowly, retrieved the ball from the back of the net, and whipped it disgustedly at one of his own fullbacks, yelling, *"Come on, Jack! You let him make an idiot out of you! If he tries that again, rip his legs off!"*

Well, they tried to stop him, and when that didn't work, they tried to knock him down, and once or twice they even tried to rip his legs off. I thought that Antonio had been showing off at our team practices. But midway through the Emerson game, I realized that he had, in fact, been holding back. Now he let it all hang out.

Emerson was a proud team, and they fought hard. But Antonio scored four beautiful goals that day, and our defense was rock-solid. It helps a defense to have an offense that can hold the ball, and score goals. When the ref finally blew his whistle, Zigler and Murray and Cavanaugh lifted Antonio on their shoulders and the team paraded back and forth in front of our bleachers, while our fans cheered.

I couldn't enjoy the hoopla. I was proud we had beaten Emerson, and that we still had a chance of making the county tournament, but these cheers, which I had waited so long to hear, only made me angry and jealous. I knew who they were for, and I knew he deserved them. I managed to congratulate Antonio and even shake his hand. "Thank you, Joseph," he responded. "See, today we played soccer. Isn't it more fun this way?" Then I watched him walk over and sling an arm around Kris's shoulder, and when she turned to see who it was, he kissed her on the lips. She blushed, but she didn't pull away.

Coach made me do an interview. "How does it feel to be the team captain of a losing team," the reporter asked me, "and then to get a star player and start winning overnight?"

"It feels . . . different," I managed to get out.

"So you guys feel really lucky, huh?" he pressed. "Like you hit the lottery?"

"Yeah," I muttered. "Excuse me."

I wandered off by myself for a while, and ended up sitting on the bench that Kris and I had had our final fight on, by the waters of Overpeck Creek. I told myself that I should go hang out with the guys, but I couldn't get up off that bench. A beautiful purple sunset unfurled across the sky above the creek, and a whole flock of gulls wheeled in from the marshes, swooping through the purple haze, hunting fish for their dinner. I listened to them screech, and watched them dive, and tried without any success to sort out my mixed-up feelings. A month ago, this victory would have meant the world to me, and now I felt like I was the one who had lost.

The gulls finally flew off in search of a better fishing spot, and I got up and headed in. I didn't know exactly how much time had passed, but I figured the guys would have showered and gone off to celebrate. I entered the school through a side exit, and sure enough, the basement hallway was empty.

As I passed one of the football team's big storage closets, I heard a most peculiar sound. It was a scream with no clear words—an anguished cry that was as close to the ghostly wail of a lost and tormented soul as I had ever heard. "*Yyyaaa-woooo.*"

The muffled wail faded to silence. I stopped and waited, a deep chill of fear prickling the back of my neck. Then I heard it again: "*Wooo . . . heee . . . helllllpppppp!*" And I heard a faint thumping sound, as if someone was kicking inside the supply closet.

I tried to open the steel door, but it was locked. So I ran off to the football training room, to see if anyone was still around. Mr. Murphy, one of the assistant football coaches, was all alone in the training room, adjusting shoulder pads. I told him what I'd heard, and he got a ring of keys, and we ran back out into the empty hallway.

"You sure about this?" he asked me.

"Someone's in there," I told him. "And they wanna get out."

We reached the storage closet. All was silent. Mr. Murphy looked at me. "This some kind of a joke, Joe?"

And then he heard it, too—first the pounding, and then a muffled, ghostly voice: "*Woo . . . hee . . . heelllpppp!*"

"Jesus Christ," he said, and fumbled with the keys. He must have tried a dozen of them before he finally found the one that fit. He yanked open the door, and we stepped into the dark supply closet.

It was a cavernous space, filled with helmets and pads

and old cartons. At first I couldn't see anything except shadowy mounds of equipment. Mr. Murphy found a light switch and flicked on an overhead bulb. Ten feet away, between two cartons, something moved.

I ran over and tugged away a carton, and then I pulled back for a second in fear and surprise. Because I hadn't uncovered a person, even though it was a human shape. There was no face or arms or legs. Rather, I saw a faceless head, an armless torso, and two thrashing bound-together legs, all trussed up like an Egyptian mummy.

Mr. Murphy saw me react and hurried over. I recovered from my shock, and the two of us reached down and hauled the mummy up. I realized that it was indeed a living person, wrapped from head to foot in yards and yards of athletic tape, his arms taped to his sides. Space had been left around his nose for him to breathe, and he had managed to bite through the tape over his mouth, so he could scream a bit. Somehow he had freed his legs enough to kick.

We unwrapped him, starting with the very top of his head. As soon as I saw his hair, I knew who it was, and I got a sick feeling in the pit of my stomach. And then I started to get angry. We kept unwrapping, and soon the Mouse's eyes gleamed back at me, filled with fear. Then we got the tape off his mouth, so he could breathe easier, and speak clearly. He was hyperventilating. *"Oh God, oh God, oh my God."*

"Easy, Mouse," I said. "You're okay now. Just take it easy and breathe. Who did this to you?"

197

"Do you need a doctor?" Mr. Murphy cut in, continuing the unwrapping. "Are you hurt? Is anything broken?"

Mouse spread his newly freed arms. "I don't think so."

We unwrapped his legs, and soon he was totally unmummified. He sat there, on a carton, buck naked, his arms wrapped around his body, shivering even though it wasn't at all cold. I found his soccer shorts in a corner and brought them to him, and he put them on. And Mr. Murphy found an old blanket and draped it over his shoulders. Just covering himself up seemed to make Mouse feel a little better.

"What happened?" I asked.

"I . . . I was with the team . . . celebrating . . . and I went out to get a drink of water . . ." Mouse gasped. "They came up from behind . . . put a bag over my head . . . told me not to scream. And they dragged me in here."

"Who did it?" I asked, ready to go get some revenge.

"Tony Borelli. Jack Hutchings. Chris Coleman. And some of their hard guy friends. Call the police."

"Sure, that's what we should do," Mr. Murphy said, and he stood up. "But, and don't take this the wrong way—but how do you know who did this to you if they put something over your head?"

Mouse looked at him. "I recognized their voices."

"All three of them? How do you know they had other friends with them?"

"I heard lots of footsteps," Mouse responded, and then

he exploded: "WHY ARE YOU ASKING ME QUESTIONS?" His squeaky voice cracked. There were red blotches on his skin where the tape had been tight, but otherwise he didn't appear seriously injured. "WHY DON'T YOU JUST CALL THE POLICE?"

"Oh, I will, I promise," Mr. Murphy said soothingly, but he didn't seem to be in a hurry to call anyone. He walked over to the propped-open closet door, gently shut it, and then came back and sat down next to us. "But first I want you to think about something very seriously. Give me thirty seconds, son. That's all I ask."

Mouse looked back at him. Mr. Murphy was in his sixties. He'd been an assistant line coach for the football team for three decades. He was a big, balding man with the physique of a water tower and a potbelly that sagged out over his belt. He helped run the school's audiovisual services, but there was no question that the football team was his real love. "See, with the new policy at this school, if you accuse people, they're gonna be expelled—"

"They should be," Mouse snapped back.

"Yeah, but here's my point. If they're expelled, there goes the football season. We're gonna be in the county championships this year, so you'll be punishing the whole team."

"Great. Punish them. Call the police," Mouse insisted.

"Just hear me out, son," Mr. Murphy said in a low, cool voice. "Once I do call the police, then we're going down that road, and there's no turning back, so this is your chance to stop and think. Even if you're right about who did this to you, can you prove it? You didn't even see them, you just heard them. Probably they'll have some friends who can provide an alibi. It will come down to your word against all of theirs. So all I'm saying is you do have a choice."

"What choice?" Mouse demanded suspiciously.

"Let me deal with this," Mr. Murphy said. "I will make sure the guys responsible are found and punished. But you won't be punishing the rest of the team. And you won't be going public with your accusations, which could do you harm."

Mr. Murphy had an arm around Ed the Mouse now, and he was rubbing Ed's shoulder, as if to restore circulation. His whisper was fast and persuasive and almost hypnotic. "Because, remember, son, you have to walk back into this school tomorrow morning. And the morning after that, too. Something like this can get out of control. You accuse somebody with a lot of friends, and you never get away from that. It follows you. And eventually it catches up to you. So mad as you are now, you gotta be sensible. Better to let me deal with this, and we'll all come out ahead."

Ed glanced at me. "Your call, Mouse," I told him. "You want the police, I'll call 'em for you right now. If somebody did this to me, I'd sure want to get back at them."

"You will be getting them back," Mr. Murphy assured

him. "I will deal with them with a heavy hand. I'll make them regret the day they were born. Joe's right, it is your call, son. Listen, I know your pride has taken a knock—"

"My pride?" Mouse looked back at the big football coach, who was still rubbing his neck and shoulders, searching for something in Mr. Murphy's eyes that he did not find. He tried to speak, but his high-pitched voice cracked again, and then the cracks widened into a ravine of anger and fear and humiliation, and I saw tears brim in my friend's eyes and start running down his cheeks. "They kidnapped me . . . They dragged me back here . . . They held me down . . . stripped me . . . I couldn't even breathe . . . I could have died . . ."

Mr. Murphy ran a hand through Mouse's hair. His voice was a friendly, wise whisper. "You gotta let that go, son. I'm gonna tell you something I never told anybody. Years ago, when I was in the Navy, there was an initiation. Bunch of guys dragged me out of my bunk. Branded me with a coat hanger, right on the butt. I screamed bloody murder. I was going to report them all. But someone talked to me the way I'm talking to you. I didn't report them. Best decision of my life, son. Some of them became my friends. I've still got the little brand mark, but I've gotten kind of fond of it over the years. It was just a prank that went a little too far. They weren't bad guys deep down. No need to ruin a whole bunch of lives over something that's already happened. Can't put the spilled milk back in the bottle, can you? Can you?"

Mouse looked back at him, hesitated for about ten seconds, and then shivered, and said so softly I could barely hear him, "No, I guess you can't."

"There you go," Mr. Murphy said. "Now, let's get you a shirt. I'm proud of you, son. I'm proud of both of you."

20

Maybe Tuesday was a slow news day. Maybe all the world leaders were on vacation at the same time, and there were temporary cease-fires in every far-flung battle zone, and no meteorites were discovered streaking toward the earth. Because on Tuesday morning, when I came down to breakfast, my father lowered his Pop-Tart and shoved the front section of the Bergen *Record* in my direction. "Hey, Captain Joe, you made the big time. You're even quoted. Check it out."

We were that rare local sports story that spills onto the front page. There was even a picture of Antonio scoring his third goal. The headline read: SOCCER PHENOM FROM BRAZIL LIGHTS UP LOCAL SOCCER FIELD. I could tell that the reporter who wrote the story was used to covering other sports. He got a lot of the soccer details wrong, but what he lacked in soccer knowledge, he made up for in hype: "The heretofore hapless Lawndale Braves, one of the perennial also-rans in Bergen soccer, have become a powerhouse overnight," the article began. "Antonio Silva, a Brazilian striker, has transferred to the school and instantly becomes one of the best players ever to grace a New Jersey school yard soccer field. He was dazzling in his debut game yesterday, scoring four phenomenal goals as Lawndale won for the first time ever against league-leading Emerson. 'We hit the lottery,' Lawndale captain Joe Brickman said gratefully.'"

I handed the paper back to my father. "The story goes on in the Sports Section," he said. "And there are more pictures. Don't you even want to see?"

"Not really," I told him. "I was there."

"But it's about your team. First time I can remember anyone saying anything good about you guys."

"True enough. Catch you later, Dad."

He heard something in the tone of my voice and grabbed my wrist. "What's wrong with you?"

I didn't want to talk about Antonio and the soccer team, so I went in another direction. "A friend of mine got ganged up on yesterday," I told him.

Physical violence was a subject that never failed to interest my father. "Yeah? They beat him up?"

I nodded. "They got him pretty bad."

"It happened at school? With all those police and security precautions?"

"Yup. Right at school. So what do I do? I know who did it. Do I go after them?"

This was one of the first times I had ever turned to my father for advice, and he didn't hesitate for a second. "Nope. You can't fight somebody else's battles," he said. "Your buddy's got to learn to fight for himself."

"What if he can't? What if he's not a fighter?"

"Then he's got to learn to get along better."

"You mean he's gotta pay respect?" I asked. "You're saying what Kevin Hutchings said the other night?"

My father didn't appreciate me likening him to his old enemy. "All I'm saying is that the way it is in school is the way it is out of school," he said. "If you can't fight, then learn to live so you don't get picked on."

I thought it over. On some level it made sense. I knew Mouse had brought it on himself. But it also didn't seem like a guy should have to walk through school for a week, bowing and scraping, just to avoid worse punishment. "And would you have fought with Kevin Hutchings Friday, if you guys had found each other in the crowd?" I asked him.

"Sure." My dad nodded. "I was ready to go."

"Even though you weren't proud of fighting with him the first time, years ago? You would have done it all over again?"

"Kevin hasn't changed," my dad said, his voice getting a little louder. "He's still a loud-mouthed punk who comes to our gym, in our town, and starts pushing people around. You can't take a back step to a guy like that, Joe, or you'll spend your whole life retreating."

"Okay," I said, "thanks for the advice."

"Anytime, Captain Joe," Dad said, and glanced back at the paper. "So, is this Brazilian guy really such a stud?"

"People seem to think so. I'll catch you later."

I wasn't surprised that Ed the Mouse didn't come to school that Tuesday. When I walked him home the previous evening, after he had showered and dressed, he hadn't even let me come into his house. I don't think it was physical pain that was bothering him—I think it was the humiliation of being set upon, and the fear of what could have happened, that had done the damage. They'd given him an airhole to breathe, but it could have been a long time before someone found him. Anything could have happened in that storage closet. He could've even died, surrounded by football pads and old helmets.

I tried to call Mouse from school, but even though I was pretty sure he was up there in that big house on Grandview Lane, he wasn't answering the phone. I darted into the school's computer lab between classes and e-mailed him, but he didn't respond. Clearly, whatever he was doing, he wanted to be left alone.

Antonio had become "the Phenom" to everyone at Lawndale High—the newspaper's nickname stuck. I guess any kid who gets on the front page of newspapers, and appears on TV, becomes a celebrity in his school. But Antonio had always acted the part of a celebrity, from the first moment I met him. Now, as other kids turned to look at him when he passed in the corridor, and as teachers and even the policemen on duty shook his hand and asked him about the game, it didn't seem that he had changed. Rather, the vibe I got from him was that he was finally getting his due. Kris was always near him, talking to him, holding his hand. Bitterly, I thought to myself that she was basking in his glory, and that they deserved each other.

That afternoon, after soccer practice, I walked by the football field and saw Mr. Murphy out there with Jack Hutchings, Tony Borelli, and Chris Coleman. The rest of the team had finished and gone in to shower, so it was just the four of them. Jack's knee had healed enough for him to come to practice again, even though he wasn't running plays. Now he wasn't running at all—he was crawling. Mr. Murphy was working the three of them like dogs, making them crawl back and forth over the hundred-yard field from goalpost to goalpost while he shouted at them and occasionally whipped footballs at them. I could tell by the way they were crawling that they were exhausted and that their arms and legs were cramping. I didn't have much sympathy.

I tried calling Mouse that night, but no one at the McBean home ever answered. I figured Ed had tuned out from the world for a while, and his father was probably working late, as usual. After leaving three messages for Mouse on the answering machine, I gave up.

He wasn't in school the next day either, and I was starting to worry. Even someone as brilliant as Ed the Mouse can't miss too much school. I remembered how he had looked, when we unwrapped him, how he'd sat on the carton, shivering. I guessed that he was still suffering, and that if he didn't come to school, I should go to him.

Mouse wasn't the only guy in pain. I passed Tony Borelli and Chris Coleman in the hall between second and third periods that Wednesday. They were shuffling along stiff-limbed, wincing with each step. They glared at me when I passed, and even though no words were spoken, I got the message that they knew I had found Ed the Mouse, and they blamed me for their punishment. I glared right back at them. What they had done to Ed made me sick. Anytime they wanted to take me on, I was, to use my father's phrase, ready to go.

And with all the other stuff going on, I still had to attend classes and force myself to pay attention and take notes. I was no longer lab partners with Kris in advanced biology—we had moved our desks apart, and except for an occasional hello or goodbye we weren't communicating too much. That Wednesday we dissected crayfish, and I paired up with Phil Elliot, a tall guy with bad acne and even worse breath. I don't mean to be gross, but his breath was so bad that it even made the formaldehyde smell good, and I was thinking they should have just let Phil breathe on the crayfish and that would have preserved it.

We were five minutes into the dissection when the fearsome Mrs. Eckes charged into our biology room with another of her dreaded summonses from the front office. The class went quiet, as everyone waited to see who was in trouble. Mr. Desoto looked at her note, and then strolled over and gave me a worried look. "They want you at the office again, Joe," he said in a low voice. "Everything okay?"

He had been nicer to me than any teacher I ever had, and was probably the only member of the Lawndale High faculty who believed that I had any promise at all. I wished I could have been more reassuring. "I hope so," I told him. "Sorry I can't finish the crayfish."

In Vice Principal Tobias's office, it was a replay of my last meeting, except the pretty young policewoman wasn't there to soften things up. It was just Coyle and Tobias, and this time they didn't keep me waiting. "Close the door," the vice principal said when I entered, so I pulled the door closed, shutting us in. "Sit down," the big man said, so I sat. "No one can hear what you say to us, and we won't tell anyone," he said. "So how about telling us the truth."

"About what?" I asked.

"About Monday. Something happened in school," Coyle said.

I shrugged. "Lots of things probably happened on Monday."

"Don't you sass me," Coyle snapped.

"Ask me a question, I'll give you an answer," I told him. "What happened? What do you want to know about?"

"If we knew what happened, you wouldn't be here,"

Coyle said in a low voice. "We do know it was long after school. In the basement. Start talking, Joe."

I was tempted to tell them. But I figured that if I did, it would get Mr. Murphy in serious hot water. And it would land Jack, Chris, and Tony in big trouble, too, and piss off the whole football team. My father had advised me to fight my own battles, and this wasn't one of them. This battle belonged to Ed the Mouse, and he had made the decision to go along with Mr. Murphy and keep the episode quiet. Besides, I didn't care too much for Tobias and Coyle, and I didn't like the way they were pressuring me.

"I don't have anything to tell."

"Just like you didn't have anything to tell about what happened on the golf course," Vice Principal Tobias said.

"Yes, sir. Just like that."

For a few seconds it was quiet in the room. They looked at me and I looked back at them. Vice Principal Tobias took a fold of flesh from his chin and rolled it between his fingers like cookie dough. "Congratulations on your soccer victory," he said. "It was very exciting. I saw the game myself. It would be a shame if the captain had to leave the team because of a discipline problem."

"We all appreciated you coming out to watch," I said back to him. "I can tell you're a real fan."

"Maybe you didn't hear what I said about leaving the team," he growled.

"I don't see why the captain would have to leave the team if he hasn't done anything wrong," I answered back.

"You wouldn't know anything about a hole in a band practice room?" Coyle asked. "Somebody punched through a wall. Damaged school property."

It wasn't a question, and I didn't answer. They had me.

" 'Cause a janitor said he saw you leaving the band room the afternoon the vandalism occurred, holding your hand like it was injured," Coyle continued. "And, later, he found a bloody paper towel in the bathroom you went into. How's the hand, by the way? Didn't break anything?"

"No," I said. "Thanks for asking. My hand's okay."

"I take it you're not a music fan?" Coyle said. "I never saw you as one, Joe, when you were drying my car. You used to do a real good job on my hubcaps and fender."

"You read any good magazines lately?" I asked him. "I remember the ones you used to keep in your patrol car."

His face tightened. "Punching through a wall is an act of criminal vandalism. You destroyed school property. Isn't that right, Stephen?"

"Yes, but even more worrying is that it's an aggressive, violent action," Vice Principal Tobias said, nodding. "Exactly the kind of thing we're trying to prevent here."

"Maybe you should put up cameras in the band practice rooms," I suggested. "Put 'em up in every room and closet in the whole school, and then there wouldn't be any trouble—"

"NOT ANOTHER WORD." Vice Principal Tobias cut me off, and slammed his desk with his meaty palm. "We're going to keep our eyes right on you, Brickman. The next time you step out of line, you can just keep going, because we'll see it, we'll catch you up, and run you out of school."

They didn't have to tell me that the meeting was over. I controlled myself, stood up, and headed for the door. But just as my hand touched the knob, Tobias fired off one last question. "Brickman. That was your father, wasn't it, who started that fight in the gym on Friday night?"

"That was his big daddy," Coyle said.

"So making trouble runs in your family?" Tobias pressed.

"Why don't you bring my father in and ask him," I suggested.

"I might just do that," Vice Principal Tobias said. "Now get out of here."

As I opened the door, Coyle got off one final shot. "Maybe when we run him out of school, he can go back to working in the car wash with his daddy. He sure was great on hubcaps."

21

I biked up to Mouse's house late Wednesday, after soccer practice. Day was darkening into a cold October dusk by the time the McBean house swam into view above the trimmed bushes and manicured hedges of Grandview Lane. The three-story mansion looked dark and cheerless as always—no lights gleamed from any of the windows that faced the street. I left my ten-speed in the driveway and walked to the front door.

Mouse did not answer my ring. He did not answer my repeated knocks. I tried kicking the door a few times, but he didn't answer my kicks either. I was pretty sure he was in there, but I decided not to try knocking the door down with my shoulder. There had to be an easier way in.

I walked around the house, peeking in all the first-floor windows. There was no Mouse in the living room. The kitchen, den, and hall looked similarly Mouse-less. I climbed a water pipe, and pulled myself up to a window ledge outside his bedroom. At first I thought I had struck out again, because his bedroom was dark. Then I saw the gleam of a computer screen and spotted Mouse at his desk, wearing headphones and taking notes on a pad.

I banged my forehead on the glass pane, but Ed didn't

stir. I held on to the ledge with one hand and rapped on the window with the other. Still no luck. Either the music was cranked up, or whatever Mouse was studying on his computer was absorbing all of his attention.

I saw that the next window over was cracked open an inch. Hanging from the narrow window ledge, with my legs dangling into space, I put years of chin-ups to use and edged sideways, handgrip to handgrip, over to the cracked-open window. I put my lips to the narrow slit between sill and window, and screamed, *"Hey, Mouse!"*

I don't know if he heard me, or if he just sensed something, but he turned around quickly. I gripped the ledge tightly with my right hand and waved frantically with my left. Ed saw me and nearly fell off his desk chair.

Then he did a strange thing. You would think Ed would have hurried over to open the window and help his old friend inside. But that wasn't his first reaction at all. He stood in front of his screen, blocking my view, and turned off his computer. Next he put the pad he had been taking notes on in a drawer, and he scooped up and put away a few other things on his desk and a nearby table. Only after completing this rushed housekeeping did he walk to the window.

"What are you doing out there?" he asked.

"Losing my grip," I told him. "Aren't you going to let me in?"

"No," he said. "I don't think so. I'm kind of busy right now."

"Mouse, I am seriously about to fall and break my legs."

"You climbed up, so I imagine you can get down."

"Ed, for God's sakes, I can't climb down! My arms are tired from hanging on! *I'm losing my grip. Mouse!*"

He must have heard the desperation in my voice, because he finally opened his bedroom window and helped me inside. Right away I got a weird vibe in his room. Not just that it was dark. He was burning a stick of incense. Whoever heard of Ed the Mouse burning incense? Beneath the sweet incense smell, I smelled another, a chemical that I couldn't identify. I wondered if he was burning the incense to mask the other odor, and if the things Ed had put away before letting me in were chemicals.

"What are you doing here?" he asked.

"I was concerned about you," I told him. "You don't answer your phone."

"That's 'cause I don't want to talk to anyone."

"You don't answer your e-mails."

"I don't want to write to anyone either."

"What do you want to do?" I asked him.

"Be alone," he said.

We weren't getting very far, but at least I was asking him questions, and he was responding. I thought any conversation was a good thing, so I kept quizzing him. "Why don't you have any lights on in here?"

"It makes it easier for me to concentrate on my games," he said. "No distractions. No shadows on the screen."

"You're gonna hurt your eyes."

"Probably."

I reached for a light switch, and Ed didn't try to stop me as I clicked it on. Light flooded the big bedroom, and we looked at each other. Ed the Mouse had changed a lot in two days, that was for sure. A mouse is a meek rodent that runs and hides to escape danger. Ed looked cornered, dangerous, and quietly ferocious. It was mostly something to do with his eyes. I'm not sure I can quite describe what I saw, except that I was sure he hadn't slept since Monday. But while lack of sleep usually makes people's eyes blurry, it had made Ed's sharp and seethingly intense. If I saw a mouse with eyes like that, I wouldn't stick my finger in his cage.

"What's with the incense?" I asked him.

"I like the way it smells."

"You become a hippie?"

"Will you please leave my room."

"Sure," I said. "Why don't we go play Ping-Pong in the basement and you can throw a paddle at my head and apologize later."

"I'm not going to throw anything at you, but will you please leave my room, right now," he asked again, perfectly politely. So I let him lead me out of his room and pull the door closed behind him. He headed for the kitchen and opened the refrigerator door. "Want some iced tea?" he asked.

"Sure."

He poured two glasses and we sat at the table and drank our iced tea as if everything was perfectly normal. "So," I said, "sounds like you've been playing that computer game a lot?"

"I can get to level five every time."

"You must be the world record holder. How many hours a day do you play it?"

"I don't know." His sleepless eyes glowed. "I'm not that conscious of time right now."

"Are you conscious that you're missing school, and there are tests and homework assignments you'll have to make up?"

"I'll come back to school soon enough," Ed the Mouse said softly, like he was making some kind of promise to himself. "But on my terms."

I took a sip of iced tea. "What does that mean?"

"It means what it means."

"I know it means what it means, but what does it mean?"

"Don't ask so many questions or it's going to be hard for me to talk to you, Joe," he said.

"Okay," I told him. "No more questions. How about I tell you some news from school? Mr. Murphy lived up to his word."

"I don't care about Mr. Murphy."

"Yeah, sure, but I thought you might want to know that he took Jack and Tony and Chris out to the practice field and busted their butts till they could barely walk . . ."

Ed the Mouse reached into the pitcher of iced tea and pulled out an ice cube and watched it slowly melt in his palm. "I really, really, really don't care," he said.

"Look, Ed, I know what happened on Monday was awful, but nobody knows about it . . ."

"I know about it," he said in a very dry whisper. "Joe, I think you have to go now. But I'm very glad that you came by. I've been thinking about you and what a good friend you've been to me, and I want you to have something. It's in the basement. I'll go get it."

I stood by the front door while he ran downstairs and fumbled around, and then ran back up with a framed picture. It was a photograph of our first Rec League soccer team, from when we were eight years old. We had won some kind of trophy, and Ed and I were kneeling side by side in the front row, grinning as only a pair of victorious eight-year-olds can grin. "Here," he said. "I think you should take this."

"Why are you giving it to me now?"

"No reason," he said. "I was just cleaning and looking at old stuff, and I was going to throw it out, and then I thought you might like to have it."

I studied his face. "Why now, Ed?"

He shrugged. "Do you want me to throw it out?"

"No," I said. "Thanks." And I took the photograph.

He opened the door and waited for me to leave. I hesitated and then stepped outside. He immediately tried to push the door closed, but I stuck the toe of my track shoe to block it. "Ed, when are you coming to school?"

"Maybe tomorrow. Definitely Friday. When I come, you'll know." I jerked my toe out of the way as he slammed the door closed and locked it, and then double-locked it.

22

I coasted down Grandview Lane, trying not to think about what I couldn't stop myself from thinking about. I told myself that I was being foolish or dramatic or a nosy busybody. Ed the Mouse would be fine. Kids are picked on in my school all the time, day in, day out, year after year, and they turn out okay. They swallow it down, just the way Mr. Murphy said, and they learn to get along better and pay respect, as my father and Kevin Hutchings believed. The process of learning how not to get beaten up is probably a valuable part of a public school education.

Mouse would be fine. Years from now, he would probably tell his kids about the time he was taped up like a mummy and thrown in a closet, and it might even be a fond and nostalgic memory, the way Mr. Murphy had gotten to like the brand on his butt.

Mouse would be fine.

I stopped pedaling under a streetlight, and just sat there on my bike.

He would be in school tomorrow, or Friday at the latest, and everything would be okay. He would be fine.

I took out the framed photograph that he had given me,

and studied it in the glow from the streetlight. There Mouse was at eight, small for his age but with a grin a mile wide. And there I was next to him, with an equally idiotic grin. Even then we were best friends.

Suddenly I knew what I had to do. I didn't want to do it, but I had absolutely no choice. It was one thing to keep silent when being grilled by Deputy Police Chief Coyle and Vice Principal Tobias, but this was a very different matter. This was my oldest and best friend.

It was more than five miles from Lawndale to Rutherford. Several times along the way I slowed, and almost turned back, because I was heading into unexplored territory. I don't mean the trip to Rutherford—I had been there before. But I had never done to anyone what I was about to do to Ed the Mouse.

I had gone to a rough elementary school, where kids fought in the sandbox, and then to an even tougher junior high school, where I saw kids get bones broken in fights while their classmates cheered. Now I was a senior at a high school so violent that police patrolled the halls, and all along the way one lesson had been drummed into me: "Don't be a squealer." I had played on dozens of sports teams, and had seen all kinds of rough stuff and intimidation and dishonest maneuvers, and I had not told tales. I had kept my lips sealed. Because everyone—from my friends to my coaches to my father—had told me there was nothing lower than a squealer.

I knew Dr. McBean's building because I had visited him with Mouse three or four times over the years. Twice he had taken us on tours of the labs, and I had been impressed by all the complicated equipment and the friendly but serious people in white lab coats. But I had never arrived alone before, on a bike, at night.

It was a big steel-and-glass building rising from a wide, grassy lawn. A sign on a slab out front proclaimed the building to be GAUCHER-KAHN CHEMICAL CORPORATION.

I locked my bike up to a signpost, and walked to the lobby. There was a fat night guard on duty, hunched over his wooden desk, breathing hard. When I got closer, I saw that he was snoring. "Pardon me, sir," I said. He stirred, but didn't wake. His snores sounded a little like groans.

"Excuse me, but it's kind of urgent," I said again, and lightly touched his shoulder.

The guard sat up very fast, and even before his eyes popped open he started saying, "I wasn't sleeping. I swear I wasn't." Then he saw me, and took control of the situation. "Who are you? What do you want?"

"I need to talk to Dr. McBean," I said.

"The building's closed."

"He's still here. I'm sure of it."

The guard looked at me, taking in my blue jeans and old corduroy shirt with the sleeves rolled up above my elbows. "What's this about?"

I hesitated. "It's private. I'm a friend. Just tell him it's Joe

Brickman, and I need to talk to him right now. It's an emergency."

"It better be," he grunted, and picked up the phone on his desk.

He made the call, and less than a minute later one of the gleaming elevators opened and Dr. McBean came hurrying out. He was a short little man—just about Ed's height—neatly dressed in a jacket and tie, with an I.D. badge swinging on a chain from his neck. Worry showed on his face. "Joe," he said, "Joe, what is it? Did something happen to Ed?"

"No, sir," I said, "everyone's fine."

"You're sure?"

"Yeah. But I need to talk to you." I glanced at the guard, who was watching and listening. "Alone."

Dr. McBean studied my face for a moment and nodded. "Of course. We can talk in my office."

The elevator took us up to the fifth floor, and a long, carpeted corridor to Dr. McBean's office. It was a nice-sized corner office with a view of an industrial park. His computer was on—he must have been working on something when the guard called. I saw that he made notes on the same type of white pad Mouse used. On the desk, near the computer, was a small, gold-framed photograph of his wife holding her baby son, Mouse, in her arms. She was looking down at her baby with a smile that lit up her face. Her smile seemed almost out of place in the otherwise sterile office.

Dr. McBean beckoned me to an empty seat. He wheeled

the leather swivel chair away from his desk to face me. "What is it, Joe?" he asked.

For several seconds I tried to tell him, but the words wouldn't come. Dr. McBean watched me, and waited patiently. "I'm worried about Ed," I finally managed to get out.

He knew it before I said it. But he didn't press too hard. "What's wrong?"

"You don't know anything?"

"I guess not, if there's something to know," he said. "I've been working hard lately. Let's see, I know he has a cold and has taken a few days off from school."

"He doesn't have a cold," I told him.

This time Dr. McBean wasn't inclined to wait. He sat forward on his chair, his hands pressed together. "What is it, Joe? Is he in danger?"

"Maybe," I said. "Or I could be completely wrong about this. I mean, I could be one hundred percent wrong. And I almost didn't come, because I wanted to be wrong. You know Ed is my closest friend—"

"Why do you think he's in danger?"

"Stuff's been happening at school," I told Dr. McBean.

"What sort of stuff?"

So I took a deep breath, and then I told him. I didn't go into the details of how and why Ed had been bullied. But I did tell him that something bad had happened to his son on Monday, and that ever since then Ed had withdrawn into himself, playing ultra-violent computer games for hours on end.

"Staying home alone is probably a normal response to being picked on in school," Dr. McBean said.

"Maybe," I agreed. "But you'd better listen to me. Because I wouldn't be here if I didn't think this was serious."

"I know that," he said. "I'm listening. I assure you."

So I told him the rest of it. I told him that I thought Ed might be building something with chemicals—something secret that he was learning about on the Internet. That got Dr. McBean's attention. I told him what Ed had said about coming back to school Thursday or Friday, on his own terms. And that when he came back to school, I would know about it. Lastly, I showed him the photograph Ed had given me. "He gave it to me like . . . a goodbye present."

Dr. McBean looked at the photograph a long time, and his hand holding the picture began to shake. Finally he handed it back to me and stood up. "You don't really think . . ."

"I don't know what to think," I said honestly.

"I see. Thank you. It was . . . it was brave of you to come here," he said, and his voice cracked just the way Mouse's did when he was highly stressed.

"I hope I did the right thing. I didn't know what else to do. I hope I'm wrong. I'm sure I'm wrong. Mouse will kill me for talking to you."

But Dr. McBean was already heading toward the door. "I need to get home right away," he said. "Do you need a lift?"

"No, I came by bike."

"Let's go," he said. When we were in the corridor, he walked very fast. Then he started sprinting for the elevator, and I was surprised how fast this serious little man could run.

23

Ed the Mouse vanished. So did his father.

I didn't expect Ed to come to school Thursday, but I did expect to see him on Friday, or for sure on Saturday afternoon, when we had a big soccer game. I also thought he might call me to curse me out for telling his dad, or that his father might call me with some news of what had happened. But no one called. The only thing I got from the McBean house was a strange silence.

On Saturday afternoon we played our third-to-last regular-season game, against a very good and determined Greenwood team. It's amazing what a front-page story and a couple of news clips will do to attract fans. I guess the small town of Lawndale was a little starved for big events. Also, I know there are towns all through northern New Jersey with large immigrant populations from countries that love soccer, and I guess some of those fans were curious to see a real live Phenom from Brazil.

Hype feeds on hype. Buzz creates buzz. Believe it or not, we had five hundred people in the stands to watch our game against Greenwood—more people than I have ever seen at one of our home football games. The bleachers on both home and away sidelines were full. The mayor of our town was there. Deputy Police Chief Coyle showed up with Vice Principal Tobias. I saw them walk up together, and they gave me cold stares.

We had to win this game and the two after it to make the county tournament. Before the game, Coach Collins made us kneel in a circle and gave us one of his less than great pep talks. I could tell how nervous he was, because he kept glancing around at the five hundred people. "You guys have a chance to do something special, but we have no margin for error. So let's get the ball to Antonio and score some goals. Defense, play hard and get the ball to Antonio. Midfield, nothing too fancy, we want to work the ball up through Antonio. Antonio, don't feel like you're carrying the whole burden, but . . . just do your thing out there. Okay, let's go!"

It didn't work out the way Coach Collins planned. The Greenwood team apparently had the same idea he had—that our only good player was Antonio. So they decided to shut him down, no matter what it took. They had two guys shadowing him all over the field, and every time he touched the ball, four or five of their players swarmed around him, kicking at his heels.

I think Antonio had faced these tactics before, because he seemed to know exactly what to do. When a ball came to him, he held it just long enough to draw their players out of position, and then he cracked off a perfect pass to one of our forwards who was left completely unguarded. He set up more clear breakaways for Zigler and Murray and Cavanaugh than I could count. Even those jokers couldn't miss forever. Zigler scored one, and then Cavanaugh, after missing what seemed like a dozen wide-open shots, finally converted. Our defense held firm, and at the half we were up two to nothing.

I sat on the bench near Antonio during halftime, and saw him roll down one sock to check a bruise. He was getting pushed and hacked on every touch, but he wasn't complaining. If anything, the rough treatment seemed to make him better. And I had to admire him for his unselfish play. Instead of getting angry and trying to take the Greenwood defense on all by himself, he was making the rest of our team look good.

In the second half, things got even rougher. The Greenwood team seemed to have decided that if they couldn't beat us with Antonio on the field, they would find a way to get rid of him. He was knocked down twice from behind, on tackles that should have drawn red cards but didn't. The players shadowing him began shoving him even when the ball was on the other side of the field. Their strategy seemed to work. Soon Antonio's uniform was so covered with mud you couldn't even read his number, and Greenwood scored a goal on us. Two to one.

But as quickly as the momentum of the game shifted, Antonio found a way to shift it back. He sprinted all the way back to our penalty box to collect a pass, opening up a little distance from the two Greenwood players who were shadowing him. And then he started to move the ball upfield. I sensed what was about to happen. I had seen him do it to our defense in practices. And that peculiar quality he had—the quality that would one day no doubt make him shine as a professional star—was practically radiating from him.

The two players who were chasing him around the field caught up to him, and one of them tried to trip him while the other tried a vicious shoulder charge. Antonio jumped sideways at the exact right moment, and they missed him and hit each other, and went down in a tangle of arms and legs. He split two of their midfielders with a burst of pure speed and darted down the right sideline.

Their left fullback tried to contain him near the sideline. He had been pushing and kicking and taunting Antonio all during the game, and I guess the Phenom had had enough. Antonio stepped over the ball twice to freeze him, and then kicked the ball right at the fullback's groin. I would swear he was aiming. The ball hit their defender with a loud ZWAP and bounced perfectly back to Antonio, while their fullback crumpled onto the grass, holding his testicles.

Their stopper was tall and gangly, and Antonio nutmegged him without breaking stride, shooting the ball right through his legs, and then running onto it. Now only their sweeper stood between Antonio and their goalie. Antonio slowed in front of their sweeper, and for a half second he seemed to consider what to do as he moved the ball from one foot to the other. Then came a series of lightning fakes, left-right-left, before Antonio finally went right, opening up enough space to take his shot.

But their sweeper wasn't giving up—he managed to grab Antonio's shirt and hold on. He was willing to yield a penalty kick but he wasn't letting go. Antonio dragged him half a step, and then reached down to the waistline of his own shirt and in one smooth motion yanked it up and over his head. Their sweeper fell on his butt in the mud, still holding Antonio's shirt, while Antonio kicked a rocket shot past the Greenwood goalie, into the net, for a three-to-one lead.

It was the most brilliant run I had ever seen. I think it was the most brilliant run anyone had ever seen on a New Jersey high school soccer field. The roar from the crowd went on for minute after minute. Antonio celebrated shirtless, pumping his arms, while the entire Greenwood team hung their heads. But that goal wasn't the thing that impressed me the most that day.

Greenwood didn't give up. They scored to make it three to two, and with ten minutes left they attacked us with everything they had. One goal would tie the game. In those final few minutes Antonio ran all the way back to help our defense, and he personally broke up four or five clear scoring threats. Twice we ended up battling the Greenwood forwards side by side, and when it came to playing tough defense, he was a warrior.

When the game ended, I knew what I had to do. I didn't participate in the celebration. And I didn't say anything to Antonio, who donned dark glasses, gave Kris a hug and a kiss, and then posed for pictures and did two interviews at a time, all the while combing his hair.

Instead I waited for Coach Collins to have a free moment, and then I walked up to him and said very quietly, "Make him co-captain."

Coach looked at me. "It's not necessary. You're sure?"

"Yeah," I told him. "I'm sure."

24

Sunday passed without any word from the Mouse. I worked a double shift in my father's car wash, and for the first time in all the years I had worked there, I found myself watching everything my dad did, and imagining myself in his place. I watched him open up in the morning, and check all the equipment before turning it on. I watched him deal with his employees. I saw how careful he was with money. I watched him chat with customers, and when things got slow he thumbed through a *Sports Illustrated*. It didn't look like such a bad life, but I have to admit, it also wasn't the most exciting thing in the world.

Mouse didn't come to school on Monday. When he didn't show up on Tuesday, I became very concerned. He had been gone a whole week. Had I destroyed our friendship by telling on him? Why didn't he or his father at least call me? I wondered where they were, and if anything bad had happened to them.

Tuesday evening was warm for late October—one of those fall nights when summer doesn't want to give way to winter. About nine o'clock I heard guitar music, and then Kris's voice drifted over. She hadn't sung outside on her balcony in a long time, so I cracked open my window to hear better, and sat back to enjoy the free concert. She sang two or three of her favorite songs, and they brought back a lot of nice memories.

Suddenly I heard a male voice start singing. I didn't understand the words, but I knew who was singing them. In addition to all of his other talents, the Phenom was a pretty good crooner. She had brought him to her balcony to play for him, and now he was singing to her. I couldn't be sure, but it sounded like a love song—an Italian love song.

I closed my window, and the sound of his voice got fainter, but when the wind blew a certain way, I could still hear him. Normally, I'm the last person in the world to get insomnia. But long after the Phenom stopped singing, his voice echoed in my head. I tossed and turned and buried my face in the pillow, and finally I gave up. I lay on my back, staring at the shelves of sports trophies that had accumulated over the years, and at my fish in their tanks. I replayed over and over in my mind my last fight with Kris and what she had said about my needing to grow up.

Some of my trophies were from grade school. Some were from sports I no longer even played. The cups and gold statuettes loomed on their shelves, glinting dully in the moonlight, a long parade of memories from sports seasons gone by. Why did I keep them there? Was I holding on to something that other people would have stored away in boxes in a closet long ago? Mouse had dug up the Rec League soccer picture from his basement—even he had put old memories away and moved on. What was wrong with me?

In the moonlight, the eyes and scales of my fish glowed with a ghostly luminescence. I could see them swimming around the coral and through the seaweed, cruising endlessly through the late night hours. Even lying there, I was fascinated by them. I don't know why, but I've always liked to watch fish swim. I like the way their bodies snake through the water, the small movements of dorsal and ventral fins. Was it a stupid child's hobby? Should I have exchanged my fish tanks for something more trendy or mature years ago?

And was I being a fool about my future? Had I tossed away an opportunity by not applying to college? Was Kris right, that I could do bigger and better things than help run a car wash? My father had a comfortable life, but not a very interesting one. I wouldn't learn anything new by working with him. I wouldn't travel to a new place, or learn a new skill, or meet new and fascinating people. It had been enough for him, but should it be enough for me? Was it another example of my holding on to something familiar and time-tested? Of not taking enough risks? Of not growing up?

The sleepless night had an unexpected aftereffect in daylight. Mouse wasn't at school Wednesday, and I wasn't totally there either—I was bleary from lack of sleep, and the thoughts that had kept me awake kept running through my mind. Finally, at lunchtime, I did something I hadn't planned on. Instead of going to the cafeteria, I headed to the Guidance Department. I hesitated outside, and nearly turned and walked away. Finally I opened the door and asked the secretary if I could make an appointment to see Mrs. Simmons.

"She's booked up solid with college application stuff," the secretary said, glancing at her schedule. "But she's here now, finishing her lunch. I could see if she's done—"

"Don't bother her," I said quickly, losing my nerve. "I'll come another time."

Mrs. Simmons must have overheard this, because she poked her head out of her office. "No bother at all," she said. "I'm done. Come on in."

The walls of her office were covered with pictures and brochures from different colleges, and posters from the Army and Navy. On one wall, I saw brochures from Harvard and Princeton, with photos of ivy-covered buildings and grassy campuses that looked like never-never land.

I think Mrs. Simmons saw how out of place I felt. "Joe," she said, "sit down. Congratulations on the soccer wins."

"Thanks," I said.

I tried to sit down, but somehow I managed to miss the chair and fall to the floor with a loud crash. It was about the clumsiest thing I had ever done in my life.

"Are you okay?" she asked, alarmed.

"Never better," I said, getting back to my feet. "Sorry. I really don't belong here. I should go . . ."

"Sit," she commanded. "That's an order. Sit carefully."

So I sat. And this time I didn't fall.

We looked at each other. She had kind but very penetrating eyes. "What's wrong?" she asked.

"I just . . . didn't sleep so well last night."

She waited for me to say more, and finally asked, "What kept you awake?"

"I . . . don't know."

"Since you came here, after your sleepless night, and you're a senior, let me take a wild guess," Mrs. Simmons said with a smile. "Are you worried about the future?"

"No," I said quickly. "I'm gonna work with my dad."

"That's why you didn't apply to college?" Somehow, my high school transcript had materialized on her desk. "You still have time, you know. You would have to take some tests, but many colleges accept late applications. Your grades are not great, but I've seen much worse. And you have strong extracurriculars, and—"

"I don't want to go to college," I told her truthfully. "I've had enough of sitting in classrooms. At least for a while."

"Fair enough." I had expected her to argue with me, and try to convince me I was wrong. But she didn't. "What do you want?" she asked.

"I wish I knew. If I did I would tell you."

"I believe you," she said. She scanned my transcript. "I see you're in advanced biology. That's your only advanced class, and you're doing well in it. That kind of jumps out at me."

"I like bio," I said. "And Mr. Desoto's a great teacher."

"What do you like about it?"

Seconds passed. "Fish," I finally said.

"Fish?"

"I like studying about animals, and plants, even down to the level of cells, but I like fish most of all. I have a lot of them."

She looked confused. "You have a lot of fish?"

"Yeah, in tanks. I know this sounds stupid, but I've been raising them since I was little and . . . Look, I really got to go."

She tried to stop me, but I knew I was talking sheer nonsense and that I didn't belong in that office with the posters from Princeton and Harvard. I made it out the door, hurried past the secretary, and ran off down the hall.

That night I slept for two or three fitful hours. Falling asleep is a strange thing—the more you think about it, the less chance you have of doing it. My meeting with Mrs. Simmons haunted me. I remembered stammering out silly answers, and falling off the chair, and telling a sophisticated woman that I liked biology because I liked fish.

When Mouse didn't come to school on Thursday, I decided it was time to take aggressive action. A week is a long time for someone to vanish. I got the number for Dr. McBean's chemical company from the operator, and tried calling him at work. When they connected me to his extension, I got a recorded message: "Hello, this is Dennis McBean. I'm sorry, but I'll be out of the office for a while, and I won't be checking messages. If you need more help, please call my colleague, Dr. Farnham."

I was surprised when he answered the phone on the first ring. "Farnham speaking." I explained that I was a friend of the family, and was concerned because father and son had vanished.

"I don't know any more than you do," Dr. Farnham said, sounding perplexed himself. "Dr. McBean has taken a leave of absence. He's never done that before, and I don't know when he's coming back. He's not even calling in for messages."

I thanked him and hung up. Mouse and his father had indeed vanished without a trace.

We won our second-to-last soccer game on Thursday afternoon, in front of a huge crowd. One more game to go and we would be in the county tournament for the first time ever.

Thursday night I finally got a little sleep, but I had awful, violent nightmares, and awoke at five in the morning in a cold sweat. All Friday, I had an ominous feeling, like something bad or dangerous or violent was about to happen. But school was quiet, and except for Mouse's absence, everything seemed to go normally.

When violence finally did break out that Friday, it did so in a most unexpected place. It didn't happen in school, or on an athletic field. The hard guys weren't to blame, and none of my soccer teammates was the victim. The violence broke out in my house, in my living room, and the only victim was my father.

It was getting late, and I was feeding my fish and dreading another sleepless night or more nightmares, when I heard a loud thud from downstairs. It sounded like someone had pushed over our dining room table. Then came two smaller crashes, like someone kicking chairs across the floor.

I ran to the top of the stairs, and heard Dianne Hutchings's outraged voice: "WHAT THE HELL DO YOU MEAN, TONE IT DOWN? YOU HAVEN'T EVEN CALLED ME! WHEN WERE YOU GOING TO CALL ME?"

"Well, I just think sometimes it's better to take things slow," I heard my father say.

BAM! Something shattered, and it sounded like glass breaking—I figured it might be the ashtray on our coffee table.

"WILL YOU QUIT DESTROYING THINGS?" my father shouted. Then, in his most reasonable voice: "I mean, for God's sakes, Dianne. We only went out a couple of weeks, and I didn't break any promises—"

But he never got any further, because Dianne Hutchings exploded: "WHAT AM I? A TOY THAT YOU HAVE FUN WITH AND THROW AWAY? YOU SON OF A BITCH! I'LL BREAK EVERYTHING IN YOUR HOUSE AND THEN I'LL BREAK EVERY BONE IN YOUR BODY."

SLAM, BAM, WHAM, CRASH! I didn't know exactly what she was doing down there, but I was pretty certain that if I didn't go down and stop her, my dad and I wouldn't have any dishes to eat out of, or any glasses to drink from. I edged down the stairs and saw a pitiful sight. My father—one of the biggest, toughest men you would ever want to meet— had crawled behind the tipped-over dining room table, and was holding a chair up as a shield.

Dianne Hutchings was standing in the middle of our dining room, throwing anything at him she could find. She hurled a sugar bowl. "YOU ARE SUCH A COWARD!" She fired a salt and pepper shaker at him. "HOW CAN YOU EVEN LOOK AT YOURSELF IN THE MIRROR? DO YOU KNOW WHY YOU STOPPED CALLING ME? BECAUSE YOU LIKE ME, AND IT SCARES YOU. YOU DON'T WANT TO GET HURT AGAIN. COWARD!"

She had run out of ammunition. She looked around wildly, and spotted our breakfront, where our china was arranged on shelves. She picked up a ceramic serving platter, and swung it like a discus. "YOU DON'T DESERVE ME!" She hurled it at him and he just managed to ward it off with the chair. It smashed into a billion pieces.

Next she grabbed a dinner plate, and drew back her hand to whip it at him, but I caught her right wrist from behind. "I think that's enough," I told her.

"I'M JUST GETTING STARTED." She was so strong I could barely hold her as she struggled. "YOUR FATHER'S A BUM. I'LL GIVE HIM A TASTE OF MY TEMPER."

"He's already got that taste," I told her softly. My own tiredness gave my voice a steady, emotionless quality that seemed to drain some of the fury out of her. "We need that plate," I told her. "Please don't break it."

She stopped struggling and let me take the dinner plate out of her hand. She tossed her head proudly, and stormed off toward the door, stopping near the overturned table to shout at him, "GO FIND SOME CHICK YOU DON'T LIKE AT ALL, AND THEN YOU CAN SCREW HER WITHOUT FEELING THREATENED. YOUR EX-WIFE'S STILL GOT YOU BY THE BALLS AFTER ALL THESE YEARS! YOU FILTH. YOU PIG. I'M OUTTA HERE!" She let herself out, slamming the door behind her so hard that it almost came off its hinges.

I walked over to where my father was cowering behind the table. "Is she gone?" he asked.

I looked out the window. "She's getting into her car. She's pulling away. No, hold it, she's driving up onto our front lawn! She knocked over our mailbox! Now she's in reverse. Okay, she's gone."

I helped my father out from behind the table. He had sugar in his hair, and chips of porcelain and ceramic over his arms and shoulders. As I helped brush him off, I said, "Dad, I've been thinking about what you said a while ago, about how well you understand women and how you could explain them to me."

"This isn't a time to try to be funny, Joe," he said. "Can't you see I'm in pain?"

"But you said you could tell me all I needed to know about women in five minutes," I continued. "I can see I have a lot to learn from you, and I'm ready whenever you are."

"Learn this," he said. "When a tornado hits, take cover."

We stood side by side, looking around at the shambles of our dining room. Hurricane Dianne had done a lot of damage in a short time. Then Dad surprised me by laughing out loud, and muttering to himself, "Jesus, what a hellcat." He didn't sound mad at her. He sounded amused, and even, in a strange way, admiring.

25

The phone call I had been waiting so long for came bright and early Saturday morning. "Yo, Brickhead," a familiar high-pitched voice said.

"Is that you, Mouse?"

"How many people call you Brickhead?" he asked, sounding like my cheerful friend of old.

"Only one, and I thought maybe he was gone for good," I told him. "Where are you?"

"Back in town, but not for long. Thought I'd give you a call. We have a little catching up to do."

"That's putting it lightly. Where have you been?"

"I've been away and I'm going away again," Mouse said. "To a place over the rainbow where there isn't any trouble."

"Mouse, what are you talking about?"

"And I'm not coming back," Mouse said. "So this might be our last chance to talk for a while. I don't have much time. Feel like a hike to Highwood Hills? We can meet at Indian Rock."

"I'm on my way," I told him. "And Mouse, bozo though you are, it's good to hear your voice."

"Mutual, Brickhead. See ya soon."

I jogged a mile and a half up the steepening back slope of the Palisades cliffs to Highwood Hills, a mile-square wooded area on the eastern fringe of Lawndale. Mouse and I had spent several summers playing cowboys and Indians in the little town forest more than a decade ago. There was a boulder we always called Indian Rock because it looked to us like an Indian brave wearing a war bonnet. As I neared the rock I saw that Mouse had beaten me there, which wasn't a surprise, since Highwood Hills was a short walk from Grandview Lane. Mouse was sitting cross-legged atop Indian Rock, looking down at the panoramic view of the town of Lawndale.

"Hey," I said walking up and trying to sound casual. "Whatcha doing on that rock, Chief Mouseman?"

"Thinking I won't miss it," he said.

"What?"

"Any of it. The school, the town, the people, the soccer team, the swamp, the teachers, the houses, the lawns, the creek. None of it. Not for one minute."

He slid down from the rock and offered his right hand. It seemed a little formal—I don't normally shake hands with my best friends—but I took his hand and looked him over to see if anything had changed. His grip was firm and he looked relaxed and happy, but serious. "I will miss you, Joe."

"Where are you going, Ed? And where have you been?"

"So many questions, so little time," he said. "Let's walk."

So we started off along one of the trails. We walked in silence for a while, pushing vines and branches out of the way. "It was weird," Mouse finally said.

"What?"

"All of it. Whatever you told my dad sure shook him up. When he came home that night, he was . . . crazed. He broke into my room. Cracked my locked desk drawer open with a hammer. Found the stuff I was working on. So much for personal privacy."

"Sorry," I told him. "I didn't want to get you into trouble."

"No, you did a great thing," Mouse said, with gratitude in his voice. "Although it wasn't what you thought. I wasn't going to hurt anybody or blow up the school. But I was going to create something that would make a major, major statement and give our school the stench it deserves. If my super stink bomb had gone off, I'm not sure they could have ever gotten the smell out. And I was also thinking about running away to New York City. Either of those would have screwed up my future. So I owe you a big thanks for ratting on me."

"You're welcome," I said. "Anytime."

Mouse laughed, and we turned onto an even narrower trail. It was a perfect fall morning to be out in the woods. The air was cold and crisp and the leaves on the trees overhead were turning red and gold and black and orange.

"So after your father found whatever he found, and confronted you, what happened?" I asked. "If you don't mind talking about it."

"Not at all," he said. "Dad went . . . berserk. I've never seen him lose control like that. It was kind of cool, in a way. He dragged me out into his car, and we took off at like a hundred miles an hour. Nothing packed. No maps or plans. We just drove away and headed north at double warp speed. We ended up in a fishing lodge high up in the Adirondacks. They had shut down for the winter, but they gave us a bungalow with a fireplace. A rowboat came with it. I guess the boat was for fishing, but we didn't fish. We just rowed out into the middle of that beautiful mountain lake and we talked. And we talked some more. Then we rowed back to the bungalow and we kept on talking."

"Sounds like a lot of talking," I observed quietly.

"Once we got started, it was like a dam breaking," Mouse said. "My dad turned out to be as unhappy as I was. He's been so lonely since my mom died he's been taking drugs for depression. It felt to him like he died, too. He kept it all inside him, and tried to deaden the pain by working long hours, but it was eating him up. He said it was like he crawled into a hole and he didn't know how to get out. He didn't know how to reach out to me. And I told him everything that happened at school. All the crap that's been going on, and who did what, and how I felt about it. He was horrified."

"I'll bet," I said.

"Yeah, things got pretty emotional," Mouse continued on, in a lower voice. "It was like the two of us, out there all alone on that lake, finally faced each other and opened the spigots and let it all come out. We cried a lot. I know that sounds stupid, but we spent one whole night with lightning and thunder flashing and crashing and rain pounding on the roof of the bungalow and the two of us sitting up talking about my mom and our screwed-up lives, and just weeping. I told him I was never going back to that school, and he said I never had to. So then we talked about options to make our lives happier. Money's not a problem. My grades aren't a problem. And he's pretty good at what he does. So there were a lot of options, once we started discussing them."

I noticed that the trail we were following was leading us toward Grandview Lane. Mouse was heading home. "We made some calls," he continued, "and visited a few schools together. We found a private school in Connecticut that I really liked, that will take me in mid-semester. It's not snooty at all—it's very relaxed, and it's got all kinds of advanced calculus and chem classes, and incredible computer equipment. They'll help me make sure that switching schools during my senior year doesn't hurt my college chances. I'm starting there Monday. Which means I'm moving in this afternoon. So there's a lot of work to do." He glanced at his watch. "My dad and I have a three-hour drive ahead of us. And then we have to unpack."

"What about your dad?" I asked.

"One of the reasons we chose Connecticut is because his company has a big lab there. He can get transferred, and rent a place near my school. And he's gonna stop working so hard, and we're gonna spend much more time together, and we promised to tell each other the truth, the whole truth, and nothing but the truth about everything, so help us God. So it's gonna be better. Much, much better."

"It sounds like it," I said. "Congratulations."

He had been gushing on about himself, but now he looked at me and I think he saw a bit of how miserable I was. "What about you, Joe? You don't look so good."

I told him about the soccer team's successes and how I couldn't feel any joy over them, and about the Phenom's singing with Kris on her balcony, and my own doubts about the future. I mentioned that I was having trouble falling asleep at night.

"Yeah," he said, "I know what that's like. I feel like I'm leaving when you need me. But maybe I can help a little."

"I doubt it," I said.

We had walked out of the woods onto Grandview Lane and were now a hundred feet from the McBean house. "Come in for a minute," he invited. "I have something I wanna give you."

"Not another photograph of us on a kiddy soccer team?"

"No," he promised. "Something you'll find more interesting."

So I followed him into his house, and waited while he ran up to his room. I spotted three bulging suitcases in the living room, ready to be loaded into his dad's car. I thought to myself how nice it would be to have an escape route—to just start over clean and fresh somewhere new.

Then Mouse came bounding down the stairs holding a big manila envelope. "Read it at your leisure," he said. "One night I was surfing the Web and I thought I'd dig up whatever there was to learn about Antonio Silva. I was a little curious why a star from the junior national team in a soccer-mad country would suddenly transfer to Lawndale, New Jersey."

"And what did you find?" I asked.

"Read it for yourself. There are lots of sports papers in Brazil that cover youth soccer. A couple even publish English editions. I downloaded an article on our buddy. Now I've got to go upstairs and pack up my computer stuff. Dad's getting nervous about the traffic if we don't leave soon."

He walked me out the front door and we stood on the top step. "When will I see you again, Mouse?" I asked.

"Maybe Christmas, or over the summer. Or come visit me in college. Or I'll come visit you . . ."

He didn't want to say it, so I helped him out. "You're gonna visit me here, Mouse? At the car wash? Somehow I don't think so."

"We'll keep in touch and we'll find each other. Joe,

you've been a great friend. I would've seriously messed up my life. You saved me." There was a moment of awkwardness.

This time I was the one who stuck out my hand. "Bye, Mouse," I said. "Try not to screw up in Connecticut. If they have a soccer team, don't show them all your moves the first day."

He grinned and we shook for a few seconds. "They do have a team, but I'll take it easy on them," he promised. "I'm sorry you're going through what you're going through, but you'll make it, Joe. You'll tough it out."

"You think so?"

"Absolutely," he said very seriously. "You're a lot tougher than I am, Joe. You're the best guy I know, but in some ways I think you're also the toughest."

"Not the smartest?" I asked.

"Don't push your luck."

We stopped shaking hands and Ed the Mouse walked back into his house and the door swung shut. I turned and walked down the steps and realized that I might not see my oldest and best friend again for months or even years. I was not holding on to my childhood anymore—it was moving away from me at high speed.

I started down the sidewalk, and then heard Mouse calling my name. I turned, but I had been wrong—it wasn't Mouse; it was his father. Dr. McBean also looked happy and relaxed. "Joe, wait, I wanted to say something to you." So I waited, and when he ran up he swallowed, and searched for the words. "You . . . you gave me my son back," he finally said. "I can never, ever thank you enough for having the courage to talk to me. But thank you."

"You're welcome," I told him. "Good luck in Connecticut."

He stood there looking at me, and his eyes started to tear up. Before I knew what he was doing he reached up, put both arms around me, and gave me a tight hug. I think he might have even kissed me if I hadn't been too tall. "God bless you," he whispered, released me, and headed home to his son.

16

Things that are hidden have great power. I didn't open that manila envelope right away on Saturday. I let it sit there, on my desk, wondering what secret Ed had uncovered.

I did some homework, and fixed and ate a big sandwich for lunch, and the envelope still sat there. When I went outside to get the mail, I ran into Kris, who was taking her friendly mutt, Suze, for a walk. Suze was a big dog, part collie and part Lab, and each time she saw a place she wanted to go, Kris had to win a tug-of-war to drag Suze away.

We hadn't talked much since our big fight on the bench, but there didn't seem any point to being rude and ignoring her. "Hey, K," I said, "who's walking who?"

"No doubt about it, she's walking me," Kris said. "How's it going?"

"Can't complain. With you?"

"Happy," she said simply. And she looked it.

"I'm glad," I told her. And then, for lack of better conversation, "Ed the Mouse is leaving school."

"You mean for good?"

I told her just a little of what had gone on, and where Ed was heading.

"Wow," she said. "Sounds like a good move for him. But tough for you. I know he was a real close friend."

"Yeah, a pretty good guy for a social zero."

Kris tugged Suze away from an attack on a squirrel. "I'm sure we both said a lot of things we regret," she told me.

"Not really," I said. "But I am glad you're happy. I heard you singing the other night, and it sounded like you were enjoying yourself."

She realized I must have heard Antonio singing also, and looked a little embarrassed. "Hope I didn't keep you awake."

"You know me," I told her. "I sleep like a rock. Looks like your dog has had enough of our talking."

"She's got more important things to do than listen to us," Kris agreed. "Bye, J."

"Bye."

I watched the big dog drag Kris off down the block. She was laughing and shouting at Suze, and I have to admit, in all the years I had known her, Kris had never seemed happier.

When I got back to my room, I opened the envelope. Seeing and talking with Kris had given me the power to break the seal, so to speak. It was a small, downloaded article from a Brazilian sports newspaper, published in São Paulo. I sat at my desk and read it through in about two minutes.

There had been a scandal at a teen soccer tournament in France. Five members of the Brazilian Junior national youth team had been accused of using drugs and alcohol in their hotel room and had been suspended indefinitely. Antonio

Silva was the first name mentioned. The article didn't say what drugs were involved, or whether the accusations had been proven. But I figured if this was why Antonio had left Brazil and the national team to resettle in Lawndale, he probably wasn't completely innocent.

I put the article back in its envelope and went out for a long run. I think I must have run ten miles. I left Lawndale far behind me, and ran through two whole towns. I ran fast, but I never felt winded—not a cramp, not even a pinch between the ribs, or a slight burning in the lungs. It felt like I could have run on and on forever.

While I ran, I thought about Mouse, and what it would be like to go to school without him. I had always taken it for granted that he would be around. I tried to imagine what it had been like when he and his father finally faced each other at that mountain lake, and spoke the truth to one another. It's sad that the two of them had to be pushed that far to open up, but I'm not sure it's that out of the ordinary. As I ran, I wondered what it would take to make my father and me have a conversation like that. I had a gut feeling it would never happen. I had been right all along about Mouse—in some ways he was very lucky.

I also thought about the Phenom and Kris, and what I should do with the information Mouse had tossed my way. I admit I had a strong urge to take the news article over to Kris's house and show it to her. In my fantasy, she would read it, and her parents would read about the drug-abusing louse

255

their daughter was dating, and I would say, "See, I told you he was no good. I may not have known much, but I knew that."

When I got back from my run, Kris's parents' station wagon was gone from her driveway, and Antonio's sports car was sitting there instead. Kris and Antonio weren't in the car. They also weren't out on her balcony, which meant they were most likely somewhere inside her house, alone together. I tried to convince myself they were watching TV in the den, or studying together at her living room table, but I admit I didn't completely succeed. My imagination tortured me. I couldn't see her bedroom from my own, and I resisted the urge to climb up on the roof.

Instead, I walked to my desk, picked up the manila envelope with the news clipping inside it, and ripped it in half. And then I tore it in quarters, and then in still smaller pieces till it was confetti.

I opened my hand and watched the bits of paper sift down into my trash can. Kris had picked the guy she wanted to go out with, and she was in love with him, and she looked very happy. I had ratted on my best friend and it had worked out for the best, but it didn't seem like such a good idea to make a habit out of being a squealer. My fantasy of exposing Antonio, of proving that he was no good, was just jealous wishful thinking.

Mouse was right. I would have to tough this one out.

17

Those were the dark days. Mouse was gone, Kris was with Antonio, and a chilling breath of November winter began to blow through Lawndale. Cold drizzle fell for days on end, at times surging into a driving rain, at other times lessening to a low-hanging mist, but never completely going away. As if washed down by persistent rain, leaves let go of the trees and dive-bombed their final kamikaze routes to the pavement.

Our school was relatively quiet—the police and metal detectors seemed to be doing their job. Most of the action took place in the center of town, at the intersection of Broad and Main, where rival parents' groups had set up tables. One group supported the security measures and was collecting names on a petition to ask the board to appoint Vice Principal Tobias as principal. These parents passed out leaflets quoting Dr. LaFarge about the necessity of what he called "Measured Intervention to Prevent the Escalation of School Violence."

Across Broad Avenue, two or three parents manned a second table from morning till night, crouching under umbrellas and passing out leaflets that claimed: "Isolated cases of violence in schools cannot be stamped out by turning those schools into armed camps." They were collecting names on a petition demanding that the School Board search for a new principal outside our system, and that they end the contract of Dr. LaFarge as a consultant.

Each side had its loudmouths and know-it-alls, so the decibel level at Broad and Main sometimes got pretty high. I was passed brochures from both tables, but I have to admit, I couldn't really find the energy to care. I wasn't sleeping more than a few hours a night, I wasn't eating much, and I just couldn't seem to find a way to enjoy my life. I started watching a lot of late-night TV, and several times I was surprised when my dad padded down the stairs in his socks and shorts to join me. "What's wrong with you?" he would ask as he plopped down on an overstuffed armchair.

"Nothing," I would reply. "Can't sleep. Upset stomach. Ate too much spaghetti. What about you?"

"Bad back," he would mumble. "Must have thrown it out at the car wash. Forget this movie, it's a dud. Find something good to watch." And we would sit there together, not talking, watching whatever old movies and stupid shows were on at two in the morning.

The wet weather continued and our soccer field became flooded, so we began practicing in the gym. One rainy night, when I had tossed and turned for hours, and couldn't bear any more mindless late-night TV, I walked out into the storm. It was just drizzling when I left home without an umbrella or a raincoat, but the drizzle stiffened to a hard rain and soon my clothes were soaked. It was a great way to catch pneumonia, but I didn't care—the colder it got and the harder it rained, the more numb I felt, and that was what I wanted. Wind howled around me but couldn't blow me over, and sheets of icy rain slapped my face and blinded me, but I wiped my eyes clear and kept walking.

I reached the business district of Lawndale and all the main intersections of my town were dark and empty, as if the driving rain had washed people and traffic into the storm drains. I walked on, to Lawndale High School—the deserted building looked ominous. Don't ask me why, but I headed right for it, and began to slog around the muddy grounds.

As I walked on alone, the storm came alive all around me. Lightning flashed through tree branches and flickered off iron-grated windows, so that horrific faces with gaping mouths appeared and disappeared on the school's walls. Peals of thunder chased me, getting closer and louder, and the wind howled angrily down at me from the open throat of a furious November night.

Lawndale High did seem haunted by tormented spirits. I can't say for sure whether they were long-dead Indian braves or Revolutionary War soldiers, or my own fears and despair at losing friends and letting go of what had been a mostly happy childhood. All I can say is that I felt something eerie and powerful swirling around me in that storm—I think somewhere on that hellish walk I said goodbye to my childhood and realized how brief life really is. One day I would be my father's age, one day even older; one day I would wake and look in the mirror and see an old man, and soon after that become as cold and empty as the night wind that whipped through the willow trees.

I don't really remember walking home that night. When I finally made it back I took a long, hot shower, but when I was done I still felt cold. I thought of getting into bed and trying to fall asleep, but the hike through the storm had left me in a strange, slightly feverish state. I looked around my room, and the sports trophies on their shelves seemed to press in on me, to mock me.

I dragged an old trunk out of my closet and packed the trophies away inside it, one by one. The first one was the hardest, but then they got easier and easier to take down and stow away. Next, I took out the photograph of my mother that I had kept hidden in my room for so many years, as if holding on to her image would somehow magically bring her back. I studied her pretty face for a few seconds, and then put the photo into the trunk with the trophies, and closed the top.

The room felt a little lonely with so many bare shelves, but also somehow less tormenting. I got into bed and pulled the blanket over my head, and mercifully soon fell into a deep and dreamless sleep.

The next morning I woke up with a slight fever, a runny nose, and a cough. My dad said I should stay home from school, but we had a game to play, so I went in anyway. On a soccer field dotted with puddles, my team won its final regular-season game, six to one, and qualified for the first time ever for the county tournament.

Antonio's mother came to that final regular-season game and sat next to his father on the front row of bleachers. She was a tall blond woman who looked like a movie star and didn't talk to anyone. Antonio scored five of our six goals, proving that a rain-soaked field could work to his advantage, as his quick moves caused opposing players to skid and slide and fall into puddles the size of ponds.

By the time the game was over, I was covered in mud from head to foot. I was heading off to the locker room to shower up when Dianne Hutchings intercepted me near our bleachers. "Hey," she said, "Joe, congratulations. You guys kicked butt."

"I didn't know you were a soccer fan."

"Never been to a game before in my life," she said. "But I've been reading about your team in the sports pages. And I was off from the hospital this afternoon. I figured if I came I might have a chance to talk to you."

"What about?" I asked.

"Just wanted to apologize for breaking all that stuff."

"My dad didn't mind too much," I told her.

"I didn't come to apologize to him," she said. "He's the one who owes me an apology. But I felt bad that you had to walk into that situation. It was pretty ugly."

"I've seen worse," I told her.

"Really?" She sounded incredulous.

"No, not really. That was by far the worst."

Dianne smiled, and then she laughed. "How can you make fun of me when you're covered in mud?"

"Actually I'm about to go shower up." I sneezed.

"Better hurry," she said. And then, "Want a ride home? I'll wait for you."

"Okay," I said. "As long as you promise not to throw anything at me in the car."

I showered, got dressed, and found her red sports car waiting in the parking lot. I sneezed again when I got in, and she handed me a scented yellow tissue. "You okay?"

"Never better."

"You look like crud," she said.

"Is that a medical term?"

"Really, you look awful. Are you sick?"

"A bit."

"Mind, body, or soul?" she asked.

"All of the above. Are we gonna just sit here?"

She headed out of the parking lot. "Want to talk about it?"

"Not really," I said.

"That's not a no," she pointed out. "Come on, let's go for a drive."

"Where to?" I asked.

"Enemy territory," she said.

We headed up Fort Lee Road, crested the Palisades, and started descending. Pretty soon we were driving through Bankside. It was a hardscrabble town that clung to the steep slope by the most precarious of grips—a lot of the small businesses we passed were closed and shut up, but a dozen bars were open for late afternoon drinkers. We passed a closed paint factory with broken windows and chains across the gate, and an auto junkyard guarded by a one-eyed German shepherd that came running to a corner of the fence to snarl ferociously at our car as Dianne waited for the light to change. "You been here much?" she asked.

"Driven through," I told her.

"It's a good town," she said. "A tight town. I wouldn't trade growing up here for anything."

"Do you still live here?"

"Are you crazy?" she replied with a laugh. "Nineteen years was enough. That's the family business."

A big faded green sign proclaimed HUTCHINGS BODY WORK AND DETAILING. The sign reminded me a lot of my dad's sign advertising BRICKMAN CAR WASH. Dianne slowed as we went by, and I saw a long, squat building made of sheet metal, with open areas where cars were being worked on.

Several men in the open yard recognized the red sports car and waved at Dianne, who waved back. I spotted Slade, wrench in hand, lift his head from behind a hood and watch us cruise past.

Dianne continued on through Bankside, to the edge of town, which was literally the west bank of the Hudson River. There was a ribbon of park down there, right by the water's edge, with a sandy baseball field I had played on a few times. One legend held that ten years ago a Bankside crowd got so angry at an umpire for making questionable calls that they stuffed him in a trash can and threw the can into the river. Supposedly, the poor guy drifted half a mile downstream before he was fished out.

Dianne pulled over near the backstop to the baseball field and shut off the engine. We sat for a while in silence. "So, you have enough plates left to eat off?" she asked.

"Barely," I told her.

"I just light up sometimes, and I can't really control my temper," she confessed. "Has your dad moved on?"

"Moved on where?"

"Has he found another girlfriend yet?"

"Not yet," I told her.

"He will," she said, staring out at the river. "He's got a smooth line."

"I guess he must."

For a long moment she was silent. Then she asked, softly,

"So he doesn't talk about me at all?" and she swung her eyes from the river to me for a second.

"No," I said truthfully.

"Good," she said. "To hell with him. So, what's bugging you, Joe? And don't you dare tell me it's just a touch of flu. I'm too smart for that."

I hadn't meant to tell her about Kris, but I guess maybe I needed to talk about her with somebody. Once I started, I couldn't stop myself from going into a lot of detail.

"Wow," Dianne said when I was finished, "sounds like you really love this girl."

"I did," I said. "For years."

"She's a fool," Dianne said, looking me over carefully.

"No," I said, "I'm the fool."

Dianne reached out a hand and ran her fingers gently through my hair, and for a fleeting moment I thought she might try to kiss me, and things might get really weird, but she only smiled sadly. "I'm sorry you're going through this. It's never fun to get your heart broken, but the first time hurts worst of all. Why don't you date someone else?"

"I've thought about it," I told her. "Our soccer team's really hot at school now. Lots of girls are coming to our games, and two or three of them have been talking to me and smiling a lot. But . . . it wouldn't be fair to them."

"Because you're still in love with Kris?"

"Whatever," I said with a shrug. "It just wouldn't be fair."

"Life's not always fair," Dianne Hutchings said, and her voice hardened as she said it.

I let out a colossal sneeze. She handed me another scented tissue, and switched on her car. "Let's get you home," she said. "And since I'm a nurse, here's my medical opinion. Drink hot liquids. No more rolling around in the mud. Get lots of sleep."

As we headed back through Bankside I muttered, "Easier said than done."

28

I didn't see the attempt to get revenge on the Phenom, but I heard all about it, and I saw the results. I wasn't surprised to hear the news—ever since the Phenom hurt Jack Hutchings, I knew some angry water rat would eventually try to make him pay. When Antonio joined our soccer team and became the school's big sports celebrity, I knew he was tempting fate. Since Bankside is a town of clans and blood bonds, I could have guessed it would be a family member who would make the attempt to get revenge.

Ray Hutchings was a star defensive back on the football team, and he was also on my wrestling team. He was a tough wrestler with strength and savvy, and if he had closed with the Phenom and taken him down, he probably could have gotten in a control position and done what he wanted. But from what I heard, when they squared off in a backyard at a party, Ray made the mistake of punching at long range. He landed a couple of clean shots, but then the Phenom threw some kind of side kick at him that knocked Ray off his feet and broke three of his ribs, and that was the end of that.

News of the fight circulated quickly through the student gossip hot line. I already knew about it when Ray Hutchings came to school the next day on crutches, with his ribs in some kind of cast. That was bad news for Ray and bad news for the Lawndale football team, which was heading into the playoff season already missing one key Hutchings.

The fight was never reported to the police, the cops guarding our school seemed clueless about it, and Principal Tobias's shadowy spy network didn't pick up the news either. I guess no kid from Bankside or Lawndale felt like sharing information with the adult world. But we all knew, and everyone was tense at school. I figured someone would go after Antonio again, or they would take it out on the soccer team, or possibly the soccer captain. When I was summoned out of history class, I figured something had happened, or that Tobias and Coyle wanted to grill me yet again. But instead of a note from the front office, I was told to head for the Guidance Department, to see Mrs. Simmons.

"Hello, Joe," she said when I entered, "congratulations on the county tournament."

"Thanks," I said, and sneezed.

"Why don't you have a seat. Are you okay?"

"Never better," I told her, sitting down carefully. I was getting tired of repeating the same lie—I would have to find a new answer to that question.

"Sorry to pull you out of class," Mrs. Simmons said, "but something's come up. I looked into possibilities for you . . ."

"You didn't have to do that."

"It's my job," she said. "I found some options. There's the Navy. There are a few unorthodox colleges with limited classroom time that you might want to consider. But there's one work-study program that we have to talk about today, because the deadline is pressing. Actually, I didn't find this program, Mr. Desoto did. I talked to him about your . . . future . . . and he suggested this right away. I guess he knows one of the men who runs the program. Mr. Desoto called him, and even though you don't fit their profile, he's willing to interview you. But it has to be soon."

"What's the program?" I asked.

"It's an old-fashioned sailing ship," Mrs. Simmons said, "called the *Sea Gypsy*. There are a few such ships these days, modeled on a famous one called the *Clearwater*. The *Sea Gypsy* takes a small crew of high school graduates with strong science backgrounds on a one-year program. You learn how to sail, and you study river and marine biology, and I guess the ship does some environmental work on the Hudson River." Mrs. Simmons passed me some pages. "Here are a few pictures and descriptions I downloaded from its Web site. Are you interested?" She grinned at me. "I would be."

I took the pages and scanned them quickly. My eyes were drawn to a color photograph of a sailing ship flying before the wind. It looked breathtakingly beautiful. There were also photos of student crew members—they all looked like they were having fun and working hard. There was even a shot of two pretty girls in bikinis. "Sure," I said. "I'm interested. But they won't be interested in me."

"Why not?" Mrs. Simmons asked.

"Because it says: 'Successful applicants will be highly motivated college-bound students with exceptional academic and extracurricular backgrounds.' That's not exactly me."

"It's not exactly not you either," she said. "Look, I can't promise they'll take you. Probably they won't. It's a very competitive program, and most applicants are rejected. But Mr. Desoto made the call for you, and he thinks it's worth a try." She saw my doubts, and leaned forward, and said in a very low voice, "When you came to see me the first time, you opened a door, Joe. You knew what you were doing. Give it a chance."

I looked back at her. "Can I keep these pages and think it over?"

"Don't think too long," she said. "Here's the name and number of the man you need to call to schedule an interview. If I were you, I'd call him tonight."

I read the pages over five or six times in school that day, always when I was alone and no one could see and make fun of me for dreaming crazy dreams. Twice I almost ripped the pages up, because crazy dreams can cause you lots of pain. But I didn't tear them up, and that night I read them one more time and then called the phone number Mrs. Simmons had written down for Dr. Rossini. I guess the first thing I did wrong was mispronounce his name, because he said, "No, it's Ross-*ini*—like the famous composer."

I didn't ask which famous composer. "I guess Mr. Desoto called me about you, I mean you about me," I stammered.

Even though I was garbling the English language horribly, Dr. Rossini didn't hang up. "Yes, of course," he said. "I've known Victor for years. He speaks very highly of you. We should meet and talk. There's only one problem."

The problem was that he had to see me in the next two days or it would be too late, and the *Sea Gypsy* was anchored up the Hudson River, nearly a hundred miles north of Manhattan. "Do you drive?" Dr. Rossini asked.

"I have my license but no car," I told him. "Let me see what I can do. I'll have to call you back."

I went downstairs, and my dad was sitting there watching a boxing match. I headed to the fridge and got him a beer, and brought it to him along with some salted peanuts. "Here," I said, "thought you might enjoy a snack and a drink."

"Hey, thanks," he said, swallowing a peanut. And then his eyes narrowed suspiciously. "What do you want?"

"Just . . . your car," I told him. "I need to borrow it."

He made me tell him the whole story. I thought he might laugh at me and my crazy dreams, but he chewed a few more peanuts and thought it over. "You can't drive my car out there alone," he said. He took a big swallow of beer to wash down the nuts, and let out a belch. "I'll take you. We can go tomorrow morning bright and early."

"What about the car wash?"

"Let people drive dirty cars for one day."

"Are you serious? It's nearly two hours' drive each way. It will take all morning."

"One of the perks of running your own business is that you can give yourself a vacation anytime you want," Dad told me. "Besides, it'll give me plenty of time to tell you all about women."

I looked back at him. "Forget it. I'll ride my bike up there."

29

My father and I left at ten the next morning, heading north on the Palisades Parkway, which runs along the Jersey side of the Hudson River. It was a mild November day, there was plenty of sunshine, and the traffic was light. Dad found a sports call-in show on the radio, sipped coffee from a plastic cup, and drove much too fast. "Slow down," I told him. "I'd like to make it to this interview in one piece."

"What are they going to ask you?"

"I have no idea," I told him. "Maybe questions about ships."

"What do you know about ships?"

"Nothing," I admitted.

"Then how are you going to pass the interview?"

"I'm not," I told him. "They're gonna laugh me off the boat."

"That's my boy," he said, and took another sip of coffee.

We crossed the Hudson River on the Rhinebeck Bridge, and I looked down but couldn't see the *Sea Gypsy*. The river was beautiful, though—it was hard to believe that this same gleaming blue water that flowed past forested banks on either side was headed out to sea, and would soon be passing under the George Washington Bridge, past the town of Bankside, and providing a backdrop for tourists' photographs of Manhattan.

As we got a few miles from the boat basin where the *Sea Gypsy* was anchored, my dad turned off the radio. "Joe, here's some advice," he said. "Just be yourself."

"How can I not be?" I asked.

He swatted me lightly on the top of the head. "I mean at the interview today. You have a lot going for you."

"Like what?"

"A great father," he said. "Who would love to work with his son at the family business. But if that son should prefer to go another way, his father will understand. There's more to life than washing cars." It was the only time I had ever heard my dad complain or say anything negative about what he did.

"Thanks," I said. "I appreciate that. Any advice about ships that I can use in this interview?"

Dad thought for a minute. "Nada," he said. "Sorry."

"That's okay. I'll wing it on my own."

We drove along a narrow road on the east bank of the river, and turned a bend, and in the distance a boat basin came into view. There were several dozen small and middle-sized sailboats and motorboats, and one much larger and unbelievably gorgeous sailing ship. Its sails were furled and it rocked gently at anchor. I couldn't stop looking at it—it belonged in some old black-and-white pirate movie.

My dad saw it, too, and he surprised me by pulling over on the side of the road. "Nice-looking tub," he muttered.

"Not too shabby," I agreed.

"Listen, Joe," my dad said, "sorry I can't help you much—I don't know squat about ships. But if I was putting together a crew for a sailing ship—even a student crew—there's one thing I would want that you are."

"What's that?"

"A lifeguard," he said.

"Yeah?" I turned it over in my mind. It made sense.

"Yeah," he said. "Go with it."

"I don't have much else. Thanks."

He pulled onto the road again, and soon we were at the boat basin. "If you don't mind," he said, "I'm gonna go find myself a diner and grab a bite to eat. And I'll come back to pick you up. That way I won't cramp your style."

"Sounds good," I said, opening the door and getting out. "Bring back something for me."

"You got it." He grabbed my shoulder. "Good luck. Oh, one more thing. If this guy does laugh at you—break his nose."

I stepped out of the car, and watched my father drive away at high speed. I think maybe he was nervous for me. In seconds his car disappeared between the trees, and I was all alone. I walked to the big boat, and saw a couple of teenagers on the deck, doing different jobs or sunbathing and reading books. They were all barefoot, wore shorts and T-shirts, and they looked relaxed and tanned and happy. Suddenly I wanted this job very much.

I reached the gangplank, and a female crew member asked me, "Can I help you?"

"My name's Joe Brickman. I'm here to see Dr. Rossini."

"Come on board. I'll get him."

I walked across the gangplank and stood on deck, feeling the sway of the ship as it rocked at anchor. A big man with a red beard came hurrying up from belowdecks, crouching slightly to get through the doorway. "Joe? You're early."

"Sorry. My father drives too fast," I told him.

He grinned and we shook hands. He had a fierce grip— maybe he had spent a lot of time coiling rope or something. "So," he said, "what do you think of my little sailboat?"

"Not too shabby," I said.

"Want the grand tour?"

"Sure."

He took me from stem to stern, explaining things as we went, till we ended up beneath the mast, which he informed me was a hundred-and-ten-foot-tall Douglas fir. "It carries a mainsail of three thousand square feet," he went on. "When that sail catches a strong wind, there's nothing like it on earth. Believe me."

Then we headed down, and he showed me the galley, and the mess, and the cabins where the crew members slept. I saw that there wasn't a lot of spare room on a sailing sloop.

Dr. Rossini talked a lot and didn't ask me anything about myself, and I started to relax. That was a mistake.

"And here's my office, which is also my cabin," he said. It wasn't much larger than the crew cabins, but it did have a desk and a couple of chairs. He motioned me to one of them, and he sat in the chair by the desk. He took out a pad and pen, and then pulled a piece of paper from a drawer, studied it, and frowned. "I didn't have a chance to really look over your transcript before. Your grades aren't so hot, Joe."

"No, sir, they're pretty cold," I said.

He smiled at my ice cube of a joke, put down the transcript, and looked at me. "What's the problem? Algebra isn't that hard."

"It is for me," I admitted. "I just don't like it."

"To tell you the truth, it wasn't my favorite subject either," Dr. Rossini said. "What about history? That can be interesting."

"Yeah. I guess I just didn't try hard enough."

We sat there and looked at each other awkwardly for a few seconds, and I thought to myself that I should have ripped up the application after all.

"I don't get it," he said. He looked thoughtful, and said to himself, and then to me, "I've known Victor Desoto for twenty years, and this is the first time he's gone out on a limb for one of his students." Dr. Rossini studied me for a few seconds. "Let's take another tack. Do you know much about sailing, Joe?"

"No, sir."

"Ever been on a sloop like this before?"

"No, sir."

"You don't have to call me sir. Call me Dan. I'm not having much luck here, Joe. What do you know a lot about?"

I looked back at him. "Nothing," I confessed. "I don't know why I'm here. I'm just wasting your time."

"Time is something one has on a boat," he told me, sitting back in his chair. "Let's take yet another tack. What are you worst at?"

"That's easy," I said. "Talking to girls."

The corners of his mouth lifted in a surprised smile, and then he burst out laughing. He rocked back and forth, roaring with laughter. You can tell a lot about someone by the way they laugh. Dr. Rossini was a good guy. Watching him laugh, I found myself grinning back at him, and I relaxed a little bit.

"That's probably the most honest answer I've ever had at an interview," he finally said, gasping for breath.

"Well, that's one thing about me. What you see is what you get. I'm not great at classroom stuff. But I'm the captain of my soccer team, and we just made the county tournament. And I'm the captain of my wrestling team. They didn't make me captain just because I was the best wrestler or soccer player. I'm good at getting people to work hard."

"That's not a bad quality on a boat," he noted. "I wrestled myself in high school. It's a tough sport."

"I love it," I told him.

"What do you like best about it?"

"Pinning somebody. Maybe that sounds too harsh, but . . ."

"That's what I liked best, too," he said. "What else, Joe? I need some more."

"I like bio," I told him. "I'm in an advanced biology class, and I've been getting B's. I know a lot about fish."

He sat forward. "What kinds of things do you know?"

"I've had my own tanks for years," I told him. "I know a lot about what fish eat, and how they swim, and how clean their water has to be, and stupid stuff like that."

"Stupid stuff like that, huh?" he said, taking some notes on his pad. "Do you know I have some tanks on board?"

"I didn't see them in the grand tour."

"I'll show them to you in a minute. What else, Joe? Anything else you want to tell me? Don't hold back."

I didn't have anything else, so I borrowed my father's line. "If I was putting together a crew of a boat, one thing I would look for is a lifeguard," I said. "I've taught junior and senior lifesaving at our town pool for years. I've pulled three people out of the water who were in trouble, and my town's police department gave me a commendation for saving one guy's life. He had a heart attack."

"Is that right, Joe?"

"Yes, sir. I mean, yes, Dan."

He put down his pad and stood up. "Fair enough," he said. "Come, let me show you my fish tanks."

He led me back through the corridor, past the galley and the mess, and peered through a doorway. "Good, it's over. Come on in." He ushered me into a large room I hadn't seen before. "This is our common room—I would have shown it to you, but there was a meeting going on here, and once I walk into a meeting I never get out. Now, come over here."

On one side of the room were three large aquariums. We walked over to them. "What do you think?" he asked.

"Nice," I said.

"Why three different ones? Why not one giant one?"

This wasn't a difficult question for me. "They're three totally different worlds," I said. "Freshwater, brackish, and marine. Different fish, different plants, different food—even different amounts of light."

"Okay," he said, walking over to the biggest of the three tanks, "tell me about this one."

"Marine," I said. "Tropical."

"Why do I give it more light than the other two?"

I had two tropical tanks myself, back home in Lawndale, so I could answer this one. " 'Cause the fish are mostly from coral reefs, in shallow water with lots of sunshine," I said. "So you're making it like home for them."

"What do you see in this tank? What kind of world are we creating?"

Every good tank has its own personality. I leaned forward and tried to sense what was going on inside the glass walls. "A busy one," I finally said. "But I guess coral reefs are busy, so that makes sense. You've got living rock at the bottom, covered with anemones and sponges. I see you've built caves with the rocks, so that your shy fish can take refuge." I ran my eyes slowly up the tank. "You picked fish that swim at all different depths, to keep things interesting all over the tank. Bottom feeders like that goby, and mid-level swimmers, and those cool squirrelfish near the top. I guess you feed them shrimp and fish flake, and I would guess some live food for that parrot fish—"

"Okay, that's enough." Dr. Rossini cut me off. "I can tell you do know a lot of stupid stuff about fish," he said with a smile. "This interview's over, except for one last test. If you want to take it. It's completely up to you."

"I'll take it," I said, "but I'm not much good at tests."

"You came from Jersey, so you probably crossed the river at the Rhinebeck Bridge," he said.

"Yeah." I nodded. "We followed your directions."

"The bridge is a little more than two miles north of here. Think you could swim to it and back?" he asked.

I looked back at him. "Now?"

"The river's cold, so I can lend you a wet suit."

"Dr. Rossini, there are things I can't do, like solve a trig problem. But when it comes to physical stuff, like swimming

281

a couple of miles in a cold river, I don't mean to boast, but that's stuff I don't have a problem with. And I don't need a wet suit."

"Good," he said. "Neither do I."

"You're coming?"

"If you run out of steam, I'll have to pull you to shore," he said.

"Does that mean I have to pull you to shore?" I asked him.

He grinned. "No," he said, "because I'll be ahead of you the whole time. C'mon, I'll lend you a bathing suit."

Two minutes later we were in bathing suits, in a motor-boat near the stern of the big sloop. Two crew members from the *Sea Gypsy* were going to trail us in the motorboat, to check up on us and keep boat traffic away. "Ready?" Dr. Rossini asked. In his bathing suit, with his big stomach, he looked like a friendly walrus.

"Whenever you are."

"I don't want you to think of this as a race, Joe," he told me. "But then again, why not think of it that way." So saying, he dove gracefully into the water and started swimming northward. I followed him in, and was surprised by how cold the water was. Maybe I should have opted for the wet suit.

I could tell right away he had done a lot of long-distance swimming. He kept a steady stroke and pace as we fought the slight current upriver. I swam on his right side, matching him stroke for stroke and kick for kick. We reached the shadow of the bridge at the same moment, and my arms and shoulders were feeling it. "You okay?" he asked.

"Never better," I lied. "You need to rest?"

"Last one back is a rotten egg," he said, and took off on the homeward leg at the same strong, steady pace.

That was a hard swim back for me. The water seemed to get colder, till it chilled me to my bones and weakened me. My arms and legs felt waterlogged, so that each stroke was an effort. I tried to breathe regularly, but small waves found their way into my mouth and nose. Finally, over the top of a wave, I saw the *Sea Gypsy*, a hundred yards ahead.

Dr. Rossini saw it, too, and increased his pace. I stayed with him. Now the sloop was fifty yards away, now forty. He kept going faster and faster—the man not only looked like a walrus, but swam like one, too. Soon the big sailing ship was just thirty yards away. I heard some people shouting from its deck, and saw that a small crowd had gathered to watch the end of the race. Somehow in that split-second glance, I spotted my father—the tallest person on the deck—cupping his hands and shouting to me.

I swam to my father. He had given me this strong body eighteen years ago, and now I put every bit of heart and soul and muscle I had in swimming back to his voice. "COME ON, JOE. BRING IT, SON. COME ON, BOY." Dr. Rossini was the far better swimmer, but I was eighteen years old and had done endless push-ups and sit-ups and run countless miles training for wrestling and soccer, and some of that stored-up stamina must have come back to me. I found a second gas tank I didn't know I had, and caught up to Dr. Rossini. We raced in side by side, straining for the finish line. I kicked and stroked with everything I had. When we got to the side of *Sea Gypsy*, I outtouched him by about a tenth of a second.

We treaded water side by side for a minute, as the motorboat headed for us, to fish us out. I was gasping for breath, but he seemed totally fine. "You okay?" he asked.

"Never better," I told him, trying not to gag.

He smiled at my bravado. "Joe, I can't promise anything for sure," he said, "but here's what I do know for sure: I don't let people on my boat with C's and D's. You're no knucklehead. Work your butt off and lift your grades."

"I'll try."

"Do more than try. And keep your nose clean," he said. "Senior year, people go a little wild. I understand from Victor that your high school's been having trouble lately. I don't like trouble on my boat. And I don't like troublemakers. I want a scholar and a gentleman. You got that?"

"Yes, sir."

The motorboat arrived and they fished us out. "Good job!" the teenage crew member who pulled me out said. "Dan swims this every day, and no one's ever beaten him before."

Back on the sloop, I headed below to change out of my wet bathing suit. When I returned to the deck, my father was shaking Dr. Rossini's hand in an exchange of viselike grips, and making small talk with him. They were an odd pair—they seemed on the surface to have absolutely nothing in common, but I could tell they enjoyed bantering. Dr. Rossini soon excused himself, and disappeared belowdecks, and my dad turned to me. "C'mon, let's go home. I got you a burger, and fries," he said. As we walked away, he put his arm across my shoulders and whispered, "Nice swimming, Marlin Man."

We drove back even faster than we had come. The sun was out and I felt good. I didn't know if I had passed the interview, or won a place on the *Sea Gypsy*, but I felt like I had given a good account of myself. Dr. Rossini understood who I was, and what I had to offer, and now it was up to him.

I finished off the burger and fries. I hadn't been in a good mood for so long that I had almost forgotten what it felt like. "So," I said to my dad, "weren't you going to tell me everything I need to know about women?"

He passed a few cars and then muttered in a low voice, "The prettier they are, the crazier they are. And I only like the pretty ones. But I can't stand the crazy ones."

The car was silent for a few minutes while I thought that over. "That must explain it," I said.

"What?"

"Why you're alone so much."

"I'm not alone so much," my dad protested. "I'm surrounded by people. And I can get a date anytime I want. You know that."

"Yes, you can. No question. You're a dating machine."

We were about fifteen miles from Lawndale now, on the top of the Palisades cliffs, with the Hudson glinting beneath in the warm sunlight. From this vantage point, it was hard to believe the gleaming blue water down below was so cold.

My father asked unexpectedly, "So you think she was right?"

"Who?"

"Dianne Hutchings. When she said that I was afraid to go out with a woman I like, 'cause I don't want to get hurt again?"

"Well, you have dated a lot of women," I observed quietly.

"What's wrong with that? So you think she was right?"

"I don't know," I said. "You were going to explain things to me."

"Here's the weird thing," Dad noted. "I haven't been able to get her words out of my mind. It's like they keep digging around, annoying the hell out of me, like termites in a house." Dad made a sour face and shook his head, as if trying to dislodge something and shake it out through his ears. "Believe it or not, I've lost sleep over them," he admitted in a soft growl. He drove in silence for a few seconds, and then went on, "And I haven't been able to forget the way she looked when she was throwing those dishes at me, with her hair flying, and her eyes blazing. I've never had a woman get that angry at me before. I figure she must have really liked me to get that pissed off at me."

"I think she did really have a thing for you," I told him.

"Ah, what does it matter," he said. "First of all, she's completely bonkers. And, second, even if I called her, she wouldn't talk to me. Not that I would do it. It would violate all my rules about women. But even if I did, she wouldn't take my call. So I won't."

"If you called her," I told him, "she would take your call."

"Yeah, to tell me I'm a bum and a coward."

"She would probably call you much worse than that," I agreed. "But she would take your call."

He looked over at me. "You think so?"

"Absolutely."

It was strange to return to Lawndale High the next morning. I felt like I had taken a long detour away from it—longer than just the one-day car trip to visit the *Sea Gypsy*—but now I was back, entering through the arms of the metal detector, looking out from behind iron-grated windows, and all the time sensing a growing, ominous anger.

The tension between Banksiders and Lawndale kids that I had felt after the Phenom broke Ray Hutchings's ribs had not diminished. It might not have been photographed by the security cameras or been noticed by any of the police patrols, but it was simmering there all the same, just beneath the surface. And I knew that somewhere, sometime soon, it would explode.

I stuck around after advanced bio on Friday to thank Mr. Desoto for saying such nice things about me to Dr. Rossini. He insisted on hearing all the details of my interview. I told him everything, and when I described the final swimming race, he chuckled. "So you beat him, did you? No mercy on old scientists, huh?"

"Should I have let him win?" I asked.

"Are you crazy? Did you know he swam for Stanford

years ago? I bet he didn't like losing to you. He might put you on his crew just to set up a rematch."

That was the biggest sports weekend of the fall for Lawndale. On Saturday morning our soccer team won our first game in the county tournament, two to one, against an angry team from Rosewood. They were angry because they were a top seed, expected to contend for the championship, and they were defeated by a bottom seed led by a Brazilian soccer Phenom who refused to back down.

The Rosewood team had read the sports pages and knew what to expect and who to go after. They tried to intimidate Antonio, hacking him and shoving him and threatening him when the ref was out of earshot. As the first half ended, they scored to go ahead one to nothing. But Antonio struck almost as soon as we ran onto the field to begin the second half, tying the score with a brilliant shot that whistled in from nearly forty yards out, and then he put us in front with a perfectly placed penalty kick after one of their fullbacks tackled him in the box. Rosewood tried desperately to tie the score, but our defense was able to hold the lead. Once again, in the final few minutes, I saw Antonio retreat to our fullback line, and we defended together shoulder to shoulder to the final whistle.

Our football team fared less well. They were a top seed, expected to win in the early rounds, but without Jack and Ray Hutchings they couldn't put the game away. They allowed a late comeback, and as the seconds ticked down, a final long field goal sailed over their desperate arms and through the crossbars, ending their season.

I was at that game, and saw how hard our team's seniors took it as they trudged off the field, helmets in their hands. They had sweated and bled and vomited for four years to win this tournament, and now it was all down the drain in the very first round. I suspected it wouldn't be long before their disappointment turned to anger at those they held responsible.

The attack came very soon, and at a most unexpected time—on Monday afternoon, during our first ever school evacuation drill. I found out later that Antonio and Andy Powell and two other guys from the Lawndale popular crowd decided it was beneath them to evacuate with everybody else. So when the bells rang and the halls started to empty, the four of them headed beneath the bleachers in the gym, to hang out and pass a cigarette around. My best guess is that some Banksiders spotted them sneaking into the gym, and somebody figured out that if the school was completely empty, there would be no one around to break up a fight.

Unfortunately, I was around. Mr. Hart, the athletic director, had collared me a few minutes before, on the way up from my gym class, to let me know that ten new soccer balls had arrived. We have a constant problem with theft—sports equipment in general and balls in particular can disappear in a matter of hours. So, just to be safe, I carried the balls over to the soccer room myself to lock them away. Coach Collins wasn't there, but I have my own key. I was just trying to open the door when the bells and siren went off.

My key is not a very good duplicate. Sometimes the lock wants to open for me, and sometimes it doesn't. On Monday afternoon it took me a minute or two to get the door open, and stow the balls in the equipment locker. By the time I got the door locked again, the school hallways were nearly empty. I didn't know if there was a penalty for being late to evacuate, but I headed down at a fast jog.

As I passed the gym, I heard the unmistakable sounds of a beating in progress. I guess I could have just kept jogging, but someone was howling in pain. Instinctively, I headed for the screams, to find out what was going on, and see if I could help.

Four hard guys from Bankside were kicking the crap out of four of the popular crowd from Lawndale. They had paired off, so the beatings were going on all over the big gym. I saw Slade pick up handsome Andy Powell, the captain of the tennis team and Jewel Healy's sometime boyfriend, and hurl him to the wooden floor as if he was slamming down a tennis racket. *"Stay down, pretty boy,"* he shouted, *"or I'll break your face."* Jack Finn was kicking Stewart Roddick, our stuck-up class treasurer, stomping on his ribs as Stewart rolled over and over and tried to cover up. Glen Barrett was screaming as

Tony Borelli squeezed him in a headlock. But the real battle was the fight between Antonio Silva and big Chris Coleman.

Chris was more than a foot taller than Antonio and must have outweighed him by fifty pounds of solid muscle. He was one of the very hardest of the hard guys, in the sense that every muscle in his body was sharply defined from thousands of weightlifting reps. Chris was best friends with Jack and Ray Hutchings, and now he wanted revenge for his football season and his two buddies. He had the Phenom backed up in a corner of the gym, and he was lashing at him with a weapon—it looked like a bicycle chain.

As I watched from the stairs, Antonio didn't make a sound or look scared. He was ducking the chain and warding it off his face, taking the blows on his elbows and thighs, waiting for an opening. And then he struck back.

I'm not sure what martial art Antonio had studied—maybe jujitsu—but it wasn't just limited to kicks. He waited his chance, and then he reached up and caught Chris's right hand just as the chain started to swing down. Antonio ducked low and pivoted sideways, and used Chris's own momentum to throw him. The big water rat literally became airborne—he sailed through the air, and landed hard on his back. He got up shakily, but Antonio was already sprinting for the stairs.

And that was when Slade moved in. You don't expect big guys to move quickly. But Slade left Andy Powell lying on the floor of the gym and intercepted Antonio at the foot of the stairs. It was like a steamroller running over a skateboard. He blindsided Antonio, who went down hard. Slade stayed right on him, wrapping him up in his huge arms. Chris came limping up with his bicycle chain, ready for a few free shots, and that was when I found myself moving.

I can't say for sure why I went down those steps. I certainly didn't like the Phenom, or owe him anything. But we had played defense side by side in several tough soccer games, and he had won my respect. I had never seen him leave a teammate or take a backward step. And there was something else. He was being ganged up on, just the way Ed the Mouse had been ganged up on. And something about the way my dad had brought me up just couldn't permit that.

I jumped the final three steps and flew into Slade from behind. The impact knocked him off his feet, but he didn't let go of Antonio. The three of us crashed to the floor. I stayed behind Slade, slipping my arms under his shoulders and knotting my hands around the back of his head, snapping on a full nelson. Then I applied enough pressure to pry him off Antonio.

"I don't want to fight you," I said to him. "Just let the two of them fight it out fair and square."

Slade recognized my voice and let out a roar. He lurched and thrashed and reared, and it was like riding a Brahma bull. His strength was unnatural, improbable. But I had him from behind, in a control position, and brute strength alone couldn't possibly help him. I pulled him sideways and tripped him up, and rode him down to the wooden floor.

And that was when a lookout yelled, *"Cops! Cops!"*

I let Slade go, and we all scattered in different directions. Even the Lawndale guys who had been covering up and taking the beating got up and began to run. I guess we had all been conditioned to avoid cops. With a zero tolerance policy, anyone involved in a fight would be automatically suspended and probably expelled.

I got out of the gym through a side exit and hid in a janitor's closet. I'm not sure how the rest of them got out, or where they hid, but it was our school and after four years we knew every door and hallway. All the cops found was a bicycle chain and a sleeve that had been ripped off a T-shirt. I guess they figured it was a false alarm, and nobody was fighting after all.

Soon the bells rang and the siren blared, and the hallways filled up with students again. Vice Principal Tobias's voice came over the loudspeaker announcing that the evacuation drill had been a success. But sitting in history class, my arms still tingling from the fight, I knew better. I had taken Slade on, I had put my hands on him in combat, and a summons to battle was coming.

It arrived just before last period, in a form I didn't expect. It wasn't the Banksiders who came for me but four of the toughest kids from my own town. There was Roger Gray, who wrestled with me, and Eric Olsen, the catcher on the baseball team, and the captain of the baseball team, Troy Baptiste, and the co-captain of the football team, Ron Evans. The four of them intercepted me in the hall and just looked at me, and I looked back at them, and I knew. "Coming?" Troy asked.

"Sure," I said. And he didn't have to say anything else, and I didn't have to ask. Because I knew why they had come, and where we were going.

31

We met in the subbasement bathroom, the four guys from Lawndale and me, and four Banksiders and Slade. As soon as the door closed in the tiny bathroom, Slade got right to business. "This is me against him," he said, pointing a finger at my chest, "for starters. Later it can be whatever you guys want, but that's what it is now. It's you and me, Brickman. We've had this coming for a long time, and now it's come, so let's go get it on."

It was the strangest thing, but I wasn't scared. I looked him in the eye and said, "I don't want to fight you, Slade."

"You already made that decision," he said.

"You were jumping in. I pulled you off. That was nothing against you."

He stepped forward. "I'll rip you apart right here," he growled.

I felt myself tense, but the eight other guys in the room got between us and held him back.

"If he says he don't want to fight, then there's no fight," Troy said. "At least right now."

"He'll fight," Slade said confidently. "I know you're a little scared, Brickman. I know your knees are knocking."

I looked back, right into his eyes. "Do I look scared?"

"Then what is it?"

"I just don't want to do it," I told him.

"Your best buddy was too scared to fight back, too," he said. "We stripped him down and taped him up and he never threw a single punch. He just cried like a girl—'Don't hurt me, don't hurt me.' You gonna start crying?"

I thought of Mouse when we had unwrapped him, and how he could have died in that closet. I felt my anger building, and I tried to swallow it down. "No, I'm not gonna cry. But I'm also not going to give you what you want right now."

He laughed in my face. "Coward and son of a coward. No wonder my uncle whipped your father's butt. And I hear your mother was a whore. What about that?"

The room got very quiet. "I didn't know my mother," I said. "And I don't think you know much about her either."

"I know all kinds of things about you," Slade said. "You're a poor, broken-hearted lover boy, huh? I heard all about it from Dianne. I was curious, so I told her we were friends, and I was worried about you. She told me the whole sob story. You were sweet on that Kris chick, but you didn't have the balls to go out with her, and you don't have the balls to let her go, even though she's getting all she can handle from that Brazilian—"

Before I knew what I was doing, I had my hands on his

throat, and he had his hands on mine. And even as we choked each other, and eight guys strained to pull us apart, he smiled. "Let's go," he whispered.

And then, as if by magic, we were outside the school, walking through the marshes. The reeds got thicker around us, the air was heavy with a salt tang, and blood was roaring through my head and behind my eyes. I had felt a tiny bit like this a few times before, when I stepped onto the mat for big wrestling matches, and heard the crowd clapping, and looked across into the eyes of my opponent. But this was of a scale that wiped everything else off the map. There were no crowds, no ref, no rules, no laws. We were warriors about to go into battle. It was kill or be killed.

The War Zone came into view. It's a place deep in the swamps, a bare circular clearing where for some reason marsh plants never grow. As we neared it, I looked around and saw that we were no longer just ten guys. Somehow word must have circulated through Lawndale High at lightning speed. Slade and I were being trailed to the War Zone by several dozen of the toughest Banksiders and Lawndale kids.

There was no sign that the police knew anything was amiss, or that Tobias or Coyle had a clue that the opening battle in a war was about to take place. Tensions had reached this boiling point, and more than thirty kids had heard about the fight and slipped out of school to watch, without any of Red Flag's sensors going off.

I looked around at the faces of my classmates, and I saw how eager they were for me to fight. Guys were calling out to me, "You'll take him, Brickman. You'll spill his blood. You'll kill him." Oddly, they reminded me of the faces that the lightning had flashed on the walls of Lawndale High when I had taken my walk in the thunderstorm. They seemed to have the same hungry, ghastly, gaping mouths, the same flashing, furious eyes. The faces and voices swirled around me, and it was plain for me to see that Lawndale High was indeed haunted.

Twenty years ago my father and Kevin Hutchings had taken this same slow march to the War Zone. Now I was only thirty yards from the barren circle of sand. My hands were away from my body, my fingers clenching and unclenching into fists, the coppery taste of fury and blood thick on my tongue. I could kill in this state. I wanted to kill.

"You'll break his face, Brickman. You'll rip his heart out."

"Tear his head off his shoulders, Slade. And then we'll get the rest of these Lawndale scum."

"We'll see who gets who."

"Yeah, you'll see. You'll see."

I slowed and then stopped walking. Slade had already entered the sandy circle and peeled off his shirt. He stood there, feet spread apart and enormous arms out wide, waiting for me. "Come on, Brickman. Let's go."

But I didn't go. I just stood there, looking at him. Time

froze up for me—froze up with my whole childhood behind me, and my whole future in front of me—into one diamond-hard crystalline instant.

If we fought, it could not be hidden, just the way my father's fight with Kevin Hutchings had become a local legend. I would be tossed out of school the way he had been expelled years ago. There would be no graduation day, no chance of moving forward to something new and different and maybe better. If we fought, I would be giving way to the same anger my father had given way to, and I would have to live with that for years. My fists were still clenched—I could feel the hatred bubbling up inside of me. If we fought, there would be a war, faction versus faction, town against town, punched out in school hallways and clawed over in locker rooms.

No metal detectors or police could stop it. No adult supervision could stop it. Those security measures were only superficial—they couldn't reach into the hearts and minds of the students involved. But I could stop it. That was the truth I came to in that long and frozen moment. This was my life. Not the life of any of the people around me, clamoring for blood, but mine. I had to make the decision, and I had to make it now, or it would be made for me. I very slowly unclenched my fists. "I'm not going to fight you," I said to Slade.

"You can't back out now," he growled.

"I can," I said. "And I am."

"YOU ALL HEARD HIM!" he shouted, as if he was being robbed of something precious. "ARE YOU GONNA LET HIM CHICKEN OUT?"

Someone reached out and tried to push me forward, but I knocked the hand away. "Where are you going?" a voice demanded.

"Back to school," I said.

Slade stepped toward me and roared, "IF YOU WANNA BACK OUT, YOU KNOW WHAT YOU GOTTA DO, BRICKMAN."

"Yeah, I know," I whispered. But I didn't know if I could do it. Looking Slade right in the eye, I very slowly began to dip my shoulders toward him. My body froze for a moment in rebellion—as if my very bones and sinew were fearful that if I bowed to him now, I would never be able to straighten up fully, ever again. But with an effort of will I forced my shoulders down, forced my head to dip. It wasn't exactly a low and humble bow, but it was still the single hardest thing I have ever done in my life.

There were gasps from guys standing near us, and I heard shouts: "Don't do it, Brickman!" "Remember your father! Remember where you're from!" "What a coward. There goes the fight!"

Then I straightened up. "There's your respect," I told Slade. "But that's it. The next time you start with me, or anybody from the soccer team, or any of my friends, I'm going straight to the police and I'll tell them everything. I'm gonna name names and not hold anything back, and the only way you can stop me is to kill me. It's over."

I don't remember much about walking back through that marsh. I have some memory of guys from Lawndale and Bankside hurling insults at me, and even spitting at me, trying desperately to goad me into fighting. But most of all I remember thinking, as Lawndale High swam into view above the reeds and cattails, that when I had walked through the thunderstorm I had been saying goodbye to my childhood, and now I was walking toward my future.

32

The first word of the disappearance of the Phenom blew into our school on a Thursday with a November sleet storm.

"He's gone," Charley the Fish told a few of us as we changed into our soccer uniforms for an indoor practice.

"Gone where?" Harlan asked.

"No one knows. But he's disappeared," Charley said.

I finished tying a lace on my indoor soccer shoes, and asked, as if I really didn't care too much, "Why did he leave?"

Zigzag Zigler supplied an answer. "He felt this school was getting too dangerous. At least, that's what I heard from somebody who heard it from Andy Powell."

Antonio Silva was gone all right. Coach Collins didn't mention it when we started practicing, but he didn't look very happy either. When we finished running wind sprints, Canoe Feet Cavanaugh came right out and asked, "Is it true the Phenom's gone?"

Coach Collins looked like he had just chewed and swallowed a lemon. "Yeah. So what?" he said. "We've got a second-round tournament game to win this Saturday. He's just one player. Hell, we've won with him, and we've won without him. And we'll win this Saturday, if you guys work hard and do what I tell you."

There was a long, grim silence, as if the team had suddenly gone into collective mourning. "Coach," Charley the Fish finally said, "the truth is we didn't win much without him."

"The truth," Maniac Murray added sadly, "is that we kinda sucked without him."

"That's five extra wind sprints!" Coach Collins shouted. "Let's go. Brickman, aren't you the captain of this team? Show some leadership!"

When practice was over, I showered and changed back into my street clothes, and I was ready to head home with the rest of the guys. But then something occurred to me, and I broke away from them and headed for the band room.

The lights were off in the main room, but I could see they were on in a practice room. I didn't hear any flute music. Instead, I heard someone crying softly.

Now, I know this is gonna sound awful, but I did tell you right at the beginning that I'm not the best person in the world, and that you could find a better one without looking too hard. I confess that when I heard that soft crying, I felt a certain satisfaction. On some level I even took pleasure in it.

I switched on the bright overhead lights above the band shell, to signal my presence, and the crying stopped. I gave her a few seconds and then knocked on the door of the practice room, and pushed it open a crack. "Hey, K," I said, "where's your flute?"

She dried her eyes and managed to whisper, "I didn't feel like playing. You heard the news?"

"Yeah, at soccer practice. You okay?"

"Sure," she said. And then Kris shivered, and the tears started again, and she shook her head from side to side and whispered, "No, no, I'm not okay."

I stepped into the practice room and pulled the door closed, and held her, and let her cry on my shoulder. She cried for a long time, her body trembling. Her tears wet the back of my shirt. "He . . . he didn't even say goodbye," she finally whispered.

"Maybe it was an emergency and he left in a hurry."

"No, he left to go to Spain," she said. "I know because his father dropped off a note for me. Wasn't that thoughtful of him, to write a note that his father could drop off?" She sounded broken-hearted and furious at the same time.

"Why Spain?" I asked.

"He said in the note he had a chance to train with a team in Barcelona, and it seemed like too good an opportunity to turn down." She took a few breaths. "He said he would try to write to me from Spain. But he said he's a really bad correspondent, so I shouldn't expect too much. And he didn't give me an address to write to him."

"Maybe he doesn't have one yet," I suggested.

"Sure, right," she said. I spotted a manila envelope on the floor, and she followed my gaze to it. "Along with the note, he sent me an autographed picture of himself. As if I'm some groupie. Which is, I guess, what I was."

Kris started crying again. I bent down and picked up the envelope, and pulled out an eight-by-ten glossy. It was, indeed, a photograph of the Phenom, suitable for framing, with his name written in script in big blue letters. No message. Just his autograph. "Nice picture," I said. "He's a good-looking guy. I didn't realize his eyes were that shade of blue."

"I loved him," she said, and her voice quivered. "I loved him so much. And he just used me . . . for his American adventure. That's all I was for him."

"Look on the bright side," I told her. "At least you got to go out with him for a while. And be one of the most popular girls in the school."

Kris pulled away from me fast, and we studied each other for about five seconds without speaking. "I hurt you," she finally said. "Is that it?"

"Every time you tell me you love him, you hurt me. And you know that, but you keep doing it."

"Well, I did love him," she said. "I'm sorry, but I did."

"I know," I said. "And don't worry. There are lots of other good-looking guys in our school for you to go to the senior prom with. And some of them also own their own cars."

She turned away from me and packed up a few things. "Thanks for comforting me, Joe," she said. "I'm going now."

"Goodbye, Kris. Get home safe."

33

I took a lot of flak for not fighting Slade. A number of guys called me a coward, or at least whispered it behind my back. Other students seemed to respect me for what I had done, or at least to be glad that a full-scale war between Lawndale and Bankside had been averted. With each day that went by, I was surer that I had done the right thing. And I had other things to think about. I was studying harder than I ever had before. Final exams were a few weeks away, and somehow I had to do better than C's and D's.

It was a strange week. The School Board voted to promote Tobias to principal, and he celebrated by announcing a whole new series of rules. Each student was given a booklet containing new regulations and penalties. Clearly the iron grates and metal detectors were not coming down anytime soon.

I ran into Kris a few times in the halls, and we nodded at each other, but neither of us said anything. Her eyes were red and she looked tired. I knew a lot about insomnia from recent experience, and my guess was that she hadn't had a good night's sleep since the Phenom disappeared.

That Saturday my soccer team played its second-round

tournament game, against a high school from Rockland Township. Even though we played at home, the crowd was much smaller than we had grown used to. There were no TV cameras, and the popular clique from Lawndale decided not to honor us with their presence.

My father surprised me by showing up just before the opening kickoff—it was the first soccer game he had ever come to in his life. He walked up hand in hand with Dianne Hutchings, and the two of them stood by our sideline, smiling and shouting. In honor of his coming to the game, and despite the fact that we had no offense at all, I managed to keep the game scoreless for the first half.

I could tell my father didn't know what to yell at soccer games. He kept shouting football stuff, like "Block him," and "Chop him down," and even "Watch the run," which really didn't make any sense at all.

A soccer team without an offense is a losing proposition, and eventually Rockland broke through. They scored five goals in the last half hour, to humiliate us and end our glorious season on a dismal note. To tell you the truth, even though I'm highly competitive, I didn't mind losing. We just weren't that good a team. I enjoyed the thumping tackles, and the cold mud that slowly congealed on my shirt, and I felt like I deserved to wear every thread of the captain's armband. And when Kris shouted from the high bleacher, I glanced at her and she looked back at me.

With about ten minutes left, I gave my father what he wanted. The biggest Rockland player made a solo run at our goal, and I stopped him with a chest-to-chest collision that knocked me back three steps and sent their big guy flying face first into the mud. I heard my father shout excitedly from the sideline, "THAT'S IT, SON. CRACK HIS RIBS!"

And I think I heard Dianne Hutchings's voice shout at the same time, "YEAH, JOE! RIP HIS GUTS OUT!"

In some ways they made a lot of sense as a couple.

The final whistle blew, and we shook their hands and then circled up for Coach Collins's final bad speech of the year. "I'm proud of you all," Coach Collins said. "Maybe we weren't as good as we thought we were, but we're not as bad as we could have been, either, and we're also not mediocre." He stopped, as if he'd run out of categories, and stood there looking around at us. "I don't know what else to say," he finally admitted, "except that I don't know what else to say. Joe, do you want to add anything?"

"Nope," I told him. "Season's over. Let's move on."

My dad and Dianne waved me over as I headed back to the locker room. "Good game," Dianne said. "You really conked that guy."

"He's a tough soccer player, but he's an even better swimmer," my father told her. "I call him Marlin Man."

I watched the two of them walk off together, and then started to run back toward school with my head still turned. I bumped into Kris, and nearly ran her over. "Sorry," I said.

"No, I'm sorry, Joe," she said. "Tough loss."

"Sometimes losing feels better than winning," I told her.

"You played great," she said. There was a long, silent beat. She asked very tentatively, "You don't want to walk home together? I mean, I wouldn't mind waiting around."

"Thanks, but don't bother," I told her. "I'm gonna walk home with the guys."

"Sure, yeah," she said, and turned away. "Bye, J."

I let her get five steps before I grabbed her from behind. "All the years we've known each other, and you still don't know when I'm pulling your leg?"

"Actually, you're standing on my foot," she said.

A half hour later Kris and I were walking home together, along the same side of the street we had always walked on, stepping over the cracks in the sidewalk.

We talked about stupid stuff for about ten blocks, but by the time we reached the big maple tree with the low-hanging branches we had run out of small talk. So we stopped and faced each other and spoke the truth. "I feel sorry for a lot of the things I said to you," Kris told me. "I was a jerk. Some of what I said must have hurt bad."

"It did. But some of it was true."

"Can you forgive me?" she asked. "Can we be friends, like we were?"

"Never friends like we were," I told her. "Maybe more than friends, or maybe less, but we have the rest of the year to figure that out. I do know I'm going to need your help."

"For what?"

"To get a B in algebra. I know it's a long shot, but there's this ship called the *Sea Gypsy*."

She looked confused. "What ship? What are you talking about?"

"I actually have you to thank for it. You made me open a door. But come on, I'll tell you all about it as we walk. It's getting late, and I have a lot of studying to do."

We walked off together into the sharpening late November wind, which for the first time held more than a hint of the coming winter. We were heading toward her house that was across from my house, so that any way you figured it, we were going home.

mL   4/05